"It's just to help you protect the ranch you love so much," he added, thinking she still needed to be convinced. "If they burn you out, you'll have nothing. What do you say, Jess?"

His tone was soft and coaxing, and she was reminded that he was the enemy.

Looking up at him, she said, "Okay, Sleet, but if you persist with this misguided notion of yours about sexual conquest, I'll call the law. That's a promise. When Hal and the others find out about it, you'll be lucky to get back to Texas with your life."

He grinned. "Now, Jess," he said. "I already gave you my word on that last night. You can trust me."

"Sure," she said, stepping away, covering her inner qualms with a jaunty tone. "About as much as I'd trust a sidewinder in my pocket."

ABOUT THE AUTHOR

Louella Nelson writes of exotic locales and life-styles
such as the salmon fishing industry of Southeast Alaska,
the rare profession of lighthouse keeping in Northern
California and the gritty glamour of the gem trade in
Los Angeles and London. With trainer Joe Heim she
published *California Cutting Horse*, a magazine
celebrating the history and heroes of the cutting horse
industry—the setting for her fifth novel, *Days of Fire*. A
former president of the Orange Country Chapter of the
Romance Writers of America, she is also a past
coordinator of the RWA's national writers' conference.

Books by Louella Nelson

HARLEQUIN AMERICAN ROMANCE
214–MAIL-ORDER MATE
379–EMERALD FORTUNE

HARLEQUIN SUPERROMANCE
96–SENTINEL AT DAWN
128–FREEDOM'S FORTUNE

LOUELLA NELSON

DAYS OF FIRE

Harlequin Books

TORONTO • NEW YORK • LONDON
AMSTERDAM • PARIS • SYDNEY • HAMBURG
STOCKHOLM • ATHENS • TOKYO • MILAN
MADRID • WARSAW • BUDAPEST • AUCKLAND

With love to Mom, ever a pioneer, and her John.
Together they reversed the course of snowbirds flying south.

Acknowledgments

With appreciation to trainer Joe Heim (NCHA Riders Hall of Fame) who rode the late Docs Okie Quixote to the 1983 NCHA Futurity World Championship, and who inspired this book. Also to Vicky Benedict of DLR Ranch, Pam of Horseman's Source, Daryl Struss, Cammy, Karyl, Carl Baggett Jr., Bill Reed of Amarillo and Lee Kissel of the NCHA. Literary license with the subtleties of cutting was sometimes necessary.

Published March 1993

ISBN 0-373-16479-3

DAYS OF FIRE

Chapter One

From the smoky shadows of the barn, a horse shrilled. The piercing whistle died to a guttural *eu-agh-agh*. Jessica Latham clung to the door of the burning barn, riveted by fear, the loss of her prize stallion flashing into her soul.

Blue-bar-Satan. The blue-black, satin-coated stallion; terrified and trapped by fire. Blue. He was the reason Jessica had given up work on *Elite Magazine* and come home to the ranch. Blue and the potential he represented to make her dreams come true.

Jess gripped the rope she'd coiled around her waist, gripped it so hard her tanned fingers turned white. The night wind pulled through wet hair as long and thick and midnight black as Blue's mane, but she did not feel the chill. A sage-scented gust ballooned her soaked green blouse, while the inferno beat its hot breath against her face, challenging her courage.

She might lose everything by going in—but would have virtually nothing left if she did not.

"Win the world, win the world," she began to chant to muster her resolve. "The world, the world, the world!"

Jerking away from the door, she dragged the soggy blanket and the rope with her into the heat and cinders. "Win the world!" she shouted, gritting her teeth.

Smoke curled around her, sucking away her breath so she could utter no sound. The roaring pressed her down. The crackling and hissing urged her to turn back. Ridiculous thought. If Blue died, what would she have to turn back *to?* The ranch was so close to failure, she could smell the rank bite of the tax man's cigar as if he were standing next to her, handing her the Notice to Vacate. The only thing that stood between her and failure was a young stallion. Blue. Only Blue. *"Win the world,"* she reiterated in desperation. *Please, God...*"

The smoke lifted near a stall door on the left, evidently pushed back by the high-desert breeze. She darted for the opening, dragging in air that smelled of torched fields and charred pinewood.

"Blue," she muttered. She raised her head, shielding her eyes. *"Blue!"*

He did not answer,

Cinders shot like comets from the rafters. A brand singed through her damp cotton sleeve. She slapped her arm and leapt away from the line of stalls, staggering, her chest pinched with the effort to breathe. For a moment, looking through yellow-orange flames and wavering shadows, she felt hopeless.

"Josepha, Noa." She talked aloud to submerge the fear. "Gone to Mexico. Not coming back 'til Friday. Where the devil are the ranchers I called?"

She'd never needed anyone like she needed them now. In the yearlong struggle to train the black colt and keep the bills paid, she'd fed her courage on Blue's talent, the legacy of her father's example, and her dream of a world championship. Now...

Equine wheezing and whinnying reverberated through the barn. The sounds echoed with familiarity, hinted at her responsibility, her hope. *"Get to Blue,"* she whispered, crawling forward. *"Get Blue out of this inferno."*

Jessica coughed. The reaction sent splinters of pain through her head and chest. Her mind felt so damned vague. She concentrated hard. The need to save the stallion drew her deeper into the barn.

Heavy thuds sounded from a stall across the aisle. Jessica's head whipped toward the latched half door. The screams came again, but not from Blue. Shadows danced in the dim interior of the stall. A patch of bay hide glowed in the firelight.

"Sienna . . ." How had she forgotten the mare, the other crucial element in her desperate plan?

Jessica fell across the hall and fumbled for the metal latch, lifted it and called, "Sienna, easy . . ."

She was swinging open the stall door when the mare's chest hit with full force, slamming the door into Jessica's shoulder. She was punched into the wall. Stunned, she slipped to the floor.

Squealing and snorting, the brown quarter horse plunged this way and that in the smoky hallway, then cantered toward the open door, her iron-shod hooves beating hollowly.

"One saved," she whispered. "Thank God."

Jessica tried to stand. Her legs wobbled. "Win the world," she muttered. With Blue, she could win.

She thought she heard men's voices over the roar of the fire, but her mind doggedly trained on the cutting-horse futurity and on the unspeakable thought of it taking place without her and Blue. The spark of anger it brought sent Jessica scrambling for the sodden blanket.

"Finally!" It felt like a moldy animal pelt as she clutched it to her stomach and rolled to her feet, pulling herself along the walls, keeping low amid the firecrackers raining down.

Ahead, hooves struck solid wood. The stallion called from beyond a curtain of flames.

Ten more feet to Blue. Blue was the only bit of heaven she knew anymore. She fought through the dull drain on her senses and crept forward.

Flames sheeted up the right side of the barn and along the ceiling, feeding on the dry fodder wedged among cracks in the planks overhead, leaving intact only a triangle of floor and stall on her left. She could clear the opening, but how would she ever get Blue back through it? He was fifteen hands of solid gleaming muscle that responded instantly when she signaled him to move—if she was mounted. His manners on the ground were another matter. Getting even a halter on him required an act of Congress. But she would have to try.

Grimly, Jess bent at the waist, threw the blanket over the right side of her face and shoulders, and set herself to run through the white-hot furnace.

She took one giant step...and felt herself grabbed around the waist, from behind. Her feet left the floor.

"What the devil—" She fought the clinging rank-smelling blanket, struggled for footing, losing much of the territory she'd struggled to cover.

"Hold still, dang you!" The command was a throaty drawl heard through the din of the fire and the muffling of the blanket. "Hold still, and we might live through this!"

Fury at being hauled from her goal by a stranger made her struggle violently. She spun, panting, twisted free and stumbled away from the man who held her. She staggered back toward the fire, the blanket forgotten.

He grabbed her wrist, spun her around. "Wildcat," he murmured, and ducked to tuck himself beneath her torso— to lift her like a sack of grain and carry her away! Away from Blue, who would die without her!

"Bastard," she snarled, whipping around, freeing her body but still tethered by the steely grip on her wrist. "Let—me—*go!*"

"Out of your mind with smoke," he said tersely, drawing her to him like a reluctant colt. She found herself flattened against a solid wall of lean man, her breasts pressed into him though she tried to arch away. He brought his other arm around her back, pinning her arms. Moving a strong hand against her hips, he snugged her to him, as if they were lovers instead of combatants. The result was so intimate, so seductive, she instinctively held her breath and looked into his face.

In the winnowing light, she glimpsed tan skin, creases driven into the long plane of his cheek, and the flash of chaff-gold hair. His eyes blazed with blue lights. His gaze raked her in what she knew was innate appreciation for her womanhood, and then challenged her with a silent command to obey. As she looked up at him, measuring his self-assurance, his virility, his dominant nature, rebellion flickered in her.

"Get out of my way. And don't tell me what to do," she said, glaring.

"You'll do as I say. Now."

"Never." She struggled, whipping to and fro.

"We'll see about that."

The arm around her back was sturdy as a new fence post and he tightened it so she could barely breathe. He began to drag her toward the doorway. Precious moments ebbed away while she scrabbled for footing.

The stallion screamed.

"Blue!" she shouted, arching and twisting to look toward the animal's stall. A dancing sheet of yellow-orange flames obscured it. "Damn you, he'll die!"

"You'll die," the stranger growled, inching her from her goal. "You're half-crazy with the smoke."

A coughing seizure bent her against his chest, stalling their progress. It angered her that he was right, she was dizzy, losing strength. . . .

She caught the scent of a breezy cologne in his brown cotton shirt. She liked it, and that angered her more. It revived her battle instincts. He probably used the scent to lure women more easily tamed. He was the rugged, macho type—the kind of man whose physical strength and Heathcliff glower made weak women feel their own weakness was a virtue, a foil to his prowess. It probably kept the other half of his harem coming back to see if they could open up his "gentle side." That he was overpowering her, forcing her to obey him, sent the heat of defiance into her bloodstream, and into her words. She flung back her head and said, "If Blue dies, I *want* to die! Dammit, there's nothing else left!"

His movement checked suddenly. In that brief stillness as he probed her eyes, amber light moved over a work-and-sun-streaked face, putting him at mid-thirties, maybe six, seven years her senior, and brightening the features enough to reveal a look of surprise. He released her.

"Which stall?" he demanded.

She cast a desperate glance over her shoulder. "Last on the left. The mare's in heat."

It wasn't necessary to explain that she'd separated Blue from Sienna to keep the ruckus between them down to a dull roar. The stranger nodded, reached down, came up with the blanket and a tangle of rope. He pushed the rope into her hands. "Let's go."

They turned and moved along the wall. His hand lay lightly along the curve of her back, intuitive, feeling every nuance, every ripple of her work-seasoned body. Something in her wanted to bend to that knowing touch—even as her defiance and Blue's peril eclipsed the thought. She knew instinctively he had ridden horses for years, and felt a foreign relief that he was with her.

As they approached the hot tentacles of flame, he threw the blanket high over his body and tucked Jessica against his left side. He dragged her through the worst of the heat. She heard him curse.

When they reached the half door of Blue's stall, she saw that the wood was split a little. Blue had tried to batter it down. Jessica tried to speak soothingly, but her voice was raw. For an instant the stallion's sleek black muzzle darted through to touch her shoulder. Then the horse was tearing around again, wheezing, kicking, whinnying.

"Halter," the man called, indicating she should grab the headgear from a nearby hook and bring it to him.

"I've got to ride him out!"

Those work-hardened fingers closed around her upper arm. He dragged her close to his chest. "That's insane! Get that rope on him and let's get out of here!"

"I've got to *ride* him, you thickheaded cowboy! He won't go any other way."

"I can handle him!" He snatched the halter from the hook and grabbed the latch to the stall.

Somewhere toward the front of the barn, a support beam crashed. The horse squealed, lunged against the door. The man leapt back as Blue's head barreled out. The gate gave in the middle, splintering, groaning, but it held. Hooves pounded on the wood.

From a long long distance came the shouts of men and metallic thumps as if someone were denting a car door with a shovel. A siren wailed. Jess's brain seemed to have stalled again. She felt a blackness hover. She rubbed her eyes. Frightened of the numbing effects of the smoke, she grabbed the man's arm and hung on.

"Listen," she said thickly. "I tell you, we'll never get Blue out of here unless I'm up on him."

"No time," he said.

"He was abused," she argued. "He's half-wild on the ground. Put that putty you call a brain into gear. Otherwise, we can kiss this rescue goodbye."

His eyes were deep smoky blue. They blazed at her, touching something buried in her, something to do with the battle for dominance between man and woman.

"Damn you," she said. "I know what I'm talking about!"

His gaze held hers for another searching moment, then cleared. "Damn me if you do," he said softly, yielding to her wisdom in this matter of the stallion.

That in itself said he had the greatest wisdom of all. Her heart sprang to him. She unlocked the best part of herself for just this moment and, through her eyes, let him see her respect and gratitude.

He nodded. "Then ride him."

Abruptly he set her free and she staggered. He caught her. A wave of reason swept her. She must hurry.

She fumbled with the lariat, coiled it, loosened the loop. "Get me up on top of the door," she ordered, already finding a grip on the side molding. His hands came up under her bottom. For an instant she knew the man was sensitive to living creatures. Instinctively she knew he was comfortable around women, and wondered if he was as gentle as he was strong. Not that she'd ever let him prove it, one way or the other. It was just the smoke, clogging her brain. She shook her head . . . and found herself balanced precariously on the edge of the stall door. The stranger's hands wrapped around her legs, steadying her.

Disoriented by the smoke and by seeing Jessica above him, Blue stood rigid against the back wall, a black silhouette against stained wood. Jess used scant seconds to cast the loop expertly over his head. It landed in a loose circle around his shoulders. "Perfect," she said. She cinched it tight and the lasso slid up along his gleaming hide 'til it tightened between chiseled head and trim arching throat. She grabbed a handful of wall and held on.

"Don't open this door 'til I yell," was all she had time to say before the stallion reared, squealing in consternation, pulling the line taut.

"Easy," soothed Jessica, wavering until she had her balance. "Blue, stand easy easy easy..."

She gauged his next move. He came down, wheeled along the back of the big enclosure, came up thudding against the side, and cut at an angle toward the half door. She was ready. Blue rammed his chest into the door. In the split instant that his head cleared the doorway, she slid out over withers slick with sweat and found her seat, collecting the rope to keep it out of his churning feet.

The tremendous strength of him, the thing that thrilled her each time she mounted him, soared through her. His body quaked once violently as his fear and wildness came up against human control. As she always did, she felt the war wage instantly, heightened by his terror. He lunged sideways. She jerked the rope and pressed brutally with her knees, willing him to obey. Blue hesitated, quivered, threw his head and quieted.

"Amazing," she breathed. It always was. Jessica smiled grimly and glanced toward the gloom of the barn.

Haze and wavering light outlined the stranger as he worked to free the warped half door.

Shadowed but for the sun mark of his hair, he braced his feet and pried at the wood, his wide shoulders muscling up. He heaved mightily, and the wood began to come apart in his hands. The cowboy was magnificent. Jessica felt a scalding inner response to him, an attraction so powerful, it jolted away the fear and filled her with a sweet, throbbing ache. But it was brief; the purely sexual reaction faded as Blue danced, commanding her attention. The man swung out of sight.

Sidling, the stallion edged toward the door, fighting the commands to obey what Jess urged through her legs and the angle of her body. Jess sat deep, trying to gain in a few seconds that edge of control over the finely trained young horse that would let her guide him through the fire. But the man, how would he get out? Could she leave him?

Damned right, her cynical side urged. Nobody had asked him to come in and foul up her plans to save Blue. Yet she might not have done it alone. And there was that moment when it had felt as if their souls had connected.

"Dammit to hell," she swore softly. Tricky at best, getting him up behind her, but she would try.

She saw firelight jag along the broken door. He'd manhandled it apart and was stepping back. Blue saw the opening, too, and started for it. She hauled on the rope and wrenched her body, feeling pride nick into her fear when the big animal obeyed, backing away. "Climb on top of the door," she ordered in a raw voice. "Ride shotgun!"

"Sounds like a plan," came the reply.

The hinges of the gate creaked, Blue backed and snorted, and then the beaten wood wobbled as the stranger climbed topside.

"You've got one chance and no guarantee," Jessica called. He nodded.

Coughing racked her; Blue crab-stepped; she fought to keep control.

"Ease him over," the man said.

She straightened. "Don't you think I'm trying? He's dancing like I put hot steel under him. Easy, Blue. Go her easy..."

Using leg commands that were jerky at best, Jess urged the animal toward the heat and the big-shouldered form hulking above them. By sheer force of will, she eased Blue past him. As she and the horse squeezed through the opening, she felt the jagged wood rip through her jeans. At the same time, the stranger's hands ran down along her shoulders, until they slid past her waist and tangled in her glossy mane. His hips snugged against her.

Then Blue bolted. Jess fell against the solid curve of the man's embrace and felt him cradle her, anchoring them both by his grip on the mane and his natural ability to sit a horse.

A few yards into his run, a smoking, red-stippled beam swung toward them and Blue planted his feet, sank to his haunches and threw his head. Solid bone struck Jess on her chin. Lightning flashed through her brain. She fought to stay conscious.

"Get a run at it," the rider behind her said against her ear.

On autopilot, she pressed with her knees.

The horse sidestepped, eyed the burning timbers littering the middle of the barn, and stood quivering, snorting ceaselessly. Jess hunched forward and kicked Blue with all her might. He veered, sinking his haunches into a spin that would win the world if he was working a rank heifer in the cutting arena. He cut to the back wall.

"Hellfire," the cowboy cursed, squirming to keep his seat.

"Damned right!" Jessica hauled on the rope, kicked viciously and sent Blue down the barn. She could feel him fighting her lead, beginning to bunch for another spin. Jess dug in her boot heels and screamed, "Go, Blue, go, *go!*"

Something primal between her and the animal connected. He lunged forward.

The sharp bite of flames. The sear of burning cotton on her shoulder. A girth of human support tightened around her waist. Powerful quarter-horse muscles honed by thousands of dips and turns and spins gathered beneath Jessica . . . sending that leap of adrenaline through her that always came with a good ride. Then they cleared the sill of the barn door.

Lights blinded her. The siren's wail seemed inches from her left ear, and a powerful engine smothered the shouts of men. Something wet splashed against her face, shoving a sliver of hope down into Jessica's brain: the barn . . . could it be saved?

The wail of the siren faded with the madness around the barn as Jess and the stranger and the horse sped through a zebra hide of light and dark. The bungalow shared by Josepha and Noa clung like a white moth to the foothills and the shadows of the main house. Yellow light framed the long veranda of the ranch house and branded the trunks of a stand of cypress, plumed tops arching toward stars and a wedge of moon. To their right, the sagging planks of the work ring flew by, and they swept around the end corral in a right turn.

The stallion thundered along the strip of dry grass edging the access road, hugging the broken fence of the foaling paddock where Jessica's father used to lean on the wood and relive his world-champion wins aboard some of the finest cutting stock in the country.

There in the paddock and among the hills behind the ranch, and in the hundreds of cutting shows in her youth, Jessica had dreamed the cutter's dream. She had dreamed of the fortune and glory that would be hers one day, as it had been her father's.

The dream was bound up with the old cowboy's memory of the past and his austere but helping hand, and made stronger for it. The fields were empty, but that fact had galvanized her intent. She meant to preserve what was left of her legacy, filling the paddock with the finest mares and foals the modern-day cutting industry had ever seen. Blue was the key to it all.

As the stallion slowed to a lope, Jess and the man behind her sucked in the sage-sweet, apple-crisp air, easing their lungs. Jessica coughed a last time. Her mind cleared, and she smiled. She and Blue had survived. God above, they had a future!

In ringing joy she embraced the movement of the horse, the moonlit path, the warmth at her back. Her knight in jeans and boots sat loose and easy—a natural horseman.

The rhythm of their bodies rising, falling, undulating in unison began to feel sensuous, reminding Jess of the years when she'd been free to explore intimacy, commitment, love—years when she had been exiled from the ranch, her dream lost. Then, since her father's death last summer, there had been no time, no opportunity to pursue romance.

It was just as well. She'd be forever grateful to this man because he'd helped her preserve her chance at glory. But acting on the powerful attraction she felt for him would surely cloud her mind, keep her from her goal. So she classified him as both dangerous and off-limits, and reined Blue toward the barn.

They'd gone halfway back at a slow lope when the man behind her murmured something.

She canted to him. "What?"

"Your stud's favoring his left fore . . . better have a look-see."

Alarmed, scolding herself for the unusual lack of attention to her mount, Jess sat deep and tugged on the rope.

Blue checked his stride and sat on his haunches. He tucked his head and stood still, snorting to catch his wind.

"Stay up, will you?" she asked the man, slipping to the ground. "Otherwise, we'll have a devil of a time mounting again."

"Enigma."

"Who?"

"This stud. The only animals I know that stop and turn like this one does, with little or no help from the rider, are cutting or fine-toned horses."

His voice sounded as if it hailed from the bottom of a canyon—it was half-lazy and deep. His words gave her a nudge of pride.

"He cuts some," she admitted.

"That's what I thought."

She ran her palms over Blue's wide, heaving chest, feeling through the wet lather to the hide, frowning at the scratches he'd gotten against the gate of his stall. He backed away, sidestepped, but let her check him out. "He's everything to me," she murmured.

"I can see that, ma'am."

He used the common courtesy of the ranching business. On his lips, it sounded like an endearment, and Jess grew wary, fell silent.

She tried to put her fingers between the V-shaped bones under Blue's muzzle to check his pulse, but the horse threw his head, pulling away. She got one hand over his nostrils, tugged him down and finally got it. Considering the stress he'd been through tonight, the pulse rate was good. His roadwork was paying off.

"Cutting horses being the most finely tuned horses in the world," the man continued, "it hardly adds up that he's green on the ground. Does it?"

His assessment of Blue's ground manners irritated her. "He was abused as a child," she said dryly, no trace of a smile.

"A shame. You rescue him from his bad daddy?"

The moon wasn't bright enough to show whether he was serious or joshing her. "Yes," she said, giving him the benefit of the doubt. "I threatened to call the Humane Society. The guy went and got Blue's registration papers on the spot. Said he won Blue and some land and other stock in a poker game, didn't care about him one way or the other. Later I called the Humane Society anyway. Hanging's too good for that jerk, what he did to his animals."

"Were you abused, too, ma'am?" The question was soft.

What she'd suffered was life's typical hardships and sorrows, no more nor less than anybody else, but that was her business. "No," she said. "Besides, Blue is—" She bent, ran her hands down the stallion's left foreleg. He picked up the foot. "Easy, Blue. He's gashed on his shin," she concluded. "But not serious. I'll just check the rest of him and then we'd better give the guys a hand with the barn."

"'Besides, Blue is' what?" he prompted.

"Besides, Blue comes from stock that are either brilliant at cutting cattle from the herd, or wild as hayseed and too ornery to train. No in-between." Blue craned around and blew warm hay breath in her face. He nuzzled her a moment. Strangely contented, Blue lowered his muzzle to rustle among the dry grasses.

"Fine-looking stud. Has he showed any cow sense?"

"Yes…" Oh, God, yes, she thought, filled with pride and hope. She felt under the damp belly and down along Blue's muscled hindquarters. He danced some, and she slapped his rump affectionately. "He's got more potential cow sense than any cutting horse I've ever known. He and I are going to whip the pants off those futurity boys in Texas come December, God willing. Then we're going to come back here and get some colts out of my mare and any other comers whose owners will pay the stud fee. Blue'll get colts that'll show the rest of the industry what real cow sense is, what a real breeding stallion is all about. Blue and I are planning—"

She stopped abruptly, head angled toward the barn. Smoke curled above the lights. She couldn't see any flame, but fire was deceptive that way. "Lord Almighty! The barn's burning and I'm standing here chewing my cud. Give me a hoist up."

"Just gettin' your wits back," he chuckled, pulling her up along a thigh as muscled-up as a stock horse. Before she could dwell on the quick thrill it gave her, he was helping her get a leg over. Blue came to attention, his ears turned back to listen for orders. "State you were in," the man said, "you wouldn't have been a drop of help to Britton and the boys."

The remark was made more irritating by his slow drawl, but she wasted no time arguing. Collecting the rope, she urged Blue toward the barnyard.

Her companion snugged himself against her tighter than before, seeming to encourage the undulating roll of their bodies. Jessica, who'd been focusing on work for too long, began to feel a lethargy in her hips, a sweet ache. He wrapped himself like a second skin around her, and her face flamed with a heat that had no connection to a burning barn or the healthy blush of exercise.

Without at first realizing it, she attuned to him, relaxing her hips, feeling the brush of the wind through her hair as if it were the caress of his fingers and all the nerve endings were aroused. A dampness accompanied the dullish ache between her thighs, and when she adjusted more closely to her companion in an instinctive act to relieve the ache, her brain tried to clang a warning. Still overloaded with the life-and-death struggle she'd survived, the synapses did not fire properly. She did not pull away. But one bit of wisdom filtered in: Oddly and suddenly, she and the stranger had bonded. It was a purely sexual connection, and though reason fought for control, for a few heartbeats, female libido ruled, and she reveled in the intimacy as a woman would in the touch of a long-beloved mate.

That isolated part of her brain still struggling toward reason tried to warn her again.

Be shocked, it tried to say. *This man is a stranger—a macho, bossy cowboy who is everything you've avoided in relationships with men. Pay attention to what's happening!*

She straightened slightly. A coolness slivered between their bodies like an ice shield, and reason returned.

She'd heard that a brush with death could make you turn toward the life-affirming connection of making love. Now she knew it was true, and she plucked a scrap of humor from beneath her jumbled emotions, and laughed aloud.

He pressed his face into her hair and said in a low voice, "What's so funny?"

"Us," she responded, feeling a jet of longing at his intimacy. "Blue! The night! We're alive. Isn't it wonderful?"

She heard him chuckle softly.

She liked the sound. Surely it meant he had a gentle side, a side that meant he could be not ruler but partner to a woman. She wondered if, after she'd attained success in the cutting world, they might find some time to get to know one another.

Then they were approaching the glare of headlights from five or six pickups and a red fire truck, whose idling engine roared into the confusion of men and equipment.

Jessica shook herself mentally and inventoried the scene. Neighbors stood watching as men in yellow fire gear hosed down the roof of the barn; another group wearing gas masks sprayed water into the smoldering interior. A ladder lay against the siding. Workers were hacking with axes and a hooked pole at the solid old timbers of the roof. No flames licked at the wood. They've saved it, she thought in relief.

And then she saw the blackened shell of the horse trailer.

Oh, no, she moaned in silent distress. Automatically she stopped Blue, bracing against the man as her horse dug in at the edge of the lights. The trailer was supposed to get Blue to the futurity and Sienna to all the local shows until then. Jessica's shoulders slumped.

The stranger peered around her. "Now what is it?" he asked, the soft drawl caressing her.

"The trailer."

"Looks like a total loss."

"I paid cash for it," she said woodenly.

"Insurance?"

"No, dammit."

"You never figured anything would happen, did you?"

Wary of the empathy, the gentleness, now that she had command of herself again, she shook her head.

"It looks like it was new," he said.

"Practically was."

"That the only one you have?"

She threw him a brittle look. "Does this ranch look like it could afford *two* like that one?"

There was a small silence. "No, ma'am, I reckon not," he said stiffly. "You could throw a coat of paint on it, a couple of retreads. Wouldn't be the first makeshift caboose a horse called home."

She grimaced. "At least I didn't lose the barn. Maybe my luck's still holding." But she knew there would be no saving the trailer.

She nudged Blue and he jumped and dug in, covering the distance across the yard.

Ranchers stood with hands on hips or lounging against the trucks, talking, smoking cigarettes, shifting their Stetson hats in dismay. A barn fire was a horseman's worst nightmare.

Hearing the thud of Blue's hooves, most of the men turned, walked a few feet into the barnyard. The mare whinnied from behind the pipe rails at the far end of the workout ring; someone had put her up.

Jessica pulled in and dismounted before the stranger could hand her down. She heard his boots hit the dirt, his low voice acknowledge some of the boys. She heard the respect they paid him.

Back to priorities, she stepped to a barrel-chested man with his paunch cinched tight over skinny legs and no rear end.

"Britton," she nodded, her tone stiff so the gratitude wouldn't show too much. These men admired strength. They expected it from her. She ran the rope through her hands. "Appreciate you all coming. I mean it—thanks. Everyone all right? Who's in charge of the fire crew?"

Hallelujah Britton tipped back a straw hat so twigs of gray hair stuck out, and jabbed a thumb toward the glare of the fire truck's lights. "Fella with the clipboard and the busy expression. 'Bout got the worse of it out already. Good crew. Nobody hurt. Say, Jess..."

"Hal?"

"Damned shame, is all. Bright side of the matter is, at least this didn't happen to your daddy in his prime. You'd 'a lost a passel 'a stock. Barn woulda' been worse 'n the L.A. freeway at rush hour. It's certain you'd 'a lost some horses—"

"Yes," she cut in, sensitive to the fact that these men felt running a ranch was man's work, and few men could come close to her late father in ability. "Yes, nobody hurt, no horses lost. I was lucky."

Except how was she going to get Blue to the futurity or the mare to the local shows without a trailer, and no money to buy another? And her tack probably wiped out. An adequate cutting saddle cost a thousand dollars, used.

"Lookin' on the bright side," Hal reminded her, squinting in concern.

She touched the sleeve of his worn denim jacket. "The bright side, Hal..." She stepped in the direction of the work ring where she'd doctor Blue before getting tied up with the fire marshal's report.

"Damned shame your brother don't fancy workin' a ranch," Hal said. "Give you a hand, put some life back into the old place."

She halted. Slowly she turned to the sage old rancher she'd known all her life. She flashed a look at the tanned faces grouped behind Hal, saw their agreement and then said flatly, "Hal, I appreciate you all coming tonight, but I don't need anybody to wet-nurse me here. I don't take it well, your suggesting I do."

"Sorry, Jess. I just know the work involved." His eyes gave her an apology, but his chin jutted. "Here, give me that sorry excuse you call a cuttin' hoss and I'll put him in the ring. What's the matter with him, anyway? He's behavin' himself. Fire take the edge off his personality?"

Softening toward him, she grinned, shook her head, handing him the coil of rope. Blue's head bounced and he crow-hopped against a cowboy, who cursed under his breath and moved out of the way. "He's just being polite because I've had a rough night, Hal. You have any ointment and bandages in that box in your truck?"

"Yep."

"Mine's in the barn. Blue's left foreleg is gashed. Scratch or two on his chest, too."

"I'll see to it, Jess. Fire marshal'll want to have a word with you."

"Thanks. Oh—" Her eyes gleamed. "Better keep out of Blue's way when you're bringing him through the gate. Spirited animal like him can't keep his personality under wraps for long no matter what his good intentions."

Hal Britton used the rope to scratch his jaw. Eyes slitted under a prickly brush of brows, he said, "The two 'a you are bound to give them futurity boys jawin' material to last a lifetime. Mark my words."

"I've never known you to be wrong about anything, Hal. Hear that, Blue—" she bent toward the horse "—we're going into the entertainment business."

Blue flicked his ears forward. A few of the boys whistled and laughed. Blue danced, stretching the rope to the limit of Hal's grip. More or less in control of the animal, Hal headed for the ring, saying gruffly over his shoulder, "Ed, bring me that medicine box and a stud chain and a flashlight."

The young ranch hand moved off.

A sheriff's car came down the access road. Maybe he'd find out how the fire started, Jess thought. Spontaneous combustion? Arson? But why, what motive? She was a rancher who kept to herself, a woman who had no enemies and only a handful of friends—decent men and women who worked the ranches. She refused to believe one of them would try to ruin her. Who, then?

Jessica's gaze skimmed to the stranger standing a head taller behind the other men. He was the only one in the group she'd never met before. Would he have sabotaged her operation and then covered his tracks by risking his life to save her and her horses?

She dismissed the wild notion. What would he stand to gain from hurting her? He was probably a new wrangler at one of the nearby ranches, told to come running when his boss said there was a fire. Yet something about the way he stood quietly talking to one of the men suggested boss, not worker. There was a casual pride in his carriage, an ease, with that thumb hooked into his back pocket and his legs braced so his rear curved in enticing lines. Who was he? She owed him thanks, but who would she be thanking?

The cowboy turned to look at her, and the character in his face riveted her. Beneath the chaff-gold hair, the tan skin bore deep slashes, weather-marks, angling up long flat high-boned cheeks. Crow's-feet radiated from eyes that shone aquamarine blue in the bright glare of the trucks. There was intimacy in the look they exchanged, and she quickly nodded to him.

Maybe more personal thanks ought to wait.

She was turning away when he stepped toward her, setting off a flock of hummingbirds in her midsection, staying her. "Miz Latham," he drawled, moving through the men until he stood looking down at her. She wanted to look away and couldn't. "Sleet Freeman," he said. "Just wanted to say—it's tough, what you've been through. The boy's 'n I'll give you a hand when we can."

"Thanks, but that's not necessary—" her eyes widened "—Sleet, did you say? Sleet Freeman?"

"That's right."

She swallowed on a suddenly dry throat. Knowing the reputation of the man who'd risked his life to help her and now stood politely introducing himself and offering to be neighborly, she felt threatened. "Hal hired *you* to train his horses?"

"Why, yes, ma'am, on a temporary basis."

She glanced toward the fire truck, the arriving sheriff's car, knowing she should go to them but reluctant to leave Sleet Freeman to wander as he pleased on her domain. He would see the ratty condition of the buildings, the falling fences, the pitifully small herd of cattle she wore to a frazzle training Blue to cut cows. He would know the once-famed Latham Ranch was half its original size, and had none of its former glory. He would also know, because she had bragged about it not twenty minutes ago, that the person who was going to attempt to unseat him from his world title in December was the owner of a hayseed operation that couldn't even afford to repair its burned barn. The shame of her situation flamed in her cheeks.

Thank God he was facing the lights and couldn't see her embarrassment. It was a small comfort.

"I'd heard a top-notch trainer was coming to the Britton Ranch," she said, turning back to him. She smiled, though the smile died before it reached her eyes. "Congratulations on your win last year, Sleet. I've been out of the world-ranked cutting racket for several years, but not so far out I don't know the world champion when I hear his name."

"Heck, a lot of it was luck." He ran a hand through his ash-blond hair. "I drew pretty chipper cows, and Checkers is a willing little mare."

Her eyes glowed for a moment with the imagined thrill and challenge of the national show. "You're being humble, of course."

"Oh, I don't know, Miz Latham. Training and conditioning count for a lot, but if you don't draw good cows, why…" Evidently sidetracked, he trailed off. His smile went from wry to speculative. "I take it you don't hold it against me, my stepping temporarily into your territory?"

"My territory?"

"You said you hope to win the futurity this year. Hal mentioned you plan to set up shop as a trainer." He gave a shrug that trailed off into the very possibility she'd just been concerned about.

Was he being arrogant, tossing down a gauntlet? Or was she being paranoid? Under the circumstances, the smart thing to do was think the worst and be forewarned.

"As to my 'territory,' as you call it," she said, "until I win the world, I don't have any territory to protect yet, do I?"

He gave her an indulgent smile—a smile that said, Aren't we the feisty little lady?

"Since you put it that way," he said. "Well—" he dipped his head in farewell "—I'd better give the boys a hand with the colt, then. Don't want one of them to get hurt while I'm pleasurin' myself talkin' to a fine-lookin' woman. My respects, ma'am."

Respects, my foot, she thought. He loved dangling his reputation in front of her nose. He wanted her to feel threatened.

Her competitive spirit burst into life. "Mr. Freeman," she called, gesturing. "Are you, that is, will you be competing this year at the futurity?"

He stopped a few paces away, squinted at her, the edge of his smile deepening the grooves in his cheeks. "Why, yes, ma'am, I will. I trained some colts this year in Texas and I'm working a couple more at Hal's place. I'll be up on one or two of them, sure enough. Better see to your shoulder, ma'am. Looks pretty sore."

She angled a look at her charred sleeve without registering a thing. When she looked up again, Sleet Freeman was walking with an easy confidence toward the cutting ring. Her cutting ring, her prize cutting horse, her hopes.

She wanted to run after him, whirl him around and slap his face. She wanted to throw him off her ranch. She could do none of those things. The men would see her weakness and judge her for it. So she clenched her hands and strode toward the arriving sheriff's car, worrying the edges of a new fear: How badly would Sleet Freeman cut into her chances to save the ranch?

Chapter Two

Sleet could see she was going to be a lot to handle, right off. Not in the professional sense—he'd never met the woman who could outride him in the cutting arena or on the trail. He was thinking strictly in personal terms. In the first two or three minutes they'd been together, in the barn, Jess had given him more sass than all the women he'd ever known rolled into one.

That didn't lessen the pleasure he was going to take in going up to the house and asking her out on their first date. It heightened it.

Meanwhile, Hal went up to have coffee with her and report on Blue's minor injuries, and Sleet delayed his departure with a project. It gave the two old friends time to commiserate over the losses Jess had suffered tonight. He was glad his boss had gone to her first. He didn't want a weepy woman on his hands when he asked her out; he wanted a woman humbled by a close brush with death, perhaps beholden to him for helping her save the thing she held above life itself—her stallion.

As Sleet led the bay mare into the barnyard, en route to the paddock, the other men were breaking up a jawing session near their trucks.

"Hey, Freeman," called a thickset cutter named Charlie. "You showing this weekend in Riverside?"

"Yeah. You?"

"Guess I will. You need a hand with that mare or anything?"

"I've got it handled, thanks. See y'all on Saturday."

They drifted to the trucks, powered them up and drove off the ranch.

When the dust had cleared, Sleet grabbed a flashlight from the seat of his pickup and walked the mare toward the paddock, thinking about the stud colt and Jessica Latham. Fine stallion; fine, fine woman. Two of a kind. Brute force would break their spirits, he knew instinctively. You had to judge them by what was in their hearts, trust what was wise in them, and ease them into the rest, politely but firmly.

The purely male side of him felt challenged by her, like his trainer side was by the young colt. She was the most strong-willed, sexy, courageous woman he'd ever run across. She was the kind of woman you courted, broke gentle and respected. Why, you could take a woman to bed and still show her respect, he mused.

The steady clop-clop of the mare's hooves on sun-baked hard-pack was comforting to him, familiar, and he let his fantasies of Jess ripen.

He went back to those moments when the two of them had rocked together at a canter, rising and falling like the wind in prairie grass. She rose and settled with the grace of a bird, fitting his embrace with heat and softness and feminine curves. When he buried his face in her black, swirling hair, he was breathing the scent of a real woman. When he looked into her eyes, he saw the early squalls of a passionate storm. He could swear, remembering, that she'd responded to him as a woman responds to her lover, and he wanted that feeling again.

He hoped she liked country music. He planned to take her dancing. Anybody who rode like she did would have a natural rhythm at his other favorite pastime.

Sleet had no doubt at all he'd gentle her. He wouldn't be moving on 'til after the national futurity, and that was nearly three months away—all the time it took to break a hot-blooded colt.

ABOUT TWO HUNDRED FEET down the side of the paddock, the top rail of the fence was down. As he played his light over the break, Sleet shook his head. The whole damned place was run-down. It screamed like a newspaper headline that Jessica Latham didn't have a man in her life. No mate worth his salt would let a woman face such staggering work alone, or let things get so far gone.

He felt sorry for her, and eager to step in, temporarily, to give her a hand. A woman liked a man handy with his hands, he thought, tying the mare to the rails and hiking back to his truck to get a hammer and some nails. More than a few times, his willingness to do a few chores had led straight to the bedroom and the fair maiden's waiting, grateful arms. Sleet congratulated himself. His social plans were beginning to take shape.

He found a blackened pine board near the barn, one of those ripped away by the fire crew so they could hose water onto the support timbers. The air near the barn smelled charred, deathlike. It gave Sleet the heebie-jeebies. He hurried back to the paddock, where the breeze brought him the lusty scents of dry grass and loam, and nailed the board between the two halves of the broken rail.

"That ought to keep you in," he told the mare, bringing her to the gate, slapping her on the rump as she trotted into the field. She nickered and began to nuzzle the chaff. He hung the lead rope on the gate latch where it could be found.

As he rinsed his hands and face at the water hose, he thought about how she'd react to him. She'd probably had time to realize she could have died tonight. Hal had spent quite a while with her. Maybe she was badly shaken, humbled, even vulnerable. He'd be doing her a favor, offering her a distraction, a night out on the town.

The matter reasoned with, he pushed his hands down his jeans to dry them, and ducked into the truck to get his gray Stetson. He snugged it down over his hair and glanced in the side-view mirror. Tipped it lower. The hat perked up his confidence.

Crossing the quarter-acre between house and barn, he gained the porch and knocked on the screen door.

"Evenin', ma'am," he said when she opened the inner door and the screen. "Just stopped by to—" And then he got a good look at Jessica Latham, and words failed him.

She wore self-possession like a robe of royalty. She was staring at him, perhaps slightly curious but very, very reserved. How had he ever imagined she'd be vulnerable?

He would have preferred her tears. They would have given him an excuse to pull her close and feel the softness promised by the teal-blue lamb's wool sweater and faded jeans she wore over that incredible body.

She was slightly built, with generous breasts and a tiny waist nipped in above gently rounded hips and slender legs. Her eyes were blue-green like her sweater, large and full of wisdom like the women in Mexican velvet paintings, yet as keenly watchful as a hunting hawk. And just to finish off a picture already etched into his memory because of its singular beauty—her black hair, gleaming with blue lights and still slightly damp at the ends from bathing, cascaded in thick endless waves around her shoulders. A man could get lost in all that luxury... if he could get past her invincibility.

He wanted to see a vulnerable, grateful woman, not this regal-looking landowner standing ramrod straight, gilded in lamplight, her chin tilted at him.

"Yes, Mr. Freeman?" she asked, probing for the reason for his visit.

"I see you've recovered from your ordeal," he said, grazing her curves with his hungry gaze.

Her eyes gleamed with challenge. "Did you think I would be crushed to pieces by a little old fire?" she asked. "If so, you're mistaken, Mr. Freeman. Flint doesn't burn. It chips to a fine cutting edge."

The horse trainer/wanderer, rawhide tough and confident to a fault, cocksure of his appeal to the many women who had preceded her, began to wonder who would gentle whom, this time around.

JESSICA'S EXHAUSTION, released by the hot shower and deepened in the quiet time after Hal's visit, now fled completely. The sight of the rugged cowboy framed in her doorway—and the knowledge of his commanding masculinity—made her tilt her chin and spar with him.

He could not see the inner, devastating impact of his presence. The memory of his courage, his sudden capitulation to her goal to save the stallion, the frightening magnetism of his gaze and his tall, rough-hewn body—these were secrets she contained by forcing them deep into her heart, where they vibrated like golden wasps caught in a net. She felt the vibrations and ignored them, letting the image of flint bore like a sting into his confidence.

For a long moment he stood still as a cast bronze. Then he said, "Flint breaks, Miz Latham. It can be chipped to smithereens. As to your cutting edge, I presume you meant against me. I'll take on any comers, any day." He rubbed an arm languidly and smiled. "I'm always glad of the chance to prove my mettle. Even against you."

She remained stoic. "Is that praise or insult, Mr. Freeman?"

"Neither, Miz. Latham." He glanced over his shoulder toward the arena, showing her the graceful curve of his Stetson and a slice of firm jaw. He hooked a thumb in his back pocket and swung back to her. He let his gaze savor the sweater she wore before returning to face her. "I wasn't speaking professionally."

Her pulse tripled its already heady pace.

"Your womanly charms are...formidable," he said, and her legs went a little weak.

He was wooing her. That she was falling for it sent anger sizzling beneath her weakening self-control. If she did not owe him so much, she would tell him to take his dance-hall sweet nothings and his apple-hard butt the hell off her ranch, and offer them to some poor woman who was hard-up enough to appreciate them. Instead she curled her fingers into a ball, controlled her breathing, and gave him a stony unyielding stare.

"I regret you weren't speaking professionally," she said, levelly. "It's the only area open to discussion."

"That's disappointing."

"I'm sorry for you."

"Oh, don't be, Miz Latham," he returned casually. He inspected a tiny scrape on one knuckle, then grinned at her. "The bigger the challenge, the stronger my resolve."

Smiling in leonine pride, he dragged his hat from his head. Lamp glow from the porch filled his hair with white-gold threads. Moisture gleamed in the stubble of a pale beard. Rim lighting accented the high bones and the long grooves of his cheeks, and it ruddied his generous mouth. Jess's own resolve faltered; she caught her breath.

His gaze flicked to her mouth and held. "Now, if memory serves," he drawled with maddening charm, "your daddy was a fine-mannered man as well as a world champion in his own right. Did you inherit his manners, or turn out to be wild hayseed like that stud of yours?" The smile turned teasing but it was laced with sexual come-on.

Thank the man and say good-night, she commanded herself. This was madness.

"Would you like a cup of coffee?" she found herself asking, lifting her hair away from her neck in an unconscious gesture to cool the heat of his gaze.

Sleet followed the gesture, then locked his eyes with hers. Her breath began to shallow out. Her breasts lifted, fell; the wasps began to escape their delicate net.

"Aren't we a pair," she murmured wryly, to lighten the moment. "Something stronger than coffee? I think there's a bottle of Jack Daniel's in the cupboard. My dad used to have a shot of it after what he called 'a killer day.'"

"That being?"

"A difficult foaling or a good workout with the colts."

"I guess a barn fire qualifies," he said.

"Yes. Yes, I guess it does."

"Coffee'll be fine, ma'am. I'm obliged."

Then it was too late to send him on his way. "Jess," she corrected in a resigned tone, stepping aside to let him in.

"Call me Sleet," he murmured, walking into the living room and looking around with keen interest.

Instantly she regretted it. The fact that he filled the large room so completely, his masculine presence radiating out to every corner, made temporary escape urgently necessary. "Hat rack on the wall across the room," she said, walking away. "Be comfortable. Throw a chunk of wood on the fire if you're chilled. I'll get the coffee."

She turned and hurried across the braided rug, past the huge fieldstone fireplace with its glowing coals, into the hall that forked left toward the dining room and kitchen, and right toward the bedrooms—every step away from him building back her normal self-containment.

Lord Almighty! she thought, the man was positively spellbinding. She knew what his arms felt like around her, what his physical magnetism did to her when she was snuggled against his hips. But to look into his eyes when nothing else was distracting her—well, she just couldn't do it anymore, that was all. Then there was that canyon-low voice and the gentle way he called her "ma'am." It ate right into her heart. Opened her right up. She lost herself in Sleet Freeman, and that wasn't even remotely smart.

Not if she wanted to win the world. To be the best in the world at anything, you had to be brutally, selfishly focused on your goal, striving toward it with every cell of your being. That's what her father had said, and nothing he'd ever done when he was winning world championships had taught her any different. With the cursory check she'd made of the barn, feed and tack, the loss of the horse trailer, it was going to be nothing short of a miracle to pull off that win. One more derailment, even a slight one, could cost her everything—the ranch, Blue and Sienna, the Latham name, her dreams.

And Sleet, with his Marlboro Man looks and his manly ways, was standing in her living room, promising to be the derailment of a lifetime. He was her competition. For crying out loud, he was the enemy!

Determined to stop the distraction before it crushed her chances to win, she gathered cream, sugar, chocolate-chip cookies and the coffees on a tray, and vowed to get him out of the house as quickly as possible. She strode back into the living room, her face a mask of self-confidence.

When she saw him, despite her intentions, she stopped and stared.

The fire was blazing and Sleet was curved above it, his back to her, warming his hands. His physical strength was like a magnet to her; the firelight outlined his wide shoulders and lean hips, and it gilded his blond hair. She'd always admired fine muscle tone. It was what you strove for in equine champions. Coupled with attractive—no, ruggedly handsome—features, he was a real challenge to her determination.

Evidently he sensed her looking at him. He angled around and grinned. "I didn't realize I was cold. Fire feels good."

She made herself look away from him, say coolly, "The coffee will help, too."

The immense, carved coffee table and the oxblood leather couch were as old as she was and somehow comforting. Sliding the tray to the table, she set out napkins, steaming cups, the plate of cookies.

"I put the mare in the paddock," he said. "Figured you'd want her away from the colt."

Inwardly, she bridled at his meddling. But she owed him that courtesy he'd dragged out of her. She owed him more, but she couldn't give it.

"I nailed a board to the break down past the gate."

"You needn't have done that," she said sharply. Then, realizing her tone was rude, she tempered the abrasion, softened it. "She'll be out by morning anyway. South corner is down."

"Hell," he said in dismay. "Where do you want her, then?"

"Oh, for goodness' sakes, Sleet," she said, exasperated. "I turn her loose in the yard sometimes just to have her around. She's like an old dog. You can't get rid of her. And I don't need the help you seem bent on giving!"

He stilled. Wiping his mouth, he stared at her. "Jesus," he said. "You are a cactus ball. I'm trying my damnedest to be neighborly."

"You're trying your damnedest to be a lot more than that!" She turned her back on him, bit her lip, exhaled. "I don't mean to be rude," she amended, regretting the personal note she'd blurted into the conversation. "I just don't . . . want that."

He came to her, touched her arm. She eased away. "Don't want what?" he asked softly. Again he touched her, and this time, it was a delicate caress. Her eyelids trembled downward; her knees went a little numb.

"It's getting late," she said, bringing her hands up to rub her arms. "I have an early day tomorrow."

"Would you like to have some supper and go dancing one night?" he asked.

Her heart bolted, running wild. The moment was already too intimate to be angry. She could only maintain the polite facade, and strive for a level tone. "Sleet, I—don't really have the time. Thank you anyway."

She glanced up at him. He saw through the facade. He gave her a look that was half lazy lion and half predator. "You can't work cattle at night."

She looked away. "I read at night."

"Read what?"

"Carpentry books, plumbing, fix-it kinds of things. I've shored up the dowels in the kitchen chairs. I've learned how to take apart the sink when it's stopped up or I've lost something down it. That kind of thing."

His eyes cut to the distant wall and the big rolltop desk by one of the front windows. It was piled high with how-to books, bills, backlogged correspondence. She felt revealed.

"You don't have anyone helping you keep things up?" he asked.

"I've got the best stockman in southern California. Noa's good with the horses and cattle and that's all I care about." She didn't tell him he wasn't too handy with a saw or a crescent wrench, or that there was no money for wood, paint or new plumbing. "His wife, Josepha, cooks for us and does the housekeeping," she added, to bolster her fortress. "They'll be back from Mexico tomorrow night or the next."

"And your brother? He doesn't like ranching?"

"Josh is married to a woman who's allergic to animal hair, and he's devoted to her. He has a professorship in chemical engineering. That's his life. This is mine."

If he was going to do the "little woman" routine, she would draw blood.

He didn't continue that vein. He said, "You have to get away from it once in a while or it'll kill your spirit."

He was showing his colors. She lunged at the flag. "I imagine you're an expert at that."

Instead of taking umbrage at her accusation, he said, "Bull's-eye. I'm a long ways from the farm where I was raised."

His honesty took her off guard. "Where?" she asked, curious.

"Missouri."

"Why'd you leave?"

He frowned. "Why do you want to know?"

So he was vulnerable there. She logged in the news. "You make it sound like a big deal. It's not." She shrugged, maintaining an offhand mood. "My daddy did teach me a few manners, Sleet. Or Josepha did, more accurately. I'm simply being polite. If you're uncomfortable discussing why you left..."

It was pure sarcasm and he ignored it. "I had to leave," he said in a flat voice.

He paced to the fire, set his mug on the massive rose granite mantle. For a moment he studied a portrait of Jess and her father and Josh, taken during her senior year in high school, when Josh had visited from college. "What are you afraid of, Jess?"

She stiffened. "What kind of remark is that?"

He turned, gave her that commanding look he did so well. "Answer me," he said softly.

The hair on the back of her neck prickled. "How dare you ask?"

"I dare because we're attracted. I'll admit it. Why won't you?"

"Dammit," she exploded, fisting her hands. "You're out of line. Way out."

He came back and stood before her. She felt very threatened, but she angled her chin and gave him her iciest glare. He spoke very low, so she could barely hear. "Angry looks good on you, Jess. Damned good."

It heightened the tension between them.

"Look," she snapped, stepping backward. "You may know when to rein your horse away from a dull cow but you don't know when to quit with me. Cut the macho moves, cowboy. I'm not interested."

Suddenly he was angry. His lips tightened. A smolder came to his eyes. He was close enough that she could see the stubble on his chin, and smell the breezy scent he wore. He was close enough that she knew she'd made a serious mistake.

She began to back away, but he grasped her arms and brought her up against him. It was rough treatment made erotic by an equal measure of sexual desire. He realized it the moment she did, and she saw the shift in his expression.

Her heart lifted as it had before and fell into a thousand shimmering shards. "Sleet," she breathed, pleaded.

"Damn, Jess," he muttered.

He lowered his head, and his mouth caressed her lips so suddenly, with such insistent, velvet command, that she gave in to him instantly, gave in to the kiss, to his dominance and incredible timing. It was madness again, madness, and when she understood what she was giving up, she struggled. He pinioned her arms with his own and she tried to free her mouth but he would not let her. She fought him, heart racing, the winged creatures that were her secrets vibrating with the need to be free, careening madly against her fury and her...desire.

Suddenly his lovemaking gentled. He was wooing her. Those knowing, capable hands circled her back, her neck, explored the still-damp silk of her hair.

She fell into the spell, lost her bearings, her defiance. And then she gave in to him. Her trembling hands wandered feverishly, needing expression, needing anchorage, and she found purchase on the living rock of his shoulders. Their tongues slid and collided in a sweet race to savor and possess. He tasted like wheat and sunshine. His strength was tinder to her long-dormant hunger.

Please, she wanted to moan. *Don't stop, ever.* A sense of destiny gripped her, an urgency propelled her. Her torso gave in to his touch, moved with it, every hungry breath she took bringing her closer, harder against that granite chest. Liquid silver trailed through her and the tips of her breasts hardened. Still he kissed her mouth and circled his hips against her, commanding her to give more. He pushed a leg between her thighs and spanned her buttocks with an urgent hand, pressing her closer, drawing forth the silver liquid of her need. Her thighs quivered with a sugary hotness.

The kiss, the intense intimacy and her surging responses confirmed the truth she'd known and feared since they'd collided in the fire. There was destiny between them. They melded like the creek feeds the river, rushing to blend, and blending, no longer distinct entities but forever inseparable. She moaned in abandon.

Abruptly he stopped and moved her back—inches, but it felt like a chasm—and let her go. "Oh, Jess," he said again, grating it from some smoky recess of arousal.

Her eyelids fluttered open. She was barely aware of his murmured words. The lava still climbed her limbs, turned her insides molten, seared her mind. "Sleet," she whispered.

"I've never met a woman who fires me like you do," he said.

The sound of his voice, the wonder and hunger she saw in his eyes...

What did he see when he looked at her? Her chest was heaving. Her legs felt...weak. Her hair was wild. Her eyes...God only knew what they told him.

What had she done? Where had she gone? She shuddered and came to. Backing away, forcing sound through reedy breath, she said, "What right had you—"

"None," he said, "but don't hang me out for this, Jess. Give in to it." He reached for her.

When she pulled away, speechless at her actions, at his, he made a sound of impatience. "Look, I'm sorry. I had no right. All I intended was to invite y'all to dinner, dancing, some laughs."

"Laughs? Sleet, please." She felt heartsick. "Dinner is out of the question."

"Oh, come on, Jess. What have you got to lose? Come dancing with me."

She drew herself tall—as tall as five-four allowed—and put that mask of hauteur on her face that she'd worn to greet him tonight. What she had to lose was her dream. She felt grateful for the reminder. "I've got a ranch to run and a horse to train," she said. "If you even think about getting in my way, I'll find a way to make the sheriff believe you lit my barn. For all I know, you did."

He straightened. A brittle quality came to his eyes and his voice lowered, slowed, the words chosen to intimidate.

"You do something that low-down and I'll burn your backside with the flat of my hand." He showed her the callused hand he would use. Then he dropped it. "Ah, hell," he said in evident self-disgust. "I've never hit a woman in my life. What kind of she-devil are you, that you'd bring that out in me?"

She put a steel rod of resolve between her shoulder blades. "The kind who'd do anything, *anything* to get what she wants. Now I'm asking you to leave, Mr. Freeman. I'm insisting on it."

He regarded her for a split second. He caught the corner of his lower lip between pearly teeth. "You got it," he said abruptly. Crossing the room to pull his hat from the rack, he muttered something about others waiting in line.

The telephone rang. It startled both of them. They jumped, looked at each other. His eyes were bright with anger.

The second ring as good as pulled a shade down over his eyes. "I'll be going," he said. "Thanks for the hospitality."

There was no trace of sarcasm in his words. There was distance.

Regret flooded her. The timing, the circumstances—everything was wrong for them. He was a decent man, as strong-willed as she, more confident, perhaps more capable, and world-class sexy to boot. He was just about perfect—and dangerous as hell to her plans. She had insulted him, lied to him about accusing him of arson; in retaliation he had threatened her with the back of his hand, for the love of God! She was sorry she'd had to ruin what could have been at least friendship between rivals.

She stepped toward the rolltop, smoothing her hair, restoring her dignity. "It may be the sheriff," she said, gesturing. "He was going to get back to me."

"No problem." Sleet snugged his hat low over his eyes. "Somebody will check in on you tomorrow. See how things stand with the barn."

"That isn't really convenient. I have appointments and I'll be tied up most of the day."

"Suit yourself." He reached for the doorknob.

She turned and went to the phone. Picking up the receiver, she said hello. It was Hal.

"Yes, better, thanks," she said to the rancher, her ears tuned to the closing of the door.

But it didn't close. "Hold on a second, Hal."

She put the receiver against her hip and looked up. Sleet was staring at her, the door open and one boot on the sill. The lamplight caught his expression. His gaze smoldered with intent, with *possession*.

Jessica's knees went rubbery and her heart fluttered.

"Some folks don't try as hard as y'all to get what they want, Jess Latham," he said in a quiet voice. "I do. Be warned."

Then Sleet tipped the brim of his hat and stepped out into the night.

Jess stared, still seeing the big-shouldered, lean-hipped man who'd just filled the doorway. What she'd read in his eyes was unmistakable. What he wanted was her.

Tonight had been only a sun-shower compared to the storm that was coming.

Chapter Three

Pursuit by Sleet Freeman wasn't the only thing to worry Jess. Next morning at 7:00 a.m., she took a look at her budget. It confirmed what she feared: she had enough in savings for three months of bare necessities, including entry fees for the cutting shows this fall, but that was all.

The futurity, exclusive and prestigious domain of untried three-year-old colts like Blue, was two months and fifteen days away. She'd already paid the steep entry fee for that, taking advantage of a cash discount, but there were other concerns. Come December, she'd need money for gas and living expenses for the trip to Texas. She'd have to stall the tax collector, and find funds for repairs, new tack, equine supplies and a used trailer. It looked as if, to make ends meet, she'd have to win a significant number of the local shows she'd planned to enter with Sienna. If that didn't work out, she'd have to get a loan somehow.

She'd tied her hair into a low ponytail with a red bandanna, and wore a red cotton shirt, scuffed brown boots and the usual faded jeans. Plucking a straw hat from the hat rack, she crossed the living room. She was dressed for work but felt reluctant to go anywhere near the barn. After studying the finances, going down to more carefully assess her losses seemed masochistic. But it had to be done.

She glanced apprehensively out one of the long double sets of windows on either side of the door. Was it all going to be worth it? she wondered, gazing at her domain.

In the distance, The Dutchman's Dairy and great oblongs of green alfalfa butted up to either side of the Ramona Expressway, a two-lane road that connected Hemet with the I-5 freeway and cities like Riverside and San Diego. Rows of cottonwood and apricot quartered up the land closest to her ranch, the roofs of thoroughbred breeders and backyard farmers glinting in the early sun.

A massive gnarled live oak and the rusted overhead Latham Ranch sign marked her southern boundary. A long rutted access road led up from the oak toward a collection of rusted wire cattle pens—no longer usable—and the pipe corrals and an oval arena that stood slightly downhill from the main house. The track ran between the corrals and arena on one side, and the tan fields of the foaling paddock on the other, its chipped white paint warmed by the sun that peaked over the ridge of high foothills behind the house.

Hemet's banks, funeral homes, flower shops, groceries and retirement communities sprawled away to the left of her vision, eating up more of the valley every year. Near her ranch, the red tile roofs of the huge new Sundance Community—which used to be Latham land—gleamed in the light. Jessica looked away to more familiar, less galling sights.

Her truck was parked near the arena. The turquoise-blue Chevy was eight years old and faded, but in good working order. She'd been lucky to get it, lucky not to lose it in the fire.

To the right of the truck stood the charred horse trailer. Next to that rose the mammoth, smoke-blackened barn, backed by the barren hills. *"My barn,"* Jess mourned, the regret an ache in her belly. She felt as if her own home had been destroyed.

Only last week, she'd begun to keep the horses in the stalls at night because mid-September marked the beginning of the cool nights. Cold air encouraged the horses to grow their winter coats, which would have Blue looking like a Steppe pony at the futurity. A competitor's appeal counted with the judges, even if only slightly. She and Blue needed every edge. Maybe there were two stalls still usable, she mused— if the fire marshal declared the structure safe. If. So many ifs.

Out of sight between the house and the barn stood the cottage, but she could see the twelve-foot high, open-fronted hay shed. Untouched by fire, its precious cache of hay and straw bales were sheeted in black plastic. That's something, she thought; at least I've still got roughage feed and stall bedding. She'd lost a couple of barrels of expensive grains in the fire.

The cattle stared toward the house, lowing, hungry, reminding her of duty. Nearby, Sienna ambled into view, munching weeds by the front porch steps, a slash of sun glancing off her shiny brown rump. Jess watched her for a moment, affection soothing her despair. Her glance lingered, then moved to the gleaming blue-black stallion. Blue trotted around his corral, antsy to be fed. *There* was hope, Jess thought, heartened. "You're going to make the struggle worth it," she said.

Feeling strung out on a fragile thread, Jess geared herself for another killer day.

AT MIDDAY, she rode Sienna in the arena, settling the herd so she could work some cows. She wanted to sharpen the mare for the show tomorrow.

Noa usually served as a turn-back man, chasing a stray cow back to the action when Jess was cutting. But since Noa was away, the sawhorses she'd dragged into the arena were adequate.

To outfit the horse, she'd scrounged one bridle and a bit from the barn, and an old saddle from the toolroom at the back of the hay shed. The rope cinch around Sienna's belly was about to fray apart. Jess hoped it would hold until Noa got back, when the two of them would see what could be done about repairing the smoke-damaged cutting saddle she'd used since high school.

Jess was heading Sienna toward the middle of the herd, preparing to divide and turn them and select a calf to cut, when a call came. The loud jangling bell rang from the phone just inside the barn door—it had survived the fire—but she didn't want to wade through mud and rubble in the barnyard to get to it. It was too depressing.

Frowning, wondering why the fire marshal's men hadn't shown yet, she dismounted. Tying Sienna, she trotted across the arena, climbed out and began to run toward the house, leaping mud holes in her path. She charged up the porch steps, tore through the doorway to the desk and scooped up the phone, panting. "Hello, this is Jess Latham."

"Jess, it's Josh. I catch you at a bad time?"

"Josh! Hi, I was expecting the fire marshal. His men aren't here yet."

"Fire marshal?" her brother repeated, his voice rising. "What's wrong?"

"Josh...oh, God, Josh, I was going to call." Slipping off her hat, wiping her damp forehead, she tried to draw enough air to sound calm. "There was a fire. The barn—"

"Almighty heavens, Jess, are you okay?"

"A little sore in spots—minor burns on my arm and shoulder, scrape on my leg, bruise on my chin, that kind of thing. Otherwise, I'm okay. Some rest put me back to rights.''

"What's the damage?"

"Horses, cattle, all okay," she said, sitting down. "The barn needs roof repairs and a lot of the stalls are damaged. The fire marshal and his men are due here any minute to tell me if the structure is sound. And to check out why it happened."

"You think it's arson?"

"Why would it be?" she asked, realizing her brother was voicing a concern that had nagged her, too. "Who would want to?"

"I haven't a clue, Jess. Other than maybe someone who wants the land. You had any calls from that developer Dad was dealing with before he died?"

"The guy who built Sundance?"

"Yeah, Devon, Bart Devon, I think it was. Before Dad died, Devon was pressuring him to sell more land."

She frowned, trying to remember. "Dad used to reminisce about all the pretty little valleys in San Diego having disappeared. 'Orange County looks like L.A., like a quilt crisscrossed with streets and freeways. Hemet Valley's next, but I'll be damned if I'll contribute to it any more than I already have.' Do you remember how he used to go on?"

"There you go," said Josh.

"But that was just the cancer talking, Josh. He even talked about Mom, how pretty she was when he met her. All our lives, he never talked about Mom, not 'til he was dying, and then it was rose-colored memories all the way. Not a word about how that horse threw her, or the fact that he never really came out of mourning. The land was everything to Dad. He never mentioned Devon. He was just philosophizing.''

"Well . . . you may be right. He'd had offers for the place for years. Doesn't mean they'd force him."

"That's just movie script stuff," she said, more to convince herself. She had enough to handle without worrying about conspiracies. "Anyway, I've got to get back to the mare. I just got her warmed up and I want to cut a few cows."

"You need me to come out, Jess? I could be there this weekend."

"You've only been at this new post for a year, Josh. I can handle things. I've got somebody lined up—" *Liar, Sleet offered to help out, but that was before I knew who he was, and what he really wanted.* "—to help me," she finished.

"I want to come," he said firmly.

"*No,* Josh. That's final." She realized she was sounding hard, like her dad. The barn fire and the run-in with Sleet had rekindled her taciturn will, but that wasn't Josh's fault. She softened her tone. "Thanks for offering, hon'. Give my love to Sarah and the kids. Gotta run. Sienna's waiting."

When she'd hung up, she wondered about the developer, Devon. Did he want her land badly enough to steal it in a fire sale? Ridiculous, she thought in irritation, rising to go outside. He'd given her no reason, then or since, to suspect him of foul play. He hadn't contacted her or crossed her path.

Josh had always tended to be more distrustful of people than either their father or herself. She wasn't going to buy into his paranoia now, not with work piled up to high heaven and finances at an all-time low.

She stepped down off the porch and strode toward the arena. Bart Devon was probably sitting down to a two-hundred-dollar lunch with some of his political cronies in Riverside, lobbying against a zoning restriction or something. Meanwhile, she had cows to cut.

IT WAS FRIDAY EVENING. He'd tucked in a pearl-buttoned dress shirt, buffed his Tony Lama boots and climbed into the minicab of the pickup. But instead of heading into Riverside to check out the country gals in one of the honky-tonks, Sleet had driven five miles east along the foothills, heading for the Latham place.

He'd done some checking. Jess was sticking to the run-down ranch like a burr under a pony's saddle, trying to make it hang together. Maybe that was why he'd done what he had today, talked to Hal and the guys about a barn-repair crew. Maybe, too, her loyalty to the land was the thing that was luring him out to face her prickly nature now.

Turning down the short stretch of paved road that dead-ended at the Latham Ranch access drive, he felt his skin flush at the memory of last night. He'd been mad enough to eat dirt when he left. But not so furious that he'd forgotten why he'd gone up to the ranch in the first place. The way she'd come alive in his arms, hot and wild like a prairie fire, and even her defiance, only deepened his resolve.

"'Be warned,'" he'd told her. He meant it. He was going to win her.

Hey, beautiful, he wanted to tell her. *Get ready for a courtship you'll remember 'til your dying day.*

The landmark live oak loomed around a bend. Pulling to the shoulder, Sleet looked up at the sign swinging on rusty hinges above the truck. He read the weather-blotched blue letters.

Latham Cutting Horses
Training ★* Sales ★* Doc's Satan, Standing At Stud

Hal had told him Blue was the son of Doc's Satan. Jess was trying single-handedly to update history. Her grit made her all the more valuable as a conquest.

She's going for it and you're not, an inner voice said, nasty and laced with envy. *You want your own spread at least as badly as she does, but what have you done about it? Caroused and womanized and drifted, that's what.*

Sleet struck the steering wheel. What a lousy time to be reminded of his own jaded dreams. Ten years of footloose living haunted him like a bad reputation. Hell, he'd just sloughed off those years he could have been building a string of blooded horses. He didn't even own a stud. Checkers was a mare—a world champion, for sure, and about the nicest little Appaloosa he'd ever ridden. But Checkers wasn't Blue. If Blue proved out, he was Jess's ticket to success.

He, Sleet, was thirty-five years old, had a world championship to his credit, money in the bank in Missouri, and plenty of horses to train. Jess had nothing but a broken-down spread and her courage. Yet she was going after her dream with a vengeance.

Ah, hell! Jess Latham had just ruined the second evening in a row. He'd started out in good spirits. Now, he was angry. What the devil made him drive out here? What would he say when he saw her? "Back for more abuse—can't get enough of it!"

But he knew that wasn't it. It was the side of himself he kept hidden—his forgotten dreams—that she challenged. That dream drew him, and he was going to get his butt kicked for it.

She wasn't like his other conquests. Being world champion and making good money wasn't enough to win her for that fling he'd had in mind. She'd seen right through him. Knew he was a phony. One day, she'd realize the rest: she was fighting for the dream he didn't have the discipline to fight for. She had sheer guts.

If he was going to pursue her, he'd better do it quick.

"Hellfire," he muttered, backing the truck to swing it around so he could head for Riverside. He was in no mood for courting. Willing gals out for a good time were more to his liking, anyhow. There'd be plenty of them at the country dance scene.

He got the truck facing out. Then, angry at the lure Jess was to him, he did a brodie that spurred dirt and rocks in a twenty-foot rooster tail, and drove through the rose-hued sundown toward his fate.

WHEN HE PULLED into the barnyard, he took in the charcoal smudge around the hole in the roof of the barn, but dismissed it because Jessica was up on the black stud, working cows. It gave him prickles along his arms to watch her.

The sunset poured magenta light over the foothills and down along the chipped white paint of the arena. It warmed the sawdust and loam, tinted the rising dust, daubed pink patches on the spotted cattle and burnished the black colt's hide. Most stunning of all, it put a rose glow into Jessica's chiseled face and the still, small hands that held the reins as the big horse cast to and fro, staying nose-to-nose with a young heifer. Jessica's red shirt flamed with iridescence. The tight, faded jeans were tinted pink and clung to her slim calves. He noted each detail, logged it, felt it become part of him.

But it wasn't the magnificent tableau that made Sleet's heart hover and fall, then thunder into life. It was the ride. Her grace in the saddle, the studied concentration that made her one with the horse, and the animal's pure gift, his cow sense—they thrilled him. Blue was down in the dirt where he was supposed to be, forelegs buckling, haunches bunched, swinging air-light and nose-to-nose with the heifer each time she tried to dodge him, to get back to the herd. It was a hot cut, and one of the best he'd seen on an untried colt.

Jessica evidently was so absorbed, she didn't know Sleet was watching from the cab window, so he stayed with the action, awed, then envious, then beyond envy to silent thunderous applause.

Suddenly Jess pitched left and flew off, landing in a sprawl in the dirt. Sleet jerked open the door and leapt from the truck. Blue was still working the cow, the saddle sliding sideways. He wheeled back almost on top of Jess, dodged her, cut off the calf's escape and started back to Jess.

"Hellfire," Sleet said. "He's loco."

In a few bounds he was swinging open the gate, dodging sawhorses and speeding toward the fallen woman, thinking, *Crazy stud doesn't have any ground manners. Grungy saddle hanging around his belly by a thread, stirrups flapping. Going to break a leg.* Leaping over Jess, still cutting the cow, the colt was too dumb—or too determined—to let the calf go. Unbelievable.

"Whoa, Blue!" he yelled, charging him when the horse was almost on top of Jess, who was trying to sit up.

Frightened by Sleet, the stallion went up on his hind legs, towering over Jess. Sleet kept his arms in the air and yelled again. The stud backed away and came down, looking startled. He snorted, sidled away. The calf darted into the herd.

Sleet angled a look at Jessica. Dragging a red bandanna from her hair, setting it free, she began to climb to her feet.

"You okay?" he said, bending to help her stand.

She wobbled, and he caught her against his chest.

"Easy, gal," he heard himself say gently, even as his heart careened from residual panic, even as his senses reached out to the female treasures within his grasp. And treasures they were—slim hard body rounded softly in the right places, dusty, sage-scented cascading hair, the thrum of energy, the heat of worked muscles. "Easy," he said again, as much to his male urges as to her.

"Freeman, what the devil are you doing here?" she asked, breathing hard as she tucked the bandanna into a pocket and looked up into his eyes, flashing accusations.

"Said somebody would come by to check on you."

"And I said it wasn't convenient."

"I think it was."

There were double meanings flying in that response and he knew it. So did she. She looked away and said, "My cutting saddle's burned. I found a roping saddle I thought would hold."

"I saw you ride," he said, still cradling her against him— she letting him. Her thrumming body took his mind off the fact that her stallion was suddenly a real threat to his world title. The thought hovered in his subconscious, buried there beneath the pure thrill of holding her close. That thrill made him effusive with praise. "You're good, Jess. So's the black."

Her gaze swung back to him. He read hope, surprise. "You think so?"

"I know it. He's pure poetry to watch. I saw his daddy take the futurity when he was a youngster. Blue's got win in him, Jess."

She gazed at him with a light in her eyes that crowned him king. "Thanks, Sleet," she said, barely a whisper. "I owe you again. Will I ever be done owing you?"

He grinned, still reeling in pleasure. "Not if I can help it."

The macho charm that had wooed a hundred women only put her off. She wiggled out of his arms, glanced at Blue— saw him standing, favoring the bandaged leg—then cut Sleet a wry look, pretty mouth quirked. "I don't like the turn of things, Sleet Freeman," she said. "You've caught me when I'm beholden to you again, but don't get any ideas."

"Now, ma'am—"

"Don't ma'am me, cowboy. I know what you're after."

"After?" He thought about filling his hands with her full, curving breasts. "Like what?"

"Like dancing or any such silly nonsense. I've never been a frivolous woman and I can't afford to change. There's too much at stake. I thought I made that clear last night."

"That means you don't like to dance?" *He pressed it for all it was worth.* She *was* beholden to him again—just where he wanted her—and couldn't possibly throw him off the ranch.

"It means no such thing," she said. "I like to dance fine. I just don't have the time." She tossed her hair, threw him an arch look. "Shut the gate, will you? I've got to catch Blue."

The horse craned his head around to nip at the saddle under his belly. He pawed with his bandaged leg, nickered, then pricked his ears at them, asking for help.

"Jughead," Sleet retorted. "Damned near killed her." Pleased at the progress he'd made with Jess, he strode back to the gate, threw the crossbar and returned to stare at the troublemaker. The beast wasn't moving. "Ought to hog-tie him with a loose saddle more often."

"He's just hungry, hoping to stay on my good side. I didn't feed him yet."

She was smiling. It seemed the tumble from the horse had taken the edge off her reserve. Sleet felt a nudge of hope.

Jess caught Blue's dragging rein just as he was backing away and unlashed the saddle. She caught it expertly as it fell. Sleet hurried to her and took it. It was a heavy old saddle—weighed a ton. Jess hadn't even buckled under its weight.

There was a smoke-singed halter and lead rope hanging on the fence by her hat. Sleet slung the saddle on the top rail and brought the tack to her. After a little head tossing, Blue let her remove the bridle and slip on the halter. Jess took the animal's pulse at the withers, then began to walk the horse to cool him down.

"He's favoring that leg some," Sleet pointed out, shortening his stride to walk with Jess.

"I know." She glanced down at it, frowning apprehensively. "I ran cold water on it several times today and changed the dressing. He was fine after he'd worked the cows awhile. Now it's probably stiffening up on him."

"You figure to work him every day?"

"No, I'll rest him tomorrow while I'm at the show. I just wanted to work some of the jughead out of him, after the fire last night. He was restless. Feel better, boy? Ready for chow?" She reached back to pat his damp neck affectionately. The horse jumped. Then he nickered, as if to remind himself Jess was friend, not foe. Theirs was as close as any person-and-horse partnership Sleet had seen or experienced, yet the black didn't quite trust her. Not entirely.

Sleet felt a stirring of professional interest.

He scrutinized the horse again, his trainer instincts alerted. Blue was sleek, muscled and alert—in perfect health. An idea began to tingle Sleet's backbone, as all really insightful ideas did. Blue liked Jess, no question about that. Yet in all the months she'd handled the horse, he was still ornery on the ground. Would the horse respond to techniques Sleet had learned from his years of training, and mellow out?

Sleet's backbone tingled again. Come December in Texas, would he have a better chance to hold on to his world title if he, not Jess, finished the stud's training and rode him in the futurity? He watched Jess cross the arena, leading the stud toward the gate. She glanced over her shoulder at him, interrupting his speculations. "If I can't get rid of you," she said smartly, "I'm putting you to work." She pointed to the sawhorses. "Stack 'em against the fence."

Touching his hat in mock obeisance, he let his brainstorm ride. There would be a time and place for seeing if Blue had a price on his head. Right now, the livestock needed care. If lending a hand with Jess's chores would earn her favor, he now had a double motive for pleasing her.

While Jess fought a minor skirmish with Blue to hose him down, Sleet stacked the sawhorses at the end of the arena. It was twilight, getting nippy, and the mare, moved to the corner corral nearest the house, was pacing, anticipating supper. Sleet saw an electric cart parked outside the fence. Flakes of hay and a stiff-bristled curry brush were on it.

"You want me to drive that rig around to the back of the corrals?" he called as Jess was walking Blue in the arena. "Throw some hay into the feeders? Cows'll go into their pens easier."

"Brilliant insight," she said, a grin softening the sarcasm. She put Blue in the corral on the other side of the cattle pens, then began to walk around the herd, lifting her arms, gathering them. "You're just trying to soften me up."

"Give a man the benefit of the doubt."

"For what?" she said, raising her voice to be heard. "So you can pretend?"

A little chilled by what might be uncanny insight into his character, he put the cart into gear. "Pretend what?"

"Pretend you're clever enough to beat me in December," she said. "No chance, cowboy. You might as well give up trying. You said yourself Blue's a winner."

The little vixen. She'd even resort to psychological tactics to get her dream. The idea she was serious competition in the cutting arena was now a reality. He didn't trust himself to answer politely.

"What?" she challenged as he parked the vehicle and lifted a flake, then chucked it into Sienna's feeder. "Tossing in the towel? Good. I like a man who knows when he's whipped."

His face reddened. She wanted taming, that one. He climbed inside the mare's corral, strode to the far side, climbed through to the arena and began to run toward her.

"Sleet, what are you doing?" Jess backed into the cattle. "Sleet?" The cows lowed and moved away, leaving a nice patch of soft dirt and pine shavings all around her. And no protection. "Quit, now," she demanded, looking half angry, half scared.

He kept coming.

"Don't you *dare*," she hollered. She turned.

That was when he tackled her.

THEY FELL AGAINST a calf. It bawled and bucked away. She landed on her side, breath knocked out of her by the fall and the solid weight of the man on top of her. His face—his mouth!—lay against her breast. She shouted in dismay. Her air gone, it came out a whimper.

A thread of sexual tension darted through her. A split second of hesitation, of pleasure at the longing she felt, then she twisted, shoved, tried desperately to get free of him. She should have ordered him off the ranch the minute she'd come to her senses after the fall. Instead, she'd let down her defenses. Now she was vulnerable.

He laughed, tussled with her, grabbed her rib cage, tickling her as if she were a child.

"Stop," she said, panting, humiliated and angry. "Don't!"

"Don't ever say 'dare,'" he said, softly. "I turn into a monster." And he growled deep in his throat, lips vibrating against her neck, sending chills along her flesh. "Mmm," he teased.

He began to nibble her throat—*nibble* it, for the love of God, as if she were a snack. She was outraged. Again she struggled, and again she felt the corded muscles of his arms close around her, like a lasso cinching a mustang.

To tame it. To bring it to *heel*.

Anger surged through her, blotting out the true quality of his laughter, turning it mean, taunting. She whipped her body viciously, bucking, breath rasping. Managing to unseat him, she scrambled away, fingers clawing for purchase in the soft, horse-smelling dirt. She resented having her hair dragged in the filth, dust inhaled with every breath, sore shoulder and leg throbbing. Almost free. She would choke him to death. Tearing him limb from limb was too good for him after this humiliation.

But he caught her, dragged her back by an ankle, a *thigh*. Pleasure blazed through her anger. She fought it and shouted, "Dammit, Sleet!"

She kicked him, her boot thudding into him somewhere. He grunted. Then the sheer strength of him overpowered her, and she found herself beneath him again, his face inches away, his blue eyes alight with mirth.

"I hate you!" she said, breathing hard, spitting dust from her mouth.

"No you don't, you resent that I'm winning."

"Ridiculous."

"Is it? Most folks who like each other the way we do would consider this play. Y'all make it a battle. That means somebody has to lose."

'Like each other the way we do'? She wanted to deny it. But it was the truth. Only a few minutes ago, she'd liked him immensely. Liked his quick reflexes and raw courage when he'd gotten under the rearing stallion to protect her. Liked his rangy walk, his energy, his willingness to help. Liked the

good-natured kidding, so rare for her these days. Liked too many things to name.

She looked away, keeping her tone brisk. "I told you I wasn't a frivolous person. You must be deaf as well as rude. The animals are hungry. I have to put away the cattle and tack and brush Blue down. I have a report to fill out for the fire marshal—he was here today, checking out the barn. Responsibilities, Freeman. I have responsibilities. Now get *off* me." She tried to shove him away but he wouldn't budge.

"I'll help with the chores, Latham," he said, mimicking the use of the last name.

"I don't want—"

"That's my condition. Say you'll let me help—without shredding my manhood—and I'll let you up. By the way. Happy September fifteenth. Mexican Independence Day. I figure a serious rancher like y'all wouldn't know it was a holiday."

That was the reason Josepha and Noa had gone to Mexico, she remembered—to celebrate the holiday with family. They wouldn't be back 'til Sunday! No help now, she thought, panicked as much by the sensual heat building inside as by Sleet's confident intention to master her. She twisted, tried to jerk away.

He held her fast. "Surrender, Jess," he said, his eyes darkening.

She glared at him, resenting his charisma, his dominance, his lightning-sparked gaze.

He dipped his head and kissed her.

She was so surprised to feel his warm lips on hers, she didn't fight it. Oh, God, *again*. A jet of liquid fire shot through her. Her body responded, softened. *Stop,* a warning rang. *Before it's too late....*

Just as she'd gathered her wits enough to firm her lips, intending to twist free, he lifted his head.

He wore a look of glee. "I'll take that as a sign of surrender," he said, smiling.

And he helped her up.

That was his mistake. Jess got to her feet, stepped up to him and shoved him in the chest. His solid body only nudged an inch, but that didn't stop her from snapping, "Off the ranch. Now."

"Hey," he said, dusting his jeans and shirt. "A deal's a deal."

"You made the terms. I didn't agree."

"C'mon, Jess," he chided. "I was teasing. I'll help with the chores. No foolishness. My word on it."

She glared at him. "No."

He reached down, picked up a tan beaver hat that must have carved five hundred dollars out of his pay, and slapped the dust from it. He seated it over that chaff-colored lion's mane and angled a look at her. "I'll make a deal with you. A fair one."

"Forget it. I already know you don't play fair."

His gaze narrowed. "You'd better hear me out before you decide. Your trailer's burnt to a crisp."

She glanced at the burned hull, and back at the cowboy. The sunset glowed around him like a red halo, making her heart hover for a moment with the pure glory of the picture he painted. Damn him to hell, he was sexy enough to blow holes in her anger and her concentration. "What about the trailer?" she managed to ask with cool disdain.

"You showing this weekend?"

"I'd planned to. Why?"

"You'll need a lift."

"Not from you. I'll call Hal."

"Hal's going to be picking up a new horse early Saturday morning. He won't be showing 'til the Gelding Class so he doesn't have to be on the grounds 'til eleven. You'll need to be there first thing."

Because he was a professional trainer, Sleet would be competing in the Open Class. She would follow him in the Non-Pro, the second-best-paying event of the day. He was cornering her, but she wasn't going to allow it. "I'll call Charlie," she said, lifting her chin. "He always goes early."

"Charlie's hauling Billy's horses. His trailer's full."

Anger tinted her cheeks. She looked at the ground, thinking, I need the winnings. I need to be there. Sleet had trapped her, stolen the advantage of her independence, and she resented him for it. Yet maintaining her cutting edge and earning a purse on Saturday dictated her next move.

Folding her arms, she glanced into his sun-bronzed face. "What's on your mind?" she asked.

"A truce."

She laughed in derision.

He ignored the put-down. "I haul your horses when you don't have a ride, and you knock off the bitchiness."

Color dashed her cheeks. "You bas—"

"Ah—" he put up a cautioning finger "—no name-calling, that's one. Two, you hold back on the attitude when we're around the guys."

"What's the matter? Afraid I'll make you out to be the pushy, oversexed manipulator you are?"

His eyes glittered. "That's fine between us, Jess. You do that in public and I'll make sure you and everyone around us knows just how sexy I can be."

Her face was blazing like the sun, but she refused to let him win without defiance. "What are you going to do, strip me and get it out in broad daylight?"

"Oh, no, Jess," he said, lowering his voice to a quiet drawl. "That's for just the two of us, behind closed doors, when y'all want it bad enough to beg for it." The low, slow drawl crawled inside her and did its work, running her blood hot and stealing the strength from her limbs. Still he talked to her, touching her with his words, sending them like invisible hands across the few feet of quiet cooling air between them, to touch her intimately. "The day will come, Jess," he promised. "It'll come. And when it does, I'm going to pleasure you with every oversexed trick I know. I'm going to explore that fine body of yours 'til I know it like I know cutting. And you're going to explore mine, and love it, and make me cry your name in sweet agony—"

"Stop it!"

Closing her eyes, she brought her hands to her ears for a moment and covered the heated skin. She felt mad, steeped in eroticism, drowning in it. "Why?" she pleaded. "Why are you doing this?" She pulled away her hands and opened her eyes to see his face.

"I told you, Jess. Most folks don't try as hard as you to get what they want. I do."

"You could have your pick of women. Why *me?*" She realized she had massaged his ego mightily with that desperate cry. She drew breath, swallowed. When she was calmer, she looked at him sideways and repeated flatly, "Why me, Sleet? Why do you want me?"

He smiled. "Because you are you, Jess. It's just that simple."

"You're wasting your time. It'll never happen."

"Want to wager? Now, how about it? Do we call a truce, temporarily, and let me haul you to the shows?"

She let out a breath. She was going to have to capitulate—but how to do it with dignity? "I've known some crazy cutters in my day, Freeman," she said, shaking her head, "but never one as off the deep end as you. You must be insane. Certifiable."

"If you need to say those things to save your pride, that's okay with me. What about my deal?"

Shoving anger away because it was pointless, she squinted at him. "On one condition."

He shrugged, spread his hands.

"That you back off on the macho moves. I'm not stepping one foot inside that Dually of yours if I have to protect my honor every time I do. You claim you're good for your word. Give it on that score, then prove it."

"Done," he said, grinning that lazy grin of his. "Shall we gather the cattle?"

Throwing him a look of disgust, she strode into the gathering twilight, lifting her arms to haze the cows. She was bound to him for now because it was expedient, but he hadn't won. She was going to prove to him just how onesided this deal he'd struck was going to turn out.

Chapter Four

After Jess had rousted Sleet off her ranch, it took a chat with her brother and a long hot soak in a bubble bath to calm her vibrating nerves. The man was positively high-voltage, and she didn't mean it as a compliment. His jolt made her waver off her solitary path to success.

Finally alone, engrossed in the calming, mindless act of grooming, she could reflect on the damage his visit had wrought. She'd lost that edge of independence she cherished, at least 'til she could figure a way to get a new set of wheels under her horses. Worse, she'd been forced into agreeing to spend time with him, when every instinct in her body screamed that Sleet was more dangerous to her than a barn fire.

It all seemed too high a price to pay for getting to Saturday's show. Yet that, ultimately, was the priority.

Jess was applying a brush and blow dryer to her clean, damp hair when glass shattered at the front of the house.

Her stomach dipped in alarm. Was he back? Drunk and out of control? Was he that type?

Dropping the dryer and brush, closing a long emerald-green robe at her throat, she slipped into moccasins and ran out of the bathroom toward the living room. She halted at the doorway, skittish, wary. She hadn't lit a fire and the dim room smelled of charred wood. The scent unnerved her. Then she saw the faint glitter of glass on the rug at the front of the room, near the rolltop desk.

And the black hole in the window.

"What on earth?" She crept toward it to investigate.

A white object had lodged against the leg of the desk chair. Before she could reach for it, another sound arrested her.

An engine whined outside, distant yet distinctly automotive. "Who—?" She whirled to look out the window. It was black out, moonless. Jess ran to the door and threw it open, bounced the screen door wide and flipped on the porch light. Putting a hand to her brow, she peered past the ghostly outline of the arena to the driveway. Nothing.

Beyond the arena in the darkness, gravel crunched beneath vehicle tires, but no headlights shone. The engine whined as if the driver were winding it up to full revs in low gear, pushing it—fleeing.

Jessica bounded off the porch. At the corner where the driveway split the paddock from the main structures of the ranch, she leapt up on the pipe rails of Sienna's corral. Straining toward the engine, she searched the pale diminishing access road. Down near the gate, a strip of chrome gleamed. Light from the nearby town glanced off new paint. There was a hint of luxury in that brief clue—enough of a clue to tell her it was no flashy red-and-white Dually leaving her land. He could have switched cars, she thought. Then the vehicle growled away into the darkness.

For several seconds, Jess held to the metal rails, her heart thudding. *Teenagers? Thugs? Who had trespassed on her land?*

Something soft pushed against the knuckles of one hand. She started, jerked her hand away. "Oh, Sienna!" Jess reached out to caress Sienna's muzzle. The mare nickered.

A new fear gripped her. Blue! Jess jumped down from the corral. She hurried down the road, past the cattle that had been delivered in August and were already soured from constant workouts—and up to the backside of Blue's corral. He was munching hay—the scratchy sound of pulling it from the aluminum shell attached to the rails, the pebbly sound of his flat teeth grinding it to cud. He should have had grain tonight, but it had all been destroyed by smoke and fire.

She leaned into the enclosure. "Blue," she said softly.

The colt's chiseled head popped out of the feeder. He nickered low in his throat and went back to nuzzling alfalfa. If he'd been hurt, he'd be spooked—charging around, causing a ruckus. He was fine.

Her relief nearly weakened her. Her legs quaked. The night air penetrated the cotton robe, chilling her. Clutching the fabric close, casting an apprehensive glance over her shoulder, she made her way back to the shadowy living room.

Rage tried to winnow through, but she capped it and moved quickly. Squinting at the slash of light coming from the hallway, she crossed to the desk, bent and scooped up the white object. It crackled. Reaching to the lamp, she switched it on. Peeling away masking tape, she unwrapped white paper from a smooth round rock the size of her fist. The stone hadn't come from her property, but either from a landscape nursery that sold paving stones, or from a riverbed. She set it down on an electricity bill that should have been paid yesterday.

Unfolding the paper, noting capital letters that looked as if they'd been scrawled with a stick dipped in red paint, Jess read:

GET THE MESSAGE?

She whirled around as if seeking someone who could explain. Message? What message? Who had broken her window, invaded her fragile peace, terrorized her this way? And why?

On the heels of these questions came the need to fight back. She grabbed the phone and dialed the sheriff's office. "I've had a prowler," she said tersely—angrily—and gave particulars. "Yes, the same Jessica Latham. The barn burned last night. Sheriff Sanford is investigating. I want to know who's doing this—now!"

SATURDAY MORNING when Sleet pulled around the corrals in his truck and color-matched four-horse trailer, he saw Jess on the porch and everything in him sped up—heart, reflexes, mood, libido. Especially his libido. She wore a Western shirt, hunter's plaid with a thin ruffle of lace around the shoulder placket. Stone-washed black Wrangler jeans outlined her hips and slim legs, worn so long, they rippled over the instep of her black boots. She'd pulled her hair back with a thin red ribbon around the ponytail. A black Stetson underscored her feminine, fragile beauty. She was dressed like the women he'd danced with last night after he'd left the Latham ranch, only cleaner, fresher somehow.

For a fleeting second he wanted to throw the truck into Park, dash to the porch and sweep her into his arms. The fantasy consumed him for a moment. But something stopped him, and it wasn't the knowledge that he had no right, yet, to make a move like that. It was something else. Something was wrong.

She was standing on the porch, obviously waiting, thumbs hooked into her jeans pockets, looking unhappy. Was he late? He checked his watch. Seven-fifteen. Right on time.

As he parked between the house and the arena, he looked her over again. Sexy as hell, he concluded, but her pretty face looked paler than it had yesterday and more serious, if that was possible. She looked vulnerable.

That was it, he decided, watching her come down off the porch carrying a red nylon sports bag. She tossed it into the bed of the pickup and walked briskly to the arena fence to untie Sienna. Jess looked vulnerable, and that just wasn't her style. She might feel it, but she'd never show it. Especially to him.

"Morning," he called, stepping out of the truck.

She murmured a reply.

The stud colt was carrying on something fierce, now that the mare was leaving. Jess had turned him out in the spacious arena so he could stretch his legs. Calling shrilly, he stormed around, a horseshoe clanging against the cattle enclosure, scattering them. Sleet wondered what Jess would take for him. He was a beauty, a champion for sure.

"I'd hate it, too," he commented, smiling wryly. "Staying home, missing all the action."

The pleasantry was wasted on Jess. Not looking at him, she slung the old roping saddle over her shoulder and came toward the back of the trailer, leading the bay mare. Sleet met her there and unbolted the ramp, lowering it to the dust. In the forward stall, Checkers's chocolate-chip rump moved to one side and she popped her head up over the slant-load partition, trying to get a look at the newcomers.

"My mare, Checkers," he said by way of introduction.

"Nice lines from what I can see," Jess said. "You want my mare up next to her, or skip a stall?"

"Right next to Checkers is okay." Every word he spoke to her frosted up like the temperature was twenty above. It was beginning to irritate him.

Jess propped her saddle on the floor of the trailer. Last evening, they'd patched the rope cinch where yesterday it had frayed through, using pieces of rawhide and a strip of leather cut from the saddle's skirt. "Hope it holds," he said, indicating the saddle.

"Yeah," she said, and took her mare up the ramp. As Sleet was swinging the next partition around to secure the mare, Jess ducked past him. She walked over to her saddle and slung it over her shoulder.

"I'll take that," he said, securing the gate. He'd intended to stow it in the tack compartment in the nose of the trailer, with his, but she hauled it out of sight. He heard the saddle clunk into the back of his pickup. Left to follow like a useless puppy, Sleet felt his face begin to burn. He heaved the ramp up against the back of the trailer with enough force to spook the mares—they jumped, rocking the vehicle—and drove home the bolts.

Climbing into the driver's side of the pickup, he slammed the door. He was reaching for the keys when Jess asked tersely, "What did you do after you left last night?"

He stopped in midaction, turning his head and gazing into her eyes for the first time. The blue-green depths looked wary, angry. The hint of a yellowish bruise discolored her chin, reminding him she'd been hurt in the rescue two nights ago, but her tone killed compassion and ignited his temper. He straightened. "What are you driving at?"

She lifted off her hat and put it next to his on the seat behind him. "Did you come back to the ranch last night?"

"Come back?" He furrowed his eyebrows, and his voice conveyed his surprise. "You mean, to see you?"

"For whatever reason. Did you come back?"

"No. Hell, no." He glanced away, thinking of the women he'd held last night at the dance club—held and wished they were her. He'd wasted his energy. She was going to make him pay dearly for the bargain he'd struck with her. Spats between lovers were one thing; interfering with his concentration on a workday was entirely another. He'd better nip her little game in the bud right now.

"If I'd been here," he said with deep insinuation, "you wouldn't need to ask. Now cut the crap, Jess. We've got a show to do."

"Then it wasn't you who threw a rock through my front window." She stated it, but it was a question nonetheless.

He jerked his head toward the house, saw the brown cardboard wedged into a window frame. He swiveled back to her. "You think I would stoop to that?"

Her fingers twisted. "I don't know!"

"Jeez, I'm not a common thug."

"How would I know that? You barge into my life wreaking havoc in every direction, showing up when you're not invited and putting the moves on me when I tell you I'm not interested. What am I supposed to think?"

He choked out a sound of amazement. "That I like you? That I think you're the sexiest, most passionate creature I've ever had the hots for? Something along those lines?"

"Oh, for the love of Pete," she snapped. She twisted away and hugged herself. "The normal guy asks if he can call you. He uses a little subtlety in the game. You're like a bulldozer running on pure testosterone."

His face reddened. "You're a coward, Jess. Maybe if you bucked up your courage and went for a real man, you'd learn to appreciate the heavy equipment."

Her breath whistled out. She stilled for a moment, then turned to him. "You know, Sleet, I'm surprised you can still stand upright. That ego of yours must be a terrible weight to bear."

"Yeah, well—" he twisted the key in the ignition and fired the truck, lurching out of the yard "—it ain't half the burden of your viperous temper."

She sat stiffly in the cab as he drove, silent, white-faced. It was several miles before the thought crept in that Jess was a frightened, desperate woman. She was struggling to save a ranch that should be leveled and rebuilt from scratch, and someone was trying to force her to see it. A low-down dirty way to do business.

He glanced over. "You call the police?"

She nodded.

"And?"

"The sheriff's department sent out a young guy who took my statement. He looked around but couldn't find anything unusual. He took the note and the stone back to his office."

"Note? Somebody left you a note?"

"Not left it, like a neighbor leaving a casserole," she said, her voice flat with disgust. "Wrapped it around a stone the size of my fist and sent it through my living room window."

Fresh anger made his cheeks ruddy. He wanted to pound the punk into the dirt. "Dang it, Jess!" He cut her a look and saw her eyes widen. "Well, don't hold me in suspense. What did the danged note say?"

"It said, 'Get the message?'"

"What message? What's it supposed to—" It struck him suddenly. It was a threat. A threat to a lone woman. A threat to break the spirit that held her to her land. The anger simmered in his bloodstream. *The barn had been torched on purpose.*

She leaned forward, searching his face. "Do you think the barn and the note are connected? Do they want me off my land? Or—" Before he could answer, she cast a worried look out the rear window toward Hemet. "Were they trying to kill Blue?"

His heart kicked his ribs. "It's just a prank, Jess. Some punks kicking you when you're down, after the fire and all."

"I don't know. I shouldn't be going to the show. I need the opportunity, but I hate to leave the ranch. If anything happened to Blue—"

"Nothing's gonna happen in the light of day. Think about it."

She blinked. "You think so?"

Hell, now he was her priest. But she was scared, and it moved him. "Yeah, I do," he said. "The fire and the broken window both happened at night. Criminals are cowards. They need the cover of dark to perpetrate their cowardly acts. Whoever threw the rock will expect you to be home today, watching for culprits. Might as well come on to the show, and deal with cowards when the sun goes down."

She shivered, and he regretted saying that last. He was rambling, trying to make her feel better. He hardly believed what he'd been telling her, but it seemed to help.

Straightening up, she said, "I guess you're right. I do need to do the show. Sienna's going to be more valuable as a brood mare as long as she's winning purses and getting a record."

"There you go," he said, turning onto the northbound freeway that skirted the eastern edge of Riverside. "No need to worry about tonight, either."

She spun toward him, wary again. "Why?"

"Because 'til your friends get back from Mexico, Jess, I'll be bunking at your place."

"The hell you will." The steel was back in her voice.

"Get used to the idea," he said, wondering where in blazes the idiot idea had sprung from—it was bound to bring him big-time grief. But he'd said it, and now it made sense. She was a woman alone. Her people weren't back yet, and he was the only one in her circle of acquaintances who didn't have a family or a place of his own to look after. Perversely adamant, he closed off retreat. "You'll have to call the law to run me off."

He was suddenly fed up with the tension, the fighting. He held up a stern silencing hand. "I don't have time to deal with phony, trumped-up pride. And you don't have the luxury of creating it. We've got a show to do. Just keep the hysterics to yourself 'til after the show, and let me get my concentration."

Evidently seeing the wisdom of getting her head clear for the competition, she plopped against the seat. "This isn't over, Freeman," she said. "This time you're not pushing me around."

"Fine," he snapped. "Just keep your temper wired down 'til after my ride."

Chapter Five

At ten-thirty in South Riverside, the sun glinted on the waxy, deep-green leaves of the orange trees and simmered the mocha-colored earth of plowed bean fields. The hot air smelled sweet and musky, like baking squash. Heat beat on the tin roof and crept between the branches of the tall sycamores lining the west edge of the open-sided arena. But the area under the roof was dark and cool, protecting Jessica from the searing Indian summer sun and filling her nostrils with a loamy scent reminiscent of mushrooms.

Sienna was smooth at the lope. Weaving among other riders, Jess worked her in a wide oval around the white walls of the warm-up area, attempting to relax her own mind as effectively as she was relaxing the horse.

It was nearly impossible. Sleet's threat to stay at the ranch harassed her composure. She wasn't going to allow it, of course, but knowing another confrontation was going to be necessary had balled up her nerves.

"Damn him, anyway," she told the horse, and Sienna flicked her ears to listen. "He thinks he's God's gift to women."

Truth was, she feared another battle with him. Too often she ended up plastered against that hard body, losing the better part of her mind to the better parts of his body. Too often, he came out the winner of the contest, in fact or in essence.

"Not this time," she said under her breath, easing Sienna to a walk. "And he's not going to steal this show from us, either. He only made that threat to ruin our concentration. Well, it won't work."

She galvanized her determination. This was an important show. Though it was small compared to regional competitions, the organizers had managed to obtain sponsorship by the National Cutting Horse Association. Thus monies earned here would count in the NCHA ranking of cutters and horses throughout the nation. That was why Sleet was participating.

"Let him have the points," she muttered under her breath. "We need the money. You need it, girl."

It was true.

In the past several months of shows, Jess had added about two thousand dollars to Sienna's lifetime earnings, bringing the total to $37,081.00. She wanted to bring it to forty thousand by year's end.

"Then, next spring, you're going to have some fun with Blue," she finished softly, reaching to caress the mare's neck. Sienna's earnings, and the Reserve Championship she'd won several years ago, would strengthen the value of her foals. "Every cutting horse trainer I know wants to train next year's futurity champion. You're going to produce a winner, girl—a winner sired by *this year's* futurity champion—Blue-bar-Satan."

As if she understood, rather than simply liked the sound of Jess's voice, Sienna tossed her head.

Jess smiled, her dream once more firmly rooted in her psyche.

Releasing her worries about national rankings and financial troubles and the fact her prize stallion was home alone—

troubled only by the nagging idea that Sleet was bent on spending the night at the ranch—Jess loped the mare two more laps.

As she was finishing up the work out, she heard the announcer's summons: "Bobby Jo Williams up next on Bit'O Poco, Sandy Letterman on deck, Jess Latham in the hole." "In the hole" meant she was third in the lineup. Jess threaded the mare among waiting contestants, walked her along the portable pipe fencing that separated the warm-up area from the sawdust-and-loam-covered show arena, and went in through the gate someone held open for her.

She permitted herself only one quick glance toward the back fence. Sleet was one of two herd-holders who were keeping the cattle bunched for the next competitor. Mounted on the black-and-white speckled mare, slumped comfortably in the saddle, he was waiting for Bobby Jo to start his cut.

It made Jess's stomach drop to see Sleet sitting a horse. He wore a black-and-white plaid shirt that fitted his broad shoulders perfectly and picked up the colors of his horse. Buff chaps encased his jeans and a straw hat that had seen better days accentuated his rugged jaw.

She remembered Sleet's ride in the Open Class, the class professional trainers could enter, first thing this morning— remembered the chills that ride had sent careering down her back. He was good. Damned good, and so was his mare. Checkers had a shot at the National Derby for four-year-olds, come April. She had talent. An hour ago the whole place had erupted in cheers at the hot cut Checkers had put on a brown cow. Sleet had won his class handily. Now he looked so lazily content, sitting on the drowsing horse, you'd never guess how the pair of them could thrill a cutter's heart.

Come December in Fort Worth, she reminded herself to keep from slipping deeper into reverie, there were going to be close to four hundred cutters from all over the country, top competitors like Sleet, trying to keep her and Blue from the championship.

When he glanced up, saw Jess gazing at him, Sleet stuck his thumb in the air, for luck. Evidently he'd dismissed their earlier argument. Jess hadn't. She kept the thought of his overall threat close to her and ignored him. Turning her head, she took stock of her surroundings.

Two turn-back riders took up positions facing the cattle, ready to cut off a cow if it tried to break from the main action. The judges, sitting in folding chairs to Jess's right, readied their clipboards.

A rangy seventeen-year-old, Bobby Jo stepped his buckskin toward the herd. He lost his first cow, his horse not turning quickly enough to keep it from the herd, and though he did better on the next one, his score was low.

Sandy Letterman, the wife of a retired Riverside stockbroker, eased her big white gelding into the herd for her run, and worked two feisty cattle in a row. She went in for a third, but the buzzer sounded. Hers was the score to beat.

Jess was the eleventh and last to compete. She flexed her fingers, lifted her shoulders and settled them, waiting 'til she was called. Now adrenaline pumped through her. The clink of tack, the stomp and snuffle of impatient horses, the low talk of cutters behind her, amplified like thunder and the clash of brass.

As Letterman trotted the white out of the arena, Jess bent to smooth Sienna's mane. "You can do it," she whispered, and the mare flickered her ears in anticipation.

Static burst from the loudspeakers, but the mare didn't leap sideways, as Blue would have done. Her seasoning was balm to Jess's humming nerves. She knew Sleet would be watching her, judging her abilities, perhaps gauging whether she was a real threat to his world title.

"Let's give him a show," she told the mare, and drew a lungful of loam-scented air, listening for her cue.

"This pretty little bay mare foaled Sienna's Trix, the horse that won the Pacific Coast Amateur for her owner four years ago," the announcer crooned. "Sienna herself is a Reserve National Champion from years ago. Jess's daddy took the futurity in '81. Got a lot of win-potential out here, ladies and gentlemen. Good luck, Jess."

Nodding, letting out a breath, she nudged Sienna forward across the arena, already studying the cows. She was looking for one that hadn't been worked much. She was looking for a reasonably fresh opponent.

At the back fence she turned the horse without ever glancing at Sleet, stepped her well forward and let the cattle peel by. She saw the dark brindle at the same moment Sienna did—felt the slight flicker of interest from the mare—and dropped the reins. Show me you can do it, she wanted to tell the mare. Show *him*.

Sienna half-crouched, straining forward. As the other cattle filtered back to the herd, the molasses-colored cow eyed its adversary, swung its head to and fro, testing. Sienna mimicked the movements. The brindle lowed, trotted a few steps. Sienna followed. So far so good, Jess thought. Then the cow bolted, and Jess was absorbed, caught up in the action, and all worries fled.

Sienna crossed the center of the arena twice, three times in pursuit. She played Ping-Pong for a few hot moves, earning whistles of approval. When the brindle lowered its head in defeat and turned away, Jess picked up the reins, heading back into the herd for a second cow.

Determination and skill paid off.

Jess and Sienna won the Non-Pro Class hands down.

The announcer called a break before the Gelding, Ladies and Novice Classes would take place.

Elated and flushed with the win, Jess flashed Sleet a look of triumph and left the ring. It registered that he was grinning like a proud papa; wondering why could come later. At the moment, she had to look after Sienna. She took the mare's pulse, then cooled her down in the workout area and checked the pulse again, making a mental note to jot the numbers in the record book at home.

When she was satisfied Sienna was properly cooled down, she rode up to the announcer's concrete booth to collect her winnings. The amount was higher than she'd hoped. Subtracting entry and cattle fees, she'd netted nearly four hundred dollars—a fine purse for a local show. It would pay for some of the grain, equine vitamins and medicines she'd lost in the fire.

Hiding a grin, Jess leaned over and ran her hand up the crest of Sienna's coarse mane. "You did it, girl," she said, voice husky with the emotions that flooded her—pride, soaring relief, gratitude. "You saved us again."

Chuffing out dust, Sienna bobbed her head, tongued the bit.

Jess pulled upright, gazing toward the knot of men and horses near the show gate—searching for the crystal-blue gaze that devastated her with such ease. Now she could face him with renewed confidence.

"Let him try his intimate games," she murmured, lifting the reins, urging Sienna forward. "I'm ready for him."

He was mounted near the gate, running a length of rein through his hands, talking idly with Hal and a few other cutters. Jess nudged Sienna over to the group. She heard several congratulations, but a disloyal part of her cared about only one.

"Nice go-round, Jess," Sleet said, smiling at her—maintaining a public courtesy, and in doing so, managing to spin new arrows into her midsection. "That old mare's still got get-up-and-go."

Careful, she thought. *His charm is lethal.* Jess leaned over, ran her hand along Sienna's glossy neck. "Better believe it."

"How old is she?"

"Sixteen...going on five." She grinned at the other men, and they chuckled.

"She does step up to a cow pretty," Sleet admitted, boldly playing his gaze over Jess's body.

It was too much even for a woman whose confidence was high. She turned to Hal, asked him about the new palomino he was riding.

Warming to her interest, Hal regaled her with the stopping and turning ability of his most recent, rather hefty investment in horseflesh, which he was eager to put to the test in the upcoming Gelding Class. Jess imagined Sleet was appraising her the same way—the touch of his gaze was almost palpable—but she wasn't about to encourage him. Rather, she had a little matter of authority to settle with him.

Unfortunately, the conversation ran straight into the heart of the matter she planned to handle privately with him.

"Heard you had a prowler last night," Hal said, taking the lead.

Jess's gaze cut to Sleet. He smiled blandly. He wasn't admitting he'd reported the incident to the men, but he wasn't denying it, either.

Hal was fretting about "Hemet's influx of city types."

"The snowbirds are mostly retirees," Jess pointed out to the rancher. "They're not the type to burn barns and vandalize property."

"What about the younger ones?" Hal groused, pushing back his hat to scratch prickly gray hair. "Developers haul them citified newcomers in here by the truckloads, 'n set 'em free to raise hell with the valley's peace-lovin' folks. They're not used to our slow country ways. They're bored. Their kids is goin' to Hades faster'n professional thieves 'n cutthroats. You got to take care from now on, Jess. Your spread's the closest to town."

Jess felt apprehension eddy around her new confidence. Was it hell-raising teenagers who'd torched the barn and threatened her with a note? Young people, bringing their jaded city high jinks to Hemet, as Hal theorized? Latham Ranch was isolated but accessible, unguarded, scantily manned—the perfect target for rabble-rousers. Was she merely a victim of pranksters? Or the object of more complex and treacherous motives?

She was frowning, wrestling with these thoughts, when Sleet eased back in his saddle, the squeak of leather drawing everyone's attention. "What'd the fire marshal have to say?"

She sent a silencing message to him but he kept up the facade of polite interest.

"He find any evidence?" Hal prompted.

She turned to him. "He grilled me about the wiring in the barn. Wanted to know if I'd reworked it lately, maybe used substandard wire."

"You didn't, did you, Jess?"

She responded sharply, preferring to keep her business private. "When would I have had time?" *Or the money?* "He asked when I'd installed the timer for the outside floodlights."

"About a year back, wasn't it?" Hal asked.

She nodded. "Begley's did the work. I assumed the wiring was to code. I never thought to ask."

"It was, you can count on it. Begley's kid runs an honest shop. I'd stake my ranch on the notion that boy is as honest as his old man."

"Still, you have someone terrorizing you," came Sleet's slow observation, and the men grumbled agreement. "Can't have someone terrorizing the neighborhood and not do anything about it, can we?"

Again the men voiced agreement.

Jess snapped her head around to stare at him. "You've got no stock in this town," she said tersely, knowing what was coming. "Keep out of it."

"Now, Jess." Hal temporized with paternal concern, but she caught the gleam of amusement in his eyes; he was enjoying the sparks that were beginning to fly. "We took a vote. We think someone ought to back you 'til things settle down."

She lifted her chin. "Meaning?"

"Post a watch. At least 'til Noa gets back. Sleet, here—" he jabbed a thumb at the instigator "—said he'd be glad to do it."

"Did he, now?" Her gaze swept past the men and landed on him. She felt the hollowing in her stomach that came from being cornered by a rugged, handsome man, and though her face warmed in reaction, she hid it by saying casually, "He tell you why he was so eager to do it?"

Sleet smiled, egging her to explain.

"He ain't the one with family or a place of his own," Hal responded, taking pleasure from her rising temper.

She suddenly realized the whole group was entranced in the moment, waiting for her temper to explode. "I don't need baby-sitting," she snapped, and backed Sienna, wheeled her smartly and trotted away.

"Go after her," she heard Hal tell someone. "She'll see reason. If she don't agree, why, we'll send a lookout anyway."

"Damn him to hell," she muttered, and she wasn't referring to Hal. She headed for a dim corner of the arena where she would let Sienna rest while she got a cool drink. "Damn his timing and his interfering ways."

Sleet had the kind of timing mothers would envy if their toddler were curious about a pot full of boiling water. He'd arrived at the ranch in time to help her save Blue. He'd come back in time to see Blue make the hottest run on a cow he'd ever had. He'd had the timing, know-how and all-fired luck to draw cattle this morning that, with Checkers's talent, earned them the best run of the show. Now he'd aired her troubles in public and used Hal's and the other cutter's protective feelings for her to convince them she needed looking after—to suit his own unscrupulous ends. A man that slick, that conniving, that clever at timing his moves, was as dangerous to her, emotionally, as the unknown night visitors who'd cost her so much money and peace of mind.

And she was stuck here with him 'til he was damned good and ready to leave.

"I said I'd ride turn-back for Hal in the Gelding Class," Sleet said conversationally, riding up to her. "After that, we can go."

"I'm ready anytime." She dismounted, looped Sienna's reins over a rail and stepped to the cinch. She began to loosen it from the mare's belly. "I need to get down to the feed store this afternoon for some supplies I lost in the fire."

"We can stop on the way home if you want."

She paused, her right hand wedged between the leather strips and Sienna's warm furry barrel. He was that determined not to let her out of his sight. "You must have colts to train, Sleet."

"Yes, ma'am. But not 'til your people get back."

So he still thought he was spending the night.

She whipped around. "Who do you think you are? Striding into my life like an almighty giant on a white horse? Arthurian legend is dead. Knights don't exist. I was born and bred to be self-reliant, and the sooner you understand that, the sooner you'll be rid of the viperous temper you couldn't stand to listen to this morning."

He dismounted, tied off his mare.

"Hal makes sense," he said as he loosened Checker's cinch. "Someone ought to help you watch your place."

"'Hal' makes sense?" She laughed derisively. "Hal wouldn't even have known about the vandal if you hadn't blabbed it."

"There's where you're wrong. Hal's buddies with a law man, a deputy. He put the word out he wanted to be informed if anything else went amiss at your place. I didn't know he knew about the rock 'til I spoke to him an hour ago."

She went back to loosening the cinch. "Okay, so Hal looks after me. You still helped prod him into saying I need a baby-sitter."

"Guilty as charged. You do."

The anger flashed through her and she turned, stepped away from the horse. "I've been alone since I was sent away to college."

"Exiled, were you?" he asked with infuriating sensitivity to her use of the word *sent*.

"I wasn't exiled, I was educated. I put that education to use. I traveled worldwide for *Elite Magazine*. By myself." Actually, she'd only been to London, Toronto and Acapulco. As a cost-saving measure, the magazine had insisted she interview mostly millionaires who lived in or visited Los Angeles. But there was a point to be made here, once and for all. "I've survived this long without a white knight and you're the last person on earth I'd want pretending I'm his damsel in distress."

Chuckling, Sleet laid a lazy arm across his horse's rump and looked at her. "I believe it. Want a Coke?"

"Not from you."

He let out a long-suffering breath. Then he did what she feared most; he came to stand in front of her, blocking her view of the cluster of riders back at the gate—her safety net. That she had to inhale a faint hint of his cologne and be reminded of what he did to her when he was close, put a chink in the armor of her defiance. She tilted her head and stared at him, letting the defiance bristle back to life.

"Look, Jess," he said in a brook-no-argument tone, "it's no sign of weakness to need other people once in a while."

"I know two categories of people," she said with a contemptuous flick of her gaze. "The first are those who show they care without trying to smother me."

"Such as?"

"My brother Josh. Hal. Most of my friends in this business."

"And the other type?"

"Those who threaten what I want."

"Like me?"

She'd stepped into quicksand but she covered it with a snappish, "Yes."

"Just how do I threaten you, Jess?"

"You meddle. You take without regard for others. You make a nuisance of yourself."

There was a dangerous glint in his gaze. "That kiss we had at your place the first night makes you a liar. I didn't have to take. You gave."

Something whisked through her—it was fear. "You took it, Sleet. Like you take everything else you want, even Hal's trust."

He grabbed her arms then, and pulled her close, so the scent he wore drifted over her like a midnight fantasy. "You little coward. I admired your grit. It was the thing that drew me. Now I see it's nothing but fear."

The color faded from her face. "That's a lie."

"You're afraid, Jess. You're afraid of anyone who might unmask the need and desperation in you."

She yanked down, straining, trying to get free. "I don't fear you, Freeman. I loathe you."

Suddenly his eyes were lightning blue, electric with fury and intent. She felt an answering swish of heat through her body.

In desperation she twisted, glanced around him. The arena was empty of all but horses drowsing at the fence. No one was looking toward the dim corner where she struggled to be free of Sleet Freeman. Her heart skittered.

Quickly she calculated that defiance would only worsen the conflict. She must use her head, her assets. If feminine wiles would work, she would use them. She quit squirming and looked up into his eyes. "Let me go, Sleet," she pleaded in a stage whisper, praying he wouldn't take her back to that place where her knees and her willpower went to putty. "Let me go."

"Not 'til I've had my say."

"Then say it!"

He eased the pressure of his grip and rubbed gently. "We don't know who's coming around your place at night, harassing you. Do we?"

"No, dammit, we don't."

"We don't know how dangerous they are." He waited.

"No," she admitted.

"We don't have the sheriff setting a deputy on a twenty-four-hour watch, either."

Her temper began to ease with the logic of his words. Afraid to push her luck when he was gentling, she shook her head.

"You need to protect your place, and you're alone," he said.

A spell was being cast, but it was so much less a threat than the terrible clash of their tempers. She let herself drift into it.

Perhaps he realized she'd stopped fighting him. His gaze grazed her lips, lingered. Longing went through her. She could only stand there, inches from him, like a bee trapped in thick nectar—buzzing with feeling.

"You're alone," he repeated, but far more softly. "Hal's worried and so am I, Jess."

"No need . . ."

"The thing is, I'm the single one, more or less without ties, with the least to lose if . . ."

He trailed off, and she felt a viper of fear twist up her back. The threat to her ranch was real.

"Hal and I agree," he continued. "You're as tough as they come when it comes to protecting your own."

"You called me a coward."

"Not in regard to your ranch, I didn't. Just this once, Jess, I don't think y'all ought to be alone."

It wasn't the womanizing side of Sleet Freeman she was seeing now, she told herself. It was the cowboy who'd been raised with country values. He and her neighbors wanted to protect her. If she refused, they'd do it anyway, and she'd be the miserly ungrateful rancher holed up in a warm ranch house while her "protector" stood guard from the hard bench of a pickup truck.

"It's just to help you protect the ranch you love so much," he added, thinking she still needed to be convinced. "If they burn you out, you'll have nothing."

She wanted to win the world, she reiterated, fighting the lull of his caressing hands. To do that, she needed Blue and what was left of the ranch. She'd be foolhardy to risk it all for some primitive fear of entrapment.

"What do you say, Jess?" he murmured. "Let me stay the night?"

It was a soft, coaxing purr. She was reminded that he was the enemy.

Looking up at him, she said, "Okay, Sleet, but if you persist with this misguided notion of yours about sexual conquest, I'll call the law. That's a promise. When Hal and the others find out about it, you'll be lucky to get back to Texas with your life."

He grinned. "Now, Jess, I already gave you my word on that last night. You can trust me."

"Sure," she said, stepping away, covering her inner qualms with a jaunty tone. "About as much as I'd trust a sidewinder in my pocket."

Chapter Six

They'd been to the feed store and the grocery store—Sleet had plans for a rare steak—and now he was driving the truck and trailer in under the rustic Latham Ranch sign.

All in all, he was thinking, his plans to keep an eye on the black stud and Jessica at the same time were panning out. He'd had a dicey moment or two when Jess had accused him of manipulating Hal into the "baby-sitting" theory, as she termed it. But she hadn't pursued the notion; she couldn't possibly know he wanted to buy her horse and was concerned about the animal's safety 'til he did. Believing he was just being neighborly—he'd let her continue in that vein because it was partially true and convenient as hell—probably accounted for the mellowing of that thistledown temper of hers.

Once she got used to the idea of having him around, she behaved civilly, if with distance.

Now if he could just keep his mind out of the bedroom and strictly on the business of watching Jess's place tonight, they had the beginnings of a pleasant visit. What started as a pleasant visit could end up, in a few days, with the groundwork for a business deal that was fair to both of them: cash money to rebuild her ranch, in exchange for Sleet's name on Blue's registration papers.

Trouble was, Sleet thought, slowing down for a rut, he had a one-track mind when it came to beautiful, feisty women. All he could think about was the erotic way Jess's lithe body molded to his in a kiss, and the hunger he'd tasted on her lips the night of the fire. True to form, his libido-driven brain was trying to figure a way to turn that hunger into passion. It was urging him to throw fresh wood on the coals that lay banked beneath her all-fired self-control. There had to be a way.

Because one thing was certain: he wasn't going to stop at gaining control of the horse. When he left town in December, he intended to leave behind a woman who knew, in the biblical sense, a real man, and appreciated him.

Sleet was glancing speculatively at Jess's profile beside him, when he saw her stiffen and stare out the windshield.

"Oh, no!" she moaned, gripping the door handle as if to jump out.

His gaze darted to the dirt track ahead. Water snaked down the drive toward them, bubbling and swirling across the road and down into the paddock. He imagined the barnyard was awash.

Untroubled by the calamity of a broken water main, the stud colt threw his black head high, sent a whistling call to the approaching truck-and-trailer—to its cargo of mares— and whirled to gallop back and forth across the arena.

"What the devil happened here?" Sleet asked, slowing the rig.

"Drive on through," Jess commanded, her face bleached with worry. "Otherwise you'll never get turned around."

Good thinking. He eased the rig through a twelve-foot swath of runoff that surged around the hubs of the wheels. Sure enough, runoff had pooled in small brown lakes where the ground was sunken between house, barn, cottage and arena. Jess's faded turquoise pickup was reflected in a lake near the barn. His own heavy trailer might tilt over in that bog. Unwilling to risk broken legs or cuts on the horses, he drove straight up onto a mound of sunburned grass near a stand of cypress, by the south side of the house.

"Go on and give me the high sign when I back up," he said. "See if I can turn around without sinking into the mud."

Strung like piano wire, Jess bolted from the truck.

Who the devil was harassing her? What did they want? Sleet wondered. He liked to confront an adversary, deal with him one-on-one. This sidewinder way of getting to Jess pissed him off.

Jess waved him back, interrupting his thoughts. He reversed gears, applied pressure to the gas pedal and felt the powerful engine ease its load toward her. He cut the turn as tight as he dared, right up to the railing of the weathered front porch. Throwing the gear shift, he nudged forward to the lip of the hillock, backed to the corner of the house and finally got the rig headed downhill toward the driveway.

Once he was outside and looking down at the burbling source of the leak, he knew it was going to be a long, messy job fixing it. He'd planned to wash down the two mares, get them curried and fed, then sit down to a steak dinner with Jess and see what developed. That obviously wasn't going to happen for a while.

"At least they didn't hurt the colt," he offered by way of sympathy.

"Hurt the colt?" she asked, glancing at him with a perplexed expression.

He angled a shoulder toward the water. "Whoever did this. They didn't mess with Blue."

Her cheeks pinked like spring roses. She looked away, curled her fingers into her palms. "It was me. I did it."

"You? I took you out of here this morning myself."

"No, I mean, I fixed the leak myself. The ground's weak from the fire hoses. Your rig's heavier than mine was. Maybe that's what cracked it open again."

She was embarrassed! He remembered the fix-it books stacked on her rolltop desk. At least she'd tried. "If try was worth money, Jess, you'd be a millionaire."

Her head snapped up. "What's that supposed to mean?"

The temper was back. He bridled. "Some of us do better with livestock," he said. "You have some spare fittings?"

"I'm good at trying but I failed anyway, is that what you're saying?"

"No, Jess, it's not. I was actually paying you a compliment, but if you need to keep the wires crossed to protect yourself from me, go ahead. Meanwhile, I'll need a shovel, and we'll need to shut down the water for a few hours."

"Fine, while you're doing your manly thing, I'll just hurry into the kitchen and rustle up your supper."

"You do that," he retorted, striding off toward the hay shed, where he hoped there were a few tools and fittings. He left her standing near a mud hole, glaring after him.

"How do you take your steak?" she called snidely.

"Juicy," he said. "The same way I take my women."

JESS WHACKED BRUTALLY at the vegetables, chopping 'til the lettuce and tomatoes looked more like salsa than salad.

She'd packed the groceries into the house a good hour ago. She hadn't even asked if Sleet needed any help with the repairs or currying the horses, and didn't know how he was faring. Part of her was grateful for his help—it might have taken days to repair the leak herself. But it wasn't like her to leave the manual labor to men, and her independent side resented him touching her things, working her land, running her out of her own front yard.

It'll be worse when he's in your kitchen, a warning voice told her, *eating the meal you prepared, wondering why your hands are shaking, watching your face for clues to your hidden feelings. Where else can you run?*

She brought the salad to the table. A fork clattered to the floor. She jumped, picked it up and put it in the sink. *Nowhere, with him spending the night.* She had to think of a strategy for that part. The cottage was Josepha and Noa's private domain and she was reluctant to let a stranger invade it. Josh's old room? The couch? Nowhere seemed safe.

It was no trouble to admit she wanted Sleet Freeman—wanted him in the most primitive, submissive, free-loving way she could imagine. The trouble was in avoiding it—for the championship, the win, the world title. He was the man she had to beat. The whole idea of competition was compromised if she slept with him.

Only problem was, Sleet's all-fired meddling kept throwing them together. As soon as Josepha and Noa got back, Jess reassured herself, he would no longer have an excuse to drop by. Keeping her distance from him would be easier. It would have to be.

She was thinking of putting him in the cottage for the night, anyway, instead of in Josh's old bedroom down the hall from the master, where she slept, when she heard the front door close.

Her heart moved strangely, then fluttered to life.

"Jess?" he called.

"In here." She hurried to the stove to turn a spoon through a saucepan full of corn.

Sleet's footsteps sounded in the hall, the entrance to the kitchen, every step making her heart hurdle. He came up beside her, glanced at the red steaks on the counter, at the bubbling corn and at her heated face. There was no sign of anger in him now. His eyes were full of humor-laced flirtation. "There's something so damned sexy about a beautiful woman cooking dinner," he said. "Do I smell corn bread?"

"I'm amazed you trusted me to bake it. There's something so damned *sexy* about making the decision to poison or not."

He grinned. "Which did you decide?"

"Let's wait and see, shall we?"

She grabbed a pot holder and pulled open the oven door. Bending, she grasped the pan and rescued the corn bread. It was golden, slightly brown at the edges, and its smell reminded Jess of her childhood. Perversely pleased, she set the hot pan on a stove burner, ducked to remove two crisply baked russet potatoes, closed the oven door and turned to him with a guarded expression. "Just the steaks left to cook. I'm going to broil them."

"Sounds good to me, honey."

She gave him a look of disgust.

Ignoring it, he swept his hands through hair that glistened like wheat after a rainstorm. He'd scraped the mud off his boots and washed up in the bucket on the porch. The blond hair on his corded arms gleamed with moisture. His grooved cheeks were damp. When he smiled, her legs became wobbly stilts. "You need a hand with supper?" he asked.

"What, and let you usurp my woman's prerogative? You can watch TV in the living room."

"I'd rather bother you."

She rolled her eyes and turned away, picking up a cooking fork. "There's beer in the fridge. Help yourself."

As he got the drink from the refrigerator, Jess forked a steak to the broiler pan and retrieved the other. Bent at the waist, she hesitated.

Something told her she had an audience. She glanced over her shoulder. Sleet was taking his fill of the curve of her thigh and buttocks. Slowly, reluctantly, she thought, his gaze traveled to her face.

He should have blushed. Instead, his voice low and thready, he said, "You're a fine, fine woman, Jess Latham. Give me the chance, I'll make you mine."

She dropped the steak. Sleet recovered first, nodded his head at it. She had to look away to reposition it on the smoking grill. Flustered, she drove the broiler door home and stood up, the fork poised to protect.

He noticed. "You'll want to put that down, Jess," he said in a soft drawl, and took a slug of beer.

"I will not. I obviously need it."

"Now, Jess." That crooning drawl. It reached out and twisted her unease into something else. Something more treacherous. He winked. "Y'all know what happens when you sass me."

Her face warmed with the remembered humiliation of being tackled in the arena—and kissed. "Don't even think it, Sleet Freeman. I'm warning you."

His leonine smile sent flash fires through her. He set the beer on the counter and, through some sort of magnetic telepathy, forced her to look into his eyes. "Didn't I warn *you?*" he asked softly.

"Don't."

"Y'all know I can make you cry uncle if I want."

He paced to her, stood so close his breath fanned her cheek. He grasped the fork and set the tines against his heart. "Go ahead on and drive it home, Jessie. I'm giving you your chance."

Beginning to tremble, she glanced away. "Chance?" she asked, breath shortened. Where the devil had her anger gone? She needed it, needed the protection of it.

"Chance to stop what I'm about to do," he explained.

It was tough to maintain her anger when he was stalking her with such lethal charm. She wanted to beg him not to ignite the flame that flickered greedily in her breast.

"The steaks—they'll burn," she said, face still averted.

"Better them than me." He lowered his head to the side of hers, pressing the fork into his chest as if to tell her he was willing to suffer to be this close. "You sassed me, woman," he whispered. "Y'all know what happens when you do that."

"Nothing," she whispered, desperate to prevent the inevitable, inexorable bonfire she knew could burst between them . . . and wickedly greedy to feel its heat. Now, this moment, would be the time to find the strength to resist him, to preserve her only chance to win the world. She tensed her muscles and pushed. He didn't budge, didn't wince at the prick of the fork. Voice pitched, she said, *"Nothing's going to happen!"*

"Wait and see. Wrap those lovely arms around me, Jess."

"I swore I'd call the law on you. Why are you forcing me to do it? I will, I'll call. . . ."

He chuckled softly and put his powerful arms around her, linking them at the small of her back. She was trapped, and the bonfire hissed and curled within. "You won't call the law," he said in a loving, patient way. "You want me as much as I want you. Now, where's my kiss?"

He was lowering his lips—only inches of space, milliseconds of time stood between this last struggle for independence, and total capitulation to a man she had only dreamed of finding, and loving. She girded her resolve. "I'm telling you to back off," she said coldly.

He laughed, released her and grabbed his beer. When he'd taken a drink, he announced, "I was only teasing you. I gave my word and I meant it."

"Except you keep breaking it."

"I haven't made a macho move on you in days," he replied, all indignant innocence.

"What do you call tonight, kid's play?"

"Yeah! I haven't even made a real play to get you in the sack!"

"You're mincing words!"

"If I had," he said as if he hadn't heard her, his voice rising, "we wouldn't be standing in your kitchen discussing it. Matter of fact, you wouldn't be standing at all. You'd be prone, or nearly so, in bed. With me."

"When hell freezes over!"

"Then get your winter duds. December isn't that far off."

"Sleet, you're impossible," she said in angry disgust. "You knew I meant to keep your hands off me when we made that bargain. You're purposely twisting my words, giving them a loose interpretation. It's despicable."

He threw his hands in the air. "I'm half in love with a woman with no sense of humor!"

Silence boomed in the kitchen. Jess's heart was careening crazily. She could hear it thundering, feel it pounding.

Slowly Sleet lowered his hands, his gaze darting in evident panic, in silent horror at his own words.

And she smiled.

"Well, now," she said in growing triumph. "And I thought you were the footloose-and-fancy-free type."

"I am," he snapped. "I didn't mean that. I just thought we'd have some laughs while I was in town. Maybe run back out to Hemet now and again to say howdy, see how you're gettin' along. Why make such a big deal out of a little fun, anyway?"

"Sorry to disappoint you, Sleet, but I don't sleep around."

He glanced at his beer. Moisture gleamed on the can. The silence lengthened. She measured the time in heartbeats—two, five, ten.

When he looked back at her, challenge gleamed in his eyes. "We'll see," he said. "We got some time between now and December. Now, what do I need to do to help you get supper on the table? I've had a long day and I'm hungry."

Vastly proud of herself for finally dislodging his infuriating aplomb, she smiled with mock-sweetness. "Why don't you turn the steaks," she said. "I'll get the corn bread and potatoes."

She pushed back the thrilling, thunderous response she'd felt when he'd admitted he was half in love with her—pushed it deep into her subconscious. Winning the world was more important than anything, even love, she told herself, reaching for a pot holder.

Especially love that would eventually break her heart.

Chapter Seven

Supper was a moody, silent affair punctuated by stiff exchanges.

"Please pass the pepper," Sleet asked at one point, and she passed it without looking at him.

"The corn bread is superb," he said later, slathering a crumbly pale yellow chunk of it with butter and honey.

"Thank you," she responded, and forced herself to finish a bite of steak sweet with rare juices—tasteless when she remembered that he liked his steak just as he liked his women. Practically everything he said related to sex. There was no safe ground on which she could introduce a topic of conversation, so she ate silently, her stomach tense.

Afterward, Sleet offered to help her with the dishes, but she quipped something about it being woman's work and hustled him into the living room to watch television.

The dishes done, she peeked into the room and saw that he'd built a fire in the fireplace and ensconced himself in the corner of the big leather couch. He glanced up at her, his gaze assessing.

Wordlessly she crossed in front of him to the rolltop desk, where she spent fifteen minutes updating her training records and sorting unpayable bills. She would normally have watched the news at ten o'clock, but Sleet was sprawled in the corner in the couch, engrossed in an old Western, his handiwork at the hearth casting wavering warmth around the room. The setting was far too intimate. She rose from the desk and announced to the air in front of him as she headed for the hallway, "You can use Josh's room tonight. Second door on the left. The bed is made up."

"All right," he said in a neutral voice.

As she left the room, she could feel his eyes tracing the fitted black jeans she wore. She felt naked.

"Sleep well," he called.

She gained the hall, the tread of her boots echoing hollowly. "You too," she said stiffly.

Entering her room, she closed the door, leaned against it and drew in a deep relieved breath. Here she was reasonably safe. Now if she could only shower and get to sleep.

IT WAS A TRIBUTE to how far she'd fallen for him that Jess didn't sleep well. When she woke in the forty-year-old cherrywood four-poster, blinking in a cottony morning light, her eyes felt gritty. Someone had put sand under her lids while she slept. Someone had put a new, heavy weight inside her body, just below her heart. And someone had filled her with the clinging languor of sexual fantasy.

She'd dreamed of racing away from the burning barn on the young stallion. Sleet had been with her, cradling her, burying his face in her streaming hair, his canyon-deep voice urging, "Go, Jess, go for the world!"

Because it was so sweet, she'd replayed the dream and this time they'd swept out of the barn into a white mist. Arms entwined, bodies glistening, hearts pounding, they'd completed the ride as lovers, his voice urging, "Give to me, Jess. Give to me, give to me!"

Jess shook her head. The languor faded slightly and she reached for her emerald robe, slipping it on and putting her feet down on the oval braided rug beside the bed. She shivered. It was chilly, and she wondered if Sleet would think her miserly to have foregone the use of the gas furnace. Perhaps she should put it on to warm the house before he woke. She owed him that much. He'd had a busy night.

Twice he'd risen from his bed to conduct a security check. It had been strange to hear the small sounds he'd made in the middle of the night, leaving Josh's room, shutting the front door, tiptoeing across the porch. She'd seen the splash of his flashlight reflected on her ceiling as he patroled the ranch in the starless night, and felt secure. She'd drifted back to sleep each time, and come awake again to the groan of bedsprings when Sleet retired. As unsettling as it had been to have him in her home, it was of greater comfort to know he was near should an intruder visit.

Hearing hoofbeats, she glanced out the lace-trimmed window. It seemed she'd be saved the gesture of turning on the heat.

And then she took another look. Hatless, Sleet was wearing the black-and-white plaid shirt, jeans and chaps from yesterday, and circling Blue on a lounge line in the arena. A gray sky arched behind them, and a pale fog drifted in shreds. The scene had a dreamlike quality, and Jess shook her head again. What the devil was he doing exercizing Blue?

The sweet, piercing pleasure of consummated love had woken her. Now a sharp dagger of concern sent her to the closet, to scramble into denim jeans and an oversize cotton work shirt.

Sleet was one of the nation's top trainers. He knew what he was doing when he worked with horses. But what was he doing with her futurity champion? Checking him out, that was obvious, but why?

Jess dashed water on her face, brushed her teeth and hurried out onto the porch. He didn't hear her close the front door, didn't see her rub her arms to scrub the morning chill from her flesh. Nor did he realize she watched him for several long moments, struck dumb by his actions.

"Come here, boy," she heard him tell the colt as he gathered in the tether and urged the horse to approach him. Sleet's voice carried on the still cool air, and Jess marveled at the gentleness with which he spoke to the colt. It was as if he were wooing him.

Blue threw his head, pulling the lounge line taut. He danced sideways. "Easy, Blue," Sleet said, collecting coils of rope. He reached back to smooth his satiny neck, but the stud spooked away and lifted onto his haunches. When he came down, shaking his head, Sleet took advantage of forward momentum and snugged him closer.

Reaching behind him to pull out a six-foot leather lead that had been looped through the waistband of his chaps, Sleet walked up to Blue's head. When Blue peered down at Sleet with wary eyes, the coffee-brown irises ringed in white, the trainer unsnapped the lounge line and hooked on the lead. Slowly he raised a hand to the quivering nostrils and, holding the animal's head still, began to stroke the fine, chiseled face.

"What the devil?" Jess murmured, perplexed.

Sleet rubbed Blue's forehead, speaking low when the animal tossed his head, applying downward pressure on the lead. "Put your head down," he said gently. "That's it. Down. This is going to feel good."

Sleet massaged between the large, intelligent eyes and up into the twin muscles running from the ears to the center of the forehead.

Jess was mesmerized, watching those slim tanned fingers explore the horse's face. It wasn't a bit of trouble to imagine what it would feel like on her own skin.

The languor of the dream swept over her, and she relaxed for a moment, as if she were the one receiving his touch. It was odd. She didn't mind the fantasy.

Within minutes, Sleet had to crouch because Blue's head began to lower toward the ground. Jess was quietly amazed. Blue hardly ever allowed her to touch his face. She assumed he'd been slapped around and was hand-shy.

Suddenly jealousy rammed through her amazement. Sleet was gentling her stud, trying to confuse his loyalty, imprint his own essence on the stallion's heart.

"Damn you," she muttered, and leapt from the porch. She crossed the barnyard, climbed through the arena rails and strode up to them.

Blue's head came bolting up. Sleet murmured something and turned, taking in the anger and suspicion in her face. "Easy," he said to her, moving his right hand to Blue's neck.

"Easy, hell," she retorted, stuffing her fists into her waist. "What do you think you're doing with my stud?"

"I'm working some kinks out of him. I didn't think you'd mind."

"I do mind. I mind like you would if I took a sledgehammer to that ritzy red-and-white rig of yours. Now what the hell are you doing?"

"I told you. Blue goes rough to the left. I'm trying to find the reason. Was he injured at some point?"

A memory flashed. When she'd seen Blue for the first time, gangly and starved, his flanks had been speckled with dried blood—spur marks, and he shouldn't even have been ridden hard yet.

Jess stood still, not even attempting to cover her shock. She glanced at the colt, then back to Sleet. The man was absolutely correct. Cutting a calf to the right, Blue was quick as spiced chili. He had to work harder to get around to the left. If he lost a cow, it was to that side. She'd drilled him endlessly, and because he was young and willing to work, the left turns had improved. But not to perfection, and that was what it would take to win the world. It had worried her.

"Was he showing any signs of injury when you brought him home the first time?" Sleet prompted.

"Spur marks. He was filthy. His hipbones protruded."

"Anything else? His legs, for instance?"

She shook her head, then remembered something. "A bruise high on his right shoulder."

"Bruise?"

"Contusion, I guess you'd call it. A big lump. I iced it down for him. It receded like any other bruise after he'd had proper care."

Thinking of the weeks of rehabilitation, she felt a surge of proprietorship. She reached to grasp Blue's lead.

"That explains why he's rougher going left," Sleet said, relinquishing the lead, rubbing a hand over Blue's sleek shoulder. "He's still compensating for the injury. If you get that worked out of him, he'll probably be more balanced when he moves."

Jess was too much a trainer in her own right, with too much energy devoted to her goals, to miss the importance of what he was saying. She extended a hand to Blue's muzzle, let him inhale her scent, then ran her fingers up his face. After a few tries, Blue let her massage him for the first time since she'd owned him. He began to lower his head. Her heart jumped in hope.

"Can you fix what's wrong with him?" she asked Sleet, trying to be casual. Still, some of the hope crept in.

"Maybe. We could try."

We. The world champion was going to show her some techniques. More than she wanted to question his motives, she wanted to have what he knew and she did not. "What do we do?"

"We touch him. It's about trust. I've gained his confidence. I've proven that I won't hurt him." He paused, then said, "Horses are like dogs, or people, for that matter. Whether they admit it or not, they like to be touched." For the first time, Sleet looked directly into her eyes. He added softly, "Don't they, Jess?"

Someone hung that stone below her heart again, making it beat slowly, heavily. Her shoulders lifted in unconscious shyness.

He searched her face, focused on her lips.

They parted for him—exactly as if he'd kissed her.

He drew a catchy breath. She felt drawn into his gaze, taunted by the longing there and chastised by subtle accusation.

"Sleet, I..." Though she ached to end the controversy between them, she let the sentence trail off.

"It's hard for me, too," he said, and looked away. "Y'all hold him, then, while I work my way back." And the moment was gone.

"I'll be touching muscles that have been sore for a good part of his life," he was saying, moving around, playing his hands over superb horseflesh, expertly gauging tenderness. If Blue jumped, he soothed. It was magic. "Horses hold trauma and pain in their muscles for a lifetime. Unless it's worked out, it'll always be a misery to them, and while it's being worked out, it's uncomfortable. The trick is to start gentle, gain trust and increase the pressure until healing takes place."

As he talked, the timbre of his voice created a tight knot in Jess's belly. The knot was a longing, a longing so intense, she barely breathed. She watched Sleet wriggle the great curved muscle beneath Blue's black mane. He put his left hand against the back side of Blue's neck for support while he circled three fingers into the forward muscles. She felt each touch in her own body.

When he retreated to rework the area above the shoulder, Blue tossed his head and sidestepped. He curved his head around to investigate.

"I expected tenderness here," Sleet commented, continuing to apply circles of pressure, and Jess fought down the sexual responses so she could pay attention. "This side has been taking more stress than the side where the injury occurred."

"To compensate," she said, and it came out a thready whisper.

Sleet's head jerked around; his gaze pierced her with inquiry. She quickly averted her eyes—they would reveal too much.

"Right," he intoned, turning away again. "We'll be gentle at first. In later massages, y'all can increase the pressure. Watch his head. See how he's bobbing it?"

"I see."

"He's telling me it's sore. Telling me to take it easy. Let the horse tell you what he likes, what he can stand."

The incredible insights she was gaining finally penetrated the sexual mist into which she'd wandered. She focused her mind on the lesson, watched and listened in fascination. After thirty minutes, Blue's muzzle hung as low as Jess's knees. Suddenly she knew that she might have failed to train this colt to win the world. It was a sobering thought. Because of Sleet . . .

Jess tingled with excitement, with certainty. Blue was going to be a pussycat on the ground. Sleet had given her the way to finish Blue to perfection and win the world. Did he realize what he'd done?

Sleet's own eyes were half closed. He was enjoying the massage as much as Blue. It was hard to figure. Why would he invest himself in a competitor's horse this way?

But the fact remained, he had done it and she was grateful.

Despite the many times she'd distrusted and resented Sleet Freeman, this gift of healing was a gift to cherish. It said something very personal, very special about the man who'd given it so freely. Beneath the macho charm and wayward nature, he was a kind and gentle man.

At that moment, Sleet turned, still rolling hide to either side of the backbone, and studied Jess's face.

Something memorable happened then. Like steel heated in flame and molded to permanent shape, Jess's brain recorded the essence of Sleet Freeman. From now till death, through separations, aging and new experience, he would always be with her. The finely textured skin of his rugged, long-lined face would always be shaved, the blue eyes forever alight with intimacy, insight, and desire; his hands ceaselessly caressing away pain and bringing pleasure.

"I want to do this to y'all," he said quietly. "My gut aches with wanting it. It just about breaks my heart to imagine we never will."

His words spooked her, sent her pivoting, turning her back on him, the movement barely illiciting a head bob from Blue. She decided he was wrong. They *would* make love. Not today, not even next week—but when she'd taken this horse into the arena in Fort Worth and shown him the cows, no matter the outcome, she would hunt down Sleet Free-man and take him to her bed. Why? Why was she so sure?

She filled her eyes with the sight of the sun breaking through clouds, and knew the answer.

I want you, Sleet, she thought. *Just for one glorious night. It'll last me a lifetime.*

Until that night, the secret was hers. But she'd be damned if it would get in the way of glory. Winning the world would come first. Then, when she was at the pinnacle, she would seek out the man she had beaten and take him to her bed.

Chapter Eight

"Try that brown cow," Sleet called.

"It's too sluggish," Jess argued, and waited 'til an ugly brown-and-white spotted heifer tried to dodge past Blue. Jess loosened the reins. The colt splayed his front legs and squared off with the calf. The two began to dance.

Watching Jess only increased Sleet's inner turmoil.

She was cutting some cows with the black to see how his left turns had improved, using the sawhorses to diminish the open space of the arena. Sleet was up on Checkers, riding turn-back, trying to keep his mind on the workout. He'd promised not to pursue her, then, first chance he got, blurted out that he wanted to touch her. She'd turned her back on him. He was a danged fool.

To ease his chagrin, he watched Blue, soon to be his most promising futurity colt. Each time a calf cut left, Blue turned back over his haunches in a gleaming mass of power, ever more fluid, more effortless as he worked the kinks out of newly released muscle tissue. Sleet marveled at his prowess. He itched to ride him.

At least the overnight stay hadn't been a total loss on that account, Sleet thought. Rising early, he'd fed the livestock, a habit still clinging from his youth on the Missouri farm. Feeding early also kept the animals quiet. He'd wanted a chance to work with Blue before Jess woke up, and he'd gotten it. He'd learned what he'd wanted to know: the stud was physically sound, and he responded well to massage therapy.

The ruse that he was "just being neighborly" was working well for him, he thought, wheeling Checkers to turn Jess's cow. It was working well all right, but it was also beginning to leave a foul taste in his mouth. The sidewinder way of doing business just wasn't his style. Yet the thought of someone else taking that black stallion to the futurity made his skin crawl with foreboding. His underhanded methods felt doubly sly when he mixed in personal interest in Jess.

Relaxed in the saddle, she laughed like a kid on Christmas morning. "He's so much better," she called, clinging to the saddle horn, her hair flying in a fetching way. "His turns are quicker."

At that moment, Blue lagged behind the cow in a sprint to the far side of the arena. "Touch him with your spur," Sleet hollered. "Get after him a little."

Jess complied.

"Good. Ease up now. A little metal goes a long way with him."

"Ease up yourself, Sleet," she said, sending him a quelling look. "I'm not some greenhorn, never sat a horse before."

He grimaced. She was right. She was a regular rag doll in a dicey cut. He ought to shut up or she'd start to wonder why he was so concerned about what she did with the horse.

If seeing her mounted hadn't constantly reminded him of how badly he wanted her, Sleet would have enjoyed witnessing her pleasure in the stallion's improvement. But Jess was beginning to worry him. He'd mulled it over this morning in the chilly mist. He hadn't meant that slip of the lip last night—"half in love with a woman with no sense of humor!" Trouble was, she had worked her way under his skin, like a bothersome insect. She was threatening his long-held belief that freedom meant happiness.

"Don't get lazy on me, Blue," she said sharply, running the colt straight up to the fence and stopping him hard. Alerted, Sleet narrowed his eyes. Jess backed Blue swiftly for ten feet, and he simply ducked his head and complied, hooves clicking against rocks, kicking up clouds of dust. Sleet silently approved of her schooling; she certainly knew the basics. The spotted cow darted back to the herd, and she cut into them again, searching for another. Determination practically shimmered off of her in waves.

Sitting his horse, watching the cut, Sleet drifted back to his problem. He'd never met a woman who made him question his choices as Jess did. He'd never felt guilty for being who he was. When a woman told him no, which was rare, he simply shrugged and went on to the next opportunity.

Since he'd met Jess, something had changed. *He* was changing. Her *no* riled his temper, and, for the first time, he was actually ashamed of his footloose life-style. He'd begun rethinking his directions. He'd begun kicking himself for not buying a ranch and building his dream when he had the money to do so. But Blue was going to change all that. Buying him was the first step.

He was mulling over how to approach the subject of the sale, when a yellow cow zinged past him.

"Dang it," he muttered, wheeling Checkers. He touched her flanks with his spurs, felt the lunge she made to recapture the cow, but the yellow critter bumped a sawhorse and darted through the barrier.

At the same moment, Jess whooped.

Sleet craned around.

She was gazing toward the driveway, face alight with pleasure. He glanced in that direction, herding the stray cow as he noted an approaching station wagon. It was dented on the driver's side, a ten-year-old red rattletrap. And it was hauling a rickety one-horse trailer. Was it her people, back from Mexico?

By the time he'd gotten the cow back through the barrier, Jess had opened the cattle pen and was gathering the cows into it. He helped round them up.

"Josepha and Noa are back," she announced, leaning down to throw the bolt on the pen. Happiness and exertion put a blush in her cheeks, a smile in her eyes. She was either extremely glad to have chaperons around, or else she loved them like family. Either way, his solo time with her had ended. He was almost relieved.

"If you'll give me your reins, I'll cool out the horses while you say your hellos," he said.

"Thanks," she said, dismounting, handing them to him. As he rode off, she was already hurrying toward the gate.

In the next fifteen minutes, he walked the horses, unsaddled them, washed them down with the hose and tied them at the arena fence to let the sun dry their coats. The stud put up a little fuss but not his usual wingding. Trust was developing between them. It was more than he'd accomplished with Jess.

Meanwhile, Sleet heard the glad sounds of reunion. The trio stacked supplies on the front porch, snippets of Spanish and English drifting to him as they caught up on family news and the reason for the sodden state of the barnyard. They were a charming sight, Sleet noted.

A slight woman wearing a shapeless flowered dress, her steel-gray hair braided and knotted in a crown, Josepha fluttered around Jess, hugging her impulsively and beaming at her like a hen reunited with a lost chick.

A short, aging *caballero* with deep lines in his face, Noa wore faded jeans, thick-heeled Mexican riding boots and a denim shirt buttoned to the throat. He made short, bow-legged sprints to the porch, bent under the weight of cardboard boxes of supplies, occasionally smiling privately at the two chattering women.

With another man around, Sleet thought grumpily, he was only baggage. The quicker he got off this ranch, the better. He had to get on with his life—such as it was—and that meant taking care of his responsibilities at the Britton place. In the meantime, he'd check his finances, make a formal offer for the stud and plan his next strategy with Jess.

Suddenly, as he hefted Jess's saddle to haul it into the space he'd cleared for it in the barn, Sleet heard exclamations of horror. Evidently the couple had just noticed the blackened roof of the barn. Most of the hole in the roof was on the side you couldn't see from the driveway.

"¿Qué pasó, mi'ja?" Noa asked in a pitched voice, using the endearment "little one." "What has happen here?"

He started for the barn, then stopped, sweeping a straw *bracero's* hat from his gunmetal gray head and holding it against his chest with both butternut-brown hands. "What happen to the barn? We are only gone a few days. You, the horses, we are okay?"

Jess assured him they'd all survived. Sleet heard his name mentioned. He continued into the barn to store Jess's tack. When he emerged from the barn, he nearly ran into Josepha.

"Gracias, señor," she said, taking his left hand in hers and pressing it. Her brown eyes were misted with emotion. "You have saved our Jessica. We are very grateful, very happy. I will fix you my best *carne asada,* my famous *tortillas de masa.* You like Mexican food? *Gracias, señor."*

He chuckled, nodded, saying yes, he liked Mexican food plenty. Jess's friends charmed him, made him feel less like baggage and more like family.

Jess hurried forward to introduce them. When she had, Noa grasped Sleet's hand in an iron grip and pumped hard. "My wife say for me. Thank you, *señor*. This *muchacha*—" glancing at Jess "—she is like a daughter to us. We work for her father for many years. My wife, she raised Jessica from a little *muchacha*."

A horse shrilled, a young, clear call of inquiry, and Noa let go of Sleet's hand to glance around. He struck his forehead and said, "*¡Ay!* I forget! I bring you a gift, *mi'ja*."

"A gift? But . . ." Jess's voice trailed off.

She frowned toward the ancient single-horse trailer attached with chain and bailing wire to the red station wagon. The trailer was one of the old type; narrow and rounded like an enclosed Roman arch, with barely room for one horse.

Noa's eyes crinkled in evident mystery. Josepha raised her dark eyebrows at Jess, expressing maternal excitement. Then she crossed the barnyard with her husband, skirting the wet spots, lifting dainty hands. Jess and Sleet followed, exchanging glances.

"I can't afford to feed another horse!" Jess whispered, apprehension putting a crimp in her brow.

You can when you put my generous check in your bank account, Sleet thought.

As he neared the trailer, his curiosity was piqued. Even Jess, preoccupied with financial matters, was peering with interest at the dilapidated vehicle.

Noa was explaining something about a cousin in San Ysidro who'd lost his job at the rendering factory in Otay Mesa and had had to sell some of his stock.

"I do him a favor and take this little one off his hands," said Noa, turning to Jess, spreading his arms as if he'd had no choice in the matter. "She steal my heart, steal my Josepha's heart." He looked at his wife for confirmation.

Josepha nodded, smiled.

"Then I think," continued Noa, stepping backward, "Jessica will love she, too. The black stud will love she. They will get *caballitos*—little babies—to cut the cows!"

Jess grinned in spite of herself. Noa's enthusiasm was catching.

Noa instructed Josepha to get something out of the car while he went around to the back of the trailer and unhooked a half door. He hunched under a frayed, knotted rump rope and went forward along the body of a sorrel filly who couldn't have been more than fourteen months old, judging by the size and gangly look of her. After Noa had untied the lead, Sleet reached in and untied the rump rope. Speaking in low Spanish, Noa backed the young horse a few steps, to the edge of the trailer. There was no ramp, and she stretched her leg, testing the drop-off, then backed suddenly out of the trailer. She stood with legs splayed and stiff, craning her head at the three adults standing in a semicircle behind her.

"Ohhh," said Jess in soft amazement. "She's lovely!"

At the sound of the feminine voice, the frightened filly nickered and stepped tentatively in Jess's direction. Noa gave Jess the lead.

Holding what Sleet recognized to be American Quarter Horse registry papers, Josepha murmured, "She is called Brisa—like a soft wind."

"Brisa," Jess repeated on a note of awe.

"She comes from cattle-roping stock," Noa said, smiling as if Brisa were his gifted child. "Her papa is very famous in Mexican rodeo."

"Do you know cows, Brisa?" Jess asked, reaching out her open palm to let the animal nuzzle her. The youngster nickered, rolling her eyes balefully at the others, and stepped closer to Jess. Unaware of Sleet's eyes on her, Jess touched the white star between the filly's eyes and began to massage the muscles of her face, mimicking the techniques Sleet had taught her. He felt a stirring of pride.

In a moment, the young horse grew restless to explore her surroundings, and Jess walked her away from the group.

Blue shrilled his possessive, commanding stallion's call, and the yearling skittered sideways, seemingly frightened and thrilled at once. She was exquisite. Her head was finely molded, the dark eyes large as an Arabian's and set wide, the nose tapering to sculpted nostrils. Her legs, Sleet had already noted, were straight and unblemished, the pasterns above the hooves long and pliant, promising a cushioned ride. Though she wasn't muscled up yet, she had the slope to her haunches and the breadth of chest that promised power.

Jess spoke to her and began to trot away down the access road, and the youngster moved with her like well-oiled machinery—smooth, effortless, balanced. She was one hell of a filly. Sleet felt the familiar itch along his backbone—his trainer's instinct. Would she train up well? Stop good, turn good, show cow sense?

He didn't know how many seconds had passed before he realized Noa and Josepha were watching him silently. Starting slightly, he glanced at them and grinned sideways. Their faces showed an empathy and perceptiveness that made him feel transparent; they seemed to know something about him he didn't understand himself.

"She is very fine, is she not?" asked Josepha in a gentle way.

Did she mean horse or woman? Sleet wondered. He chose to dissuade any personal discussion. "How'd you get her over the border without the usual quarantine, the shots, the red tape?''

The man shrugged. "She mama is in San Ysidro. Across the border from Tijuana, on the American side."

"Ah. Then the dam is American?"

"*Sí.*" He murmured something to Josepha, who excused herself and brought the registration papers into the ranch house. Noa waited 'til she was gone, then took on a man-to-man tone and said to Sleet, "The *madre,* she was bred to the Mexican rodeo champion. He is very *macho.* Very strong, very quick, very big. The dam, she is strong, too, but delicate, like a dove. Brisa have both. She have the beauty and the strong. She also have, what do you call, citizenship. She is all very legal, Señor Sleet."

"I wasn't questioning that, Noa. Just curious. She's a fine quarter horse."

"*Sí.* Our Jessica try so hard to have a horse ranch, to be like she father. My wife and I talk, decide we can use our savings to help her. I wager very hard with my cousin, and he gave me Brisa and the trailer for, what do you call, a thief."

Sleet frowned.

"I steal she, *señor.* I make the excellent bargain."

"Ah," said Sleet, nodding, glad of the subject, the diversion from inner squalls. "It's a very generous gift."

Noa studied him, then asked abruptly, "Who burn the barn, Señor Sleet?"

"I don't know. The fire marshal is investigating. He seems to think someone replaced the wiring for the light on the roof of the barn. Since it comes on automatically, it could be rewired hours before it fails."

"Replaced? *¿Por que?* Was it broken?"

"No. The wire they put in was very thin. It would heat up within an hour of the light being on. It would then short out against other wires, and start a fire."

Noa ran a thoughtful hand over his smoothly shaved, lined face. "I will ask who has done this evil thing."

If the sheriff's office, the fire marshal's men and the network of ranchers who were applying their separate means of investigation to the question couldn't solve the mystery, how was a man who spoke broken English and spent his days isolated at the ranch going to solve it? Sleet studied the shorter man, saw the intensity, the spark of intelligence in his eyes and realized Noa was not to be underrated.

"I'm at the Britton Ranch, Noa," he said. "Call me if trouble comes around, will you?"

"Pues, sí," Noa replied. Then he smiled, creasing his face with half-moons of wrinkles. "When you are looking at Jessica, my wife, she poke me. She say with her eyes, this man, he like our Jessica. She say this is a good man. He save her life. We will find the *hombre* who hurt her and kick his ass, eh?"

In spite of his concerns, Sleet chuckled. Perhaps all was not so gloomy after all; he had an ally, and so did Jess.

Chapter Nine

The return of Josepha and Noa brought routine back to Jess's life. No arsonists showed up to burn her out, no thugs harassed her in the dark of night, and while the authorities were unable to close the cases, the aging couple provided peace of mind by their presence.

Hal called every day to check on her, and because he assumed she and Sleet had become friendly rivals after his service as a bodyguard, he filled her in on his whereabouts. She wanted news of his comings and goings, she fed on it, but Hal didn't know that.

Two weeks slipped by. Jess phoned Josh to bring him up-to-date on the status of the arson case, but didn't mention the note that had sailed through her window one dark night. Why worry him when he could do nothing to solve the crime?

Nor could Hal. "Sanford's office says they ain't got lead one," he fretted on a Thursday afternoon. "You'd think all that highfalutin electronic stuff they got in law enforcement would now hustle the case along a bit."

"I know it, Hal," she said. "No fingerprints, no real clues. All we know about the note is that they used oil-based house paint, with bits of cypress twig mixed in."

"That don't tell us nothin'. There's stands of cypress scattered here and there across the valley. But someone did it and it worries me, Jess."

"It was just some kids, fooling around," she told him—but she didn't believe that for a minute. She still hadn't entirely forgotten she'd once suspected Sleet. That was the scary part of the crimes: anyone, even a neighbor, could have perpetrated them. But she had no proof, and Hal was worrying himself sick over the case. She thought to change the subject. "Meanwhile, we've got a show this weekend. Your trainer going to be there to give you some tips on the palomino?"

"No, Jess, I'm on my own. Sleet's hauling to a show in northern California this weekend." Jess felt disappointment sludge her enthusiasm for the coming show. Hal went on chatting about Sleet. "He no more gets back and he's packing up for another trip. Hauling for a national points standing'll stress you, you know? That boy's burnin' the candle at both ends. Somethin' lit a fire under him, I swear."

"What do you mean?"

"I mean he's trainin' my colts, flyin' off to Texas to see clients 'n' packin' up for shows from here to hell 'n' gone. Grouchy as a—no," he amended, "not exactly grouchy. Driven, more like. Guess he's gettin' the jitters, the season bein' over in a couple months."

So he'd changed. Why? Season jitters . . . or jitters over a specific competition? She smiled. Maybe seeing the way Blue was shaping up had worried him. But then—why had he used his special massage to improve the stallion? She still couldn't figure that one out.

Hal chuckled. "I'm going to be there to see the two of you battle it out in Cowtown, girl. Now that's going to be a show."

The world champion was training Hal's futurity colts, but she had Blue. Her confidence was high. "You're pretty proud of the colts he's training for you, you say?" she taunted.

"Sure am. Planning to bring me home a bundle of money, come December."

"Don't get too set on taking home the cash, Hal. My colt's getting around in his turns these days."

"Yeah?" he asked on a higher note.

"Yeah," she responded firmly.

"Well, you're good with the horses, too. I'll give you that. Told your daddy, when you were growed 'bout up to my waist, you showed promise of being a chip off the old block. You showing this weekend?"

He'd changed the subject. The thought of losing in Texas niggled him. She grinned. "Sure am."

"Need a lift?"

"Thanks, Hal, but I'm borrowing Noa's trailer."

"Need anything else, Jess? You gettin' along okay? Sleet will want his report."

"Report?"

"He asks about ya. Wants to know about the case 'n' all. I tell him Blue's picked up a trick or two since he's been gone, and it near to chokes him to death. He can't stand the thought of a woman givin' him a run for his money in December, y'know. I have fun with that one." He chuckled.

A confusion of feelings assailed her—a strange warmth in her gut from Sleet's interest, indignation at his prejudices, curiosity about his motives for asking about her. But most of all, her competitive nature was riled.

"You have your fun, Hal," she retorted. "I'll have the satisfaction of whipping the pants off both of you, come December. I got to go. Blue's chomping at the bit to get to his cows."

"Now, Jess," Hal temporized, but she got off the phone and stormed out to the arena, where she gave Blue the workout of his career.

UNABLE TO AFFORD the entry fees for the prestigious shows in Brawley and Las Vegas that took Sleet out of town, she worked hard in the arena and around the ranch. From dawn 'til dusk, she continued to massage all three horses, taught Brisa to walk and trot on command when tethered to the lounge line, and, for the older horses, alternated ring work with endurance training in the steep foothills above the ranch. After a hearty supper, she showered and went to bed, collapsing into a dreamless sleep.

In the mornings, Jess woke with the clinging sexual languor of that time when Sleet had stayed. She spent the first few minutes of her day dreaming of his seduction. Through her shower and grooming rituals, she recalled his face, his touch, the way he could soften her with a glance.

Though the dream of winning the futurity still drove her—and knowing Sleet looked down his nose at a woman competitor enhanced her drive—the anticipation of seducing him made the dream much sweeter.

Sleet's departure from her ranch three weeks ago had been cordial. Mellowed in her treatment of him by the great gift he'd imparted in regard to Blue, Jess had thanked him warmly. When he drove away, he'd tipped his hat and said, "I'll be in touch, Jess. Take care of yourself."

She'd felt a twinge in her heart.

Three weeks had deepened the twinge to an ache. She had become obsessed with his rugged masculinity, and couldn't wait to feel that healing touch of his turn to passion on her body.

As the days shortened with coming winter, she grew edgy with unrelieved tension. Work was her only outlet. All she could do was drive herself and Blue mercilessly, and dream of her plans for Texas.

ON A WINDY OVERCAST morning in mid-October, Noa came to her in the barn and fidgeted 'til he had her attention. His hat was in his hands, a sure sign he was perturbed.

"Hey, Noa," she said, her arms full of straw for Sienna's stall. The cavernous barn still smelled charred but the two stalls toward the front had been scrubbed and now housed Sienna and Blue. Brisa had the cattle for company. Jess went into the stall and shook straw around, then came back to a wheelbarrow parked in the corridor and grabbed another armful. She eyed Noa. *"¿Qué pasa?"*

"The *Mexicano* who works for the Millers, below this place?" He curled the brim of the hat. "He say he see two *hombres* drive a big car up here the day of the fire."

"He what!" Jess threw down the hay and closed the stall door, stepping into the corridor. Her eyes bored into Noa's.

"Sí," he said. "He is only a boy, just nineteen, but he sees real good. He said the *hombres* visit this ranch. He don't know why, because I am gone to Mexico, and he say you drive away maybe half hour earlier."

"How does he know this?"

"He know because he is cleaning the corrals for Señor Miller. He say you go to town, then these two *hombres* drive up."

She dusted her hands, filled with the need to have all the facts at once. "What's the boy's name, Noa?"

"Antonio Pascale Maria-Esques. *Americanos* call him Tony Pascale."

"Pascale." Her heart was ripping around in its cage. She tried to sound calm, think of roadblocks to chasing down this lead. "Is he . . . legal? Will he be afraid to talk to the authorities?"

"No, is okay. He has a green card."

"Good. Did he say what the men looked like?"

"*Sí,* a handsome man like a *torero*—a bullfighter—with black hair and beautiful clothes. He drives the car."

"What kind of clothes?"

"A jacket, a suit. Like for Sunday."

"And the other?"

"This one, he is a small man who wears working clothes. Antonio think he work in a store. The boy could not see this man's face. But the other, he see him."

"And the car?"

Noa grinned. "Antonio, he like the cars. He know everything. Used to be *mecánico* in Mexico. He know what kind of car the *hombres* drive."

Pushing urgency below the surface because she loved Noa, she said gently, "The car, Noa. What kind of car?"

"A big Lincoln. Town Car, he say. Black with tinted windows. The driver's window was down. Antonio say it was a pleasant day, the day the barn was burn."

Jess barely heard that last. She'd seen a dark luxury car leaving her property the night someone threw a stone through her window. She's known it had been a dark vehicle because so little light had reflected from the paint. The two visits had to be connected. She strode out of the barn, tossing over her shoulder, "The wheelbarrow, Noa. Could you put it away for me?"

WITH TWENTY-EIGHT thousand dollars banked in four weeks, gleaned from client fees and a grueling run of shows, Sleet was finally able to look himself in the mirror again. Checking into his finances a month ago, he'd found them criminally depleted. There was no other word to describe it. He'd honky-tonked and caroused for months, had sunk a fortune into a new rig purely to boost his ego, and when he'd wanted to take the first step toward a life of substance, he'd found he was nearly broke. It had sobered him dramatically.

He ought to be proud of himself, he thought. He deserved a night out on the town. A night of dancing, maybe a quick take-down in the cab of his truck, would relieve the tensions built up over the past month.

But as he seated his gray Stetson and stepped down to the gravel drive that swept around the sprawling white Britton ranch house, the danged pickup seemed to have a mind of its own. It sat there with the door still open, egging him to rethink his plans.

He did, though he knew to the marrow of his bones the timing was off. He was horny as a whole legion of fighting men. He wasn't his usual pragmatic self. Jess was going to flay his business plans to confetti.

But the mud-splattered truck blasted down the Ramona Expressway anyway, heading for the Latham place. And, dammit, he was giving it its head.

She wasn't going to like him trying to swap her pride and joy for the comforts of a rebuilt ranch. She wasn't going to leap for joy, after the suffering she'd been through, when he dangled a small fortune in front of her face. It was going to take some astute bargaining to convince her it was smart to sell Blue.

Hell, Sleet fumed, tomorrow would be better timing. She was going to be off guard, thunderstruck by the surprise they were planning for her. Tonight was dicey. The picture carved into his brain the night he'd stood on her porch for the first time was still too vivid. He was vulnerable to her tonight.

He'd checked regularly, but Noa, who reported to Hal had said the ranch had been quiet. He'd heard Jess had taken a second and a fourth in local shows; word was, Si

enna was starting to show her age. The only other news was
that Noa was chasing down a lead on the arson case. Sleet
guessed he ought to see for himself if Jess was all right. Besides, he wanted to check with Noa about tomorrow, see if
everything was in place.

Finally convinced he was safely entrenched in a business
mode, Sleet drove on past the live oak.

When he pulled into the yard, her pickup was gone. He
slammed his palm into the steering wheel. Then he sat
slumped in the minicab, the stuffing taken out of him like
starch from a shirt on a Missouri summer afternoon.

"WE'VE BEEN WAITING for a break in the case and here it
is," Jess said, voice rising as she staked her palms on the
sheriff's paper-scattered desk. "He owns a Lincoln Town
Car with tinted windows. What do you mean, you can't arrest him?"

"I'm saying he has an alibi, Miss Latham. If you'll calm
down, I'll explain."

"I don't want to calm down. The arsonist nearly cost me
my ranch. My prize stallion. My life!"

The paunchy lawman sighed as if at a dull-brained child.
He ran a thick hand through sparse sandy hair and pushed
back. He stood up from the swivel chair, glanced at the
water-resistant watch pinching the flesh of his left wrist and
grimaced. "Devon was with Councilman Warner the afternoon and evening in question. They played golf, then went
back to Devon's place for some poker."

The air went out of her in a whoosh. It had been four days
since she'd called Sheriff Sanford and told him Antonio
Pascale had named Bart Devon, the wealthy developer of
Sundance and five other new housing projects in the area,
as the man he'd seen heading for her property the evening
of the fire. It was an incredible stroke of luck that Pascale,

a Mexican immigrant, had recognized one of the leading citizens of Hemet—and especially, that he'd had the courage to name him.

When he'd heard the allegation, the sheriff had laughed aloud, calling it utter nonsense. Her ears had stung from the bark of his laughter. Bart Devon was a veritable pillar of the community, he'd said, and only grudgingly had he conducted an investigation into the allegation.

Earlier tonight, the sheriff had told her that, just as he'd predicted, there wasn't a shred of a reason to arrest Devon.

His unctuousness had stoked her ire. She'd changed into slacks and a red sweater, jumped into the pickup and come charging down town to confront Sanford. She'd been so *sure* they could nail the developer and eventually get him to pay for repairs on the barn. But the sheriff was stonewalling; there was no case; he didn't believe the boy, and there was that airtight alibi.

Frustrated, Jess spun and walked the five feet between the sheriff's desk and the closed door. She came back and asked, "How do you know Devon was with Councilman Warner the whole time? Maybe he went out for some booze or something."

"I've already checked. The councilman vouches for him the whole night, 'til 11:00 p.m. It's airtight, Miss Latham."

"What about the other guy, the one who looked like a store clerk?"

"No trace of him. Devon doesn't know such a man."

"Devon would have had access to all kinds of wiring in his line of work. What about that?"

"Without proof...?" Sheriff Sanford spread his hands.

"He has motive," she argued. "He already bought half the ranch from my father. He'd stand to make a bundle if he got the rest of it in a fire sale."

"Again, he's got the alibi."

"Damned convenient." She paced. "Devon's lying, Warner's lying. I can feel it in my gut. That boy wouldn't lie. He has no reason."

"That boy is a foreigner." Sanford's tone was cold.

Jess looked up sharply, eyes narrowed. "What's that supposed to mean, Sheriff? That a Mexican's not truthful? Devon and Warner are *pillars,* after all."

"Now simmer down, Miss Latham. I'm just saying Pascale had an ax to grind with Devon and he might have found it convenient to grind it by fingering him on your barn fire."

"What ax is that?"

"Devon fired his cousin."

She stopped pacing. "For what?"

"Devon says for theft—some garden clippers and power tools. The cousin denies the theft, says because he got vocal about some injustices in Devon's operation, Devon fired him. Devon agreed not to file charges as long as the kid is deported."

"He can't force him if the cousin has legal papers."

"That's not my jurisdiction."

Jess made a short gesture of frustration. She liked less and less everything about Bart Devon. But she'd found out how Pascale happened to know who he was.

"The boys're from Mexico," the sheriff added with a hint of derision. "Pascale's only link to home is this cousin, and I figure he wants to prevent that deportation by sullying the name of a respected citizen of this town."

Respected by whom? she wanted to ask, but other questions took priority. "How's a charge of arson against Devon going to stop the deportation?"

"With the black mark of alleged arson over his head, a guy could go down for violation of human rights more easily, wouldn't you think? And it would give a laborer a tad more credibility, maybe even halt the deportation while the case is investigated." Sanford leaned a fleshy hip against the desk, making the tooled leather of his holster squeak. "More importantly," he said, "it could tie up Devon in months of litigation, become an incident on television, smear this town's good name from here to Pittsburgh and the Panama Canal." His eyes held hers with a glimmer of warning. "As a rancher," he said, "I'm sure you're aware of the sensitivity of the green card issue and its attendant civil rights ramifications. Things like that can get nasty."

Anger flashed through her. "I'm aware. But my people are legal, Sheriff. I won't be buffaloed by such talk."

His eyes glittered. His lips pressed together. Then he seemed to collect composure. "Miss Latham, Miss Latham," he cajoled. "We're working at cross-purposes here. I'm on your side. You have every right to expect my department to do all it can to prosecute whoever is harassing you, and I intend to see that it does."

"*Harassing* me?"

"All right, something more serious. Arson is a federal crime. The point is, we take your case very seriously, and we'll continue to investigate every shred of evidence available to us. In the meantime—" he came around the desk and hovered an ostensibly paternal arm above her shoulders, ushering her toward the door "—Devon hasn't been implicated, so we'll just have to continue looking for something more substantial, won't we?"

He opened the door. "Always nice to see you, Miss Latham. Henrietta—!" he barked at a thin woman with steel-blue hair and silver spectacles. "Send in Sergeant Jones, and I want the Wimbold file on the double. I'm already late for dinner."

As bodies blurred past her vision, Jess walked numbly toward the exit. Dismissed, I've been dismissed, she thought. The sheriff wasn't on her side, not really. Devon was too important to the economy of the city to allow him to be. She might as well go home and stew in her frustrations—and pray the "harassment" was over.

But then, as she stepped into the cool dusk outside the sheriff's office, an idea began to form. The more she thought about it, the less powerless she felt. Perhaps there was something she could do to ease her frustration. She hurried to the nearest pay phone, hoping Councilman Warner was listed in the directory.

Chapter Ten

The filly, Brisa, had taken over Blue's former corral, and at noon on Saturday, her high, young whinny filtered into the barn.

Jess was finishing the grain rationing for Blue and Sienna; their strenuous workouts dictated feedings several times a day, and they eagerly munched the coveted grain.

Frowning, she chucked the coffee can into the sack of corn in the corner and went to make notes on a clipboard by the door. All the grains were nearly gone; so was the hay. With the arrival of the sorrel filly, supplies seemed to run out far too fast. Each morning, Josepha and Noa stopped by the corral and fed Brisa a carrot, calling her *"mi'ja"* and petting her as they would a new baby in the family. It touched Jess to see it; but another mouth gobbling the feed, another creature requiring care, felt like a matchstick smoldering in Jess's hayseed operation. If she could just hold on another month and a half...

Finishing up the notes, she told herself to look to the future. At least the horses were in top condition, and Blue was the finest cutting horse she'd ever ridden.

When Brisa squealed again, apprehension stabbed through her. She dropped the pencil. Councilman Warner had refused to speak to her when she'd called his home last night, and his stonewalling made her suspicious. Was he involved in the criminal activities perpetrated against her? Were the criminals back to "harass" her, as Sheriff Sanford had termed it?

She didn't consider arson and the attempted murder of a cherished, valuable stallion and a trusted blue-blood mare *harassment*. But neither did she consider herself invincible. Noa and Josepha, full of private glances and secret smiles, like a couple of kids on a first date, had gone to the grocery store. She was alone. If one more incident happened to her or her property, she'd go under. As it was, she was teetering on the edge of survival.

She glanced behind her. Columns of golden sunlight shafted into the corridor from the ragged hole in the roof. The light gleamed on the work-polished handle of the rusted iron rake Noa used to muck the stalls. As a weapon, it would be heavy, lethal. She grabbed it and crept to the open double doors. Keeping well back, she poked her head outside.

The filly trotted around her corral, kicking up clouds of dust. The barnyard was empty. What was spooking her?

Jess stepped outside, ready to run back and dial 9-1-1 on the barn phone if she needed to. Brisa shook her head at Jess, then trotted to the far rail and poked her red muzzle over the top bar. She gazed toward the old live oak at the entrance to the ranch.

Walking out into the yard, Jess spotted a familiar red-and-white pickup barreling up the rutted road. Her heart clutched. The truck swept past the corrals—Brisa bucking in confusion, the cattle charging in alarm—and tore around the pens to slide to a standstill in the middle of the yard.

Jess dropped the rake. She swallowed hard.

Sleet flung himself out of the cab, grinning, saying, "Get the coffee on, Jessie. Barn-building crew's here!"

"You've spooked my cattle, Sleet Freeman," she called, striding toward him, mad because he'd finally showed up after a month, without a phone call so she could've straightened her hair and washed her face—and mad because he'd frightened her. Anger was all she could muster, her heart was pounding so hard.

She jerked to a stop five feet from the cowboy, her fists balled. "You disappear for a month, then come charging onto my land like a drunk rodeo star. Haven't you got any sense, man? You practically gave my stock heart failure!"

"That ain't all I scared, by the look of that pretty face."

Her hands punched into her waistline.

"Whoo-ee!" he hooted, ducking back into the truck. He pulled out his sweat-stained straw hat, peered into the rearview and set the hat at a rakish angle above that raw-boned face. "Jessie, darlin'," he declared, laughing, "I've missed you, too."

In midsentence he moved, that agile grace and those long legs propelling him toward the rear of the pickup. The back of it was stacked with lumber and tools. "We've come to rebuild your barn," he said, filling his hands with clean pine one-by-tens. "Better get the beans and coffee on. There'll be a whole troop of us to feed come sundown."

At a grinding of gears halfway up the drive, she jerked her head to stare.

Sleet tossed the lumber down and dusted his hands.

Hal and his wife, Betty, their white pickup bristling with stepladders, saws and two-by-fours, drove up and parked catawumpus to the red-and-white Dually. Waving to her and Sleet, the couple disappeared toward the rear of their pickup. Both of them were wearing work jeans and Western boots, like her and Sleet. Hal had on his battered straw hat. They emerged into view lugging a gunny sack between them, the weight of the contents nearly dragging the ground. Hal toted a five-foot metal rod in his left hand.

"That's the barbecue, I expect," said Sleet.

Barbecue? Jess gaped. *How many were coming?*

"Where'll we set up the spit to roast this beef?" Hal asked by way of greeting, grinning at Jess's open-jawed gaze. "You ain't going to get me up no ladder. Back of a horse is as far off the ground as I git."

"He just wants the easy part," said Betty, rolling her eyes at her husband. She was rangy, as tall as Hal, with large capable hands and an easy smile. "Sittin' in a folding chair tending the barbecue, tellin' tales, is more his style."

"Woman gets more smarts 'tween her ears ever' day," Hal said. "It's why I married her, back when. I knew she had potential."

"Oh, Hal," Betty objected, but it was a pleased sound. She glanced at Jess. "Where do you want us to set up shop, hon'?"

Jess looked up at Sleet. He swiped at the brim of his hat. "About twenty feet from the barn, would you say?"

"That would be good," she said, and before she could lead the Brittons to the spot, another vehicle arrived.

It was her nearest neighbor, Roy Miller, the round-faced banker who liked horses, and his plump wife, Angie. Their two adolescent boys and Antonio Pascale climbed out of the bed of the pickup and began unloading materials. Bullrider Ed, Hal's skinny ranch hand, came next, toting a huge silver radio. Then the fire marshal showed up in jeans and a denim shirt, paid his respects, and joined a team of men hauling Jess's sawhorses out of the arena. She moved Blue and Sienna there so the crew could work in the barn. More trucks arrived, some with tools and lumber, others with friendly wisecracks and a willingness to work. Someone broke out a case of beer. Bullrider Ed flipped the dial on his

radio. Country music, laughter and talk filled the barnyard.

For a while Jess acted as greeter while Sleet took charge
of the work crew, ordering the stacking of the lumber by size
and type. He had the men place cans and boxes full of nails
on a slab of plywood he propped up on sawhorses for a table; two Skilsaws, clamps, hammers and a miter box were
ranged next to them. Someone slung coils of rope on the
table, another, snakes of orange electrical cord and a couple of work lights. It would have cost Jess thousands of
dollars to collect these tools and supplies. She was stunned
wordless by the generosity she witnessed.

"Charlie," she heard Sleet say in a chatty tone, and she
turned to see him hunch a shoulder at a burly ranch hand,
"I heard you could wield a claw hammer pretty good. How
do you feel about heights?" And he asked Pascale to fetch
the twenty-foot ladder Jess kept propped against the hay
shed.

At a lull in his management duties, Sleet cut Jess a preoccupied look. "You got any lemons?" he asked, tucking a
carpenter's pencil behind his ear.

"I—Lemons?" Jess dragged her gaze from his to watch
a stock of fresh lumber rising by the arena. Something was
filling her, making her want to cry.

Blue screamed his stallion's call, and the filly, who'd developed an adolescent crush on the handsome stud, whinnied back. Suddenly a lump formed in Jess's throat. It was
the horses who always reminded her of the importance of
things. Just when she'd thought life was too tough, a yard-
ful of friends showed up to prove otherwise. There were
cutters saying hello to her whom she'd only seen at shows
last spring. She barely knew them. "I don't know what to
say," she murmured, dazed.

"Either you do or you don't," Sleet said.

She put a hand to her throat. "Do or don't what?"

"The lemons. Do you have some? Building a barn's thirsty work."

Angie Miller popped her cheerful, plump face into view. "I've got two ever-bearing lemon trees in my front yard. I'll just run down home and get a sackful, alright?"

Wordlessly, Jess nodded. The plump face went away. "Sleet, I—"

"No need, Jess," he said, waving toward the barnyard full of activity. "Plans for this were underway the day after the fire. At least three of us had the same idea at the same time. If it were Hal's barn, you'd be with us, wouldn't you?"

"Oh, yes. I just didn't expect . . . the barn's so old . . . I didn't think anybody but me would think it was worth saving."

"If you treasure a thing, people who care about you see the stock you put in it and think highly of it, too."

She blinked at the irritating moisture that clouded her view of his eyes, and wondered if others treasured his face, his eyes, his healing touch as she did. He was being generous, giving credit to the others for organizing this day. *He'd* organized it; the way the men asked his opinion on the simplest things proved it. Wanting him filled her with such feeling she couldn't speak.

"Hey, Freeman," hollered a cutter from the west end of town, hoisting a bubble-level. "You need this?"

There it was again. That deference they paid him. She owed them all, but most of all him.

Sleet didn't answer the man, but gazed down at her, studying her features. She knew he saw the way her eyes filled, but he didn't mention it. "Why don't y'all figure out a way to feed this mob some supper." He winked. "Some of that corn bread you whipped up t'other night wouldn't go down half-bad with Hal's barbecue.''

"T'other night"—as if it hadn't been more than four weeks—a lifetime. But the "little woman" routine was a welcome irritation.

"I'll speak to Josepha about it, then help with the barn," she said, walking away. "Wouldn't want to give anybody the idea I can't hold my own with a claw hammer and saw." She started for the house, intending to get Josepha to organize a cooking crew.

HE WATCHED HER GO. She didn't see the longing that washed his face, but he felt it clear into his loins. The coals haven't gone out, he thought. Not in a month, not ever, perhaps. But he'd covered it well.

When he'd driven up today, it had taken every macho ploy in his repertoire to swagger around and talk loud and grin and wink, when all he'd wanted to do was grab her and kiss her senseless. Swagger and bluster. God, he'd felt like a danged sophomore around the prom queen.

But he'd had to handle it that way. She was a landowner, a woman with roots as deep in the soil as that live oak down at the property line. He was a dreamer, a drifter, a man who loved hard and cared a lot—for a night, a week, a part of a year. It had never been in him to put down roots and weather the storms—something always beckoned along the double yellow line—until he'd met Jess. Now he wanted what she had, and it felt like a stiff new beaver hat.

Why did it tear at his guts to see tears of gratitude in her eyes? To see how much it meant, a little neighborliness? Why did she take half of him with her when she simply walked away? He didn't know. He only knew he wanted her worse than he'd ever wanted any woman, and that his own ambition stood in the way.

Only a low-down sidewinder would use her and toss her away, he reiterated for the thousandth time. He was better than that. Wasn't he?

It was probably just as well he hadn't run into her last night during his impromptu visit. He'd conducted his business with Noa, who'd been clearing out the last of the debris in the barn in preparation for today, and skedaddled off her ranch. But Lord, a man ached to make love to her, she was so beautiful....

"Freeman?" called the cutter, staring at him oddly.

"Yo," he said with a wave of his hand. "Let's have a look at that level."

These next few hours while they worked on the barn, he was going to have to keep damned busy to prevent making a fool of himself.

SEVEN HOURS LATER, after feeding the livestock with Noa, Jess ducked into the kitchen. Between bouts of pounding nails and clearing charred roofing, she'd taken time to bathe and stir up some corn bread. Josepha and some of the wives were pulling tins of it from the oven, tossing salad, stirring a ten-quart pot of beans and chattering about twenty things at once.

Josepha wore a faded, neatly pressed flowered dress that made her look years younger. Her hair was braided and coiled into a crown that revealed expressive eyes. For as long as Jess could recall, she'd worn her hair just that way. *How I love her,* she thought, coming up beside her to inhale the scent of the corn bread.

The woman smiled with affection and slid the last of the hot tins to the stovetop. "Is all finished, your corn bread," she said. "It smells good, no?"

"Mmm," said Jess. "Thanks for rescuing it for me. Your tortillas ready?"

"*Sí*. I wrapped them in towels to keep warm."

"Great." The relaxed chatter of women engaged in familiar tasks rose in the old kitchen, and again Jess felt emotions rise like a flock of geese from a summering pond. It had been years since friends had congregated here, other than right after her father's funeral, which had been a deeply sad occasion. She realized she'd been isolated too long. Her neighbors had been longing to show they cared, and it had taken the meddling ways of a stranger in a red-and-white Dually to give them the opportunity. She fought to keep the feelings contained, to hide, to submerge them, as she knew she must. There must be a diversion....

Josepha provided it. She and Noa had been in on the surprise. Jess hugged her foster mom briefly. "Next time you and Noa drive off on a two-hour shopping spree," she said, "I'm going to know something is up."

"A long time since we have company, no?"

"Too long," Jess responded, eyes roving the crowded kitchen. "I've missed them."

"This I know." She leaned close. "Señor Sleet, he know what's good for you, *mi'ja*. He's a good man, that one."

Josepha was perceptive. She'd just delivered a heavy hint to share what Jess had been unwilling to discuss for weeks. Josepha hadn't missed the way Jess gazed after the cowboy, and fell into long silences around the ranch. The seamed face turned to her; the dark doe's eyes gauged her mood. "You like him, *querida?*" she asked softly, so no one else could hear.

"Sometimes," Jess admitted, and it felt good to tell a confidante. "But he's moving on in December, Josepha. Going back to Texas."

"Maybe. Maybe not. He have the big heart for you, *mi'ja*. He like you very much. Maybe he stay... if you let him."

"Blue, you, Noa and the ranch are the only things that matter to me, Josepha. That's a plateful. I've got no time for romance."

"My Noa, he could say something, you know, a hint."

Jess's eyes widened. "No way, Josepha. Not a *word*."

Josepha smiled. "Okay, but he already know."

"The only thing Sleet Freeman knows," she returned smartly, to reinforce what she hoped was true, "is the viperous lash of my temper. He's a wandering cowboy, for heaven's sake. No roots, no one spot he calls home. What good could possibly come of an alliance like that?" Now, one night of passion was another matter. A once-in-a-lifetime opportunity shouldn't be wasted! He should have no problem with that. He's spent at least a decade doing the same thing to women.

"He could change," said her confidante. "You could change him, *mi'ja*."

"No thanks. Rebuilding Rome isn't my calling in life."

Angie Miller cocked her head to overhear what they were discussing so intently, and Jess straightened.

"I got a slice of plywood from the guys," she announced to them all, raising her voice to be heard. "I put the red tablecloth over it. It'll do for a table to set everything on. I'll get the setups."

"You need some help with those things?" asked Betty Britton, indicating the picnic supplies while she washed some dishes.

"I've got them," Jess said, gathering an armful of paper plates and napkins and plastic forks from the cluttered counter—supplies Josepha had purchased with "collection money." "I'll check the coffee and lemonade while I'm out, too, and send one of the men in to carry the beans. Ten minutes to countdown, ladies. Those men are hungry enough to eat rattlesnake."

Arms full, she sent a silencing glance to Josepha, then
followed the black extension cord that lay on the floor. It led
beneath the screen door and out across the porch, where it
connected to a huge coffeepot. She tapped the base with her
toe. It was still two-thirds full; they'd filled it three times
already. The second jug of lemonade hadn't gone down an
inch since they'd set it on the porch. Evidently the crowd
was holding out for supper.

Jess stepped to the lip of the top step, then hesitated,
struck by the rustic scene before her.

Near the barn, smoke drifted from the roasting spit across
the weather-beaten faces of thirty-odd men and women. The
people ranged in clusters against the barn door, the trucks,
sat on sawhorses and folding chairs, smoking, jawing. A
knot of them hunkered near Hal, who was using a mop and
bucket to slosh sauce on the spit of beef. Noa and Antonio
and a couple of cutters were pitching pennies against the
barn wall. The Miller kids squatted on their haunches
nearby, gesturing, offering advice.

Strains of music drifted to Jess, an oldie by local country
favorite Jann Browne, "You Ain't Down Home," and she
thought with a full heart, *down home is as good as it gets.*

She looked for the man who'd made this miracle happen.

At the hay shed, Sleet was ducking a hailstorm of straw
cast by children. He swung out wildly, pretending to be
blind. A child in a red shirt and overalls ran in and tackled
one of his legs. With a soft growl, Sleet scooped the boy into
his arms and swung him around.

Jess's heart turned with them. She knew what it felt like
to be hugged close to that hard, manly body. She knew what
he looked like up close, with his hair slicked back and his
skin moist from the wash bucket—all thundering blue eyes
and sexy mouth and lean man face. *You sassed me, woman,*

he'd warned her weeks ago, *y'all know what happens when you do that.*

It ruffled her feathers to know he treated her, now, as platonically as a sister. Not once today, in the countless times they'd spoken or passed by one another, had he let that smoldering sex appeal reach out to melt her to putty.

Wrap those lovely arms around me, Jess. It seemed split seconds ago, it was still so vivid.

She made herself look away. Stepping down from the porch, she went to the makeshift table near the spit, and stacked the utensils. She didn't need him to court her, she told herself. She had neighbors and friends to make her feel wanted, and the unbelievable luck of the restored barn.

She gazed through the open doors. Smoke and sizzle from the barbecue mingled with the sharp resin scent of pine and wood stain. Not satisfied to just replace the burned wood, Sleet had had the men stain it to prevent termite damage. The charred stalls had been shored up and painted, and much of the burned smell had dissipated. The fire marshal had rustled around in his tool chest, found some spare electrical wire and fixed the lighting system. Although the light at the top of the barn now shone permanently into the barnyard, Jess didn't begrudge the extra expense. With Councilman Warner and Sheriff Sanford united, stonewalling, acting paranoid about one of the city fathers being impugned by an immigrant laborer with an alleged grudge, she was more vulnerable than ever. Nighttime illumination would at least give her more peace of mind. A couple of interior lights had been jury-rigged, too, affording just enough illumination to see to the horses in a midnight crisis.

Sleet had also sent a crew down to the paddock to repair the fence, and two men had retacked the wire mesh around a couple of the dilapidated cattle pens on the west side of the arena. At a rough guess, Jess estimated her rebuilt facilities would hold up to ten mares and foals plus a whole remuda of mature horses. Sleet had given her this gift. *Why was he being so generous?*

"Not bad for an afternoon's work, huh?" he said from a pace or two behind her.

She pivoted in surprise. Looked into his eyes. Felt her blood turn to warm milk. "Sleet . . ."

She cut a look toward the gaggle of kids standing around him, and gathered her composure. She tried a tentative smile. It came out crooked, and she expanded it to include the children. "It's a wonderful job. You all did such first-class work today."

"I helped," piped a four-year-old, stepping to Sleet to grasp a handful of jeans near his knee. "I brought Mr. Britton the wood for his barbecue fire. Mr. Freeman said I could."

"Yes," she said, crouching to speak to him—conscious of Sleet's gaze, glad she'd washed up and put on clean Wrangler jeans and tied her hair neatly at her nape. "You brought Mr. Britton all that wood, Jimmy, and the barbecue's going to taste so good! Are you hungry?"

"Yup. When're we going to eat?"

"As soon as I can find a big strong man to carry out the pot of beans. It's heavy."

Four pairs of eyes rolled up to fix on Sleet's face. He smiled, swiped the brim of his hat. "Guess I'm hired," he said.

A small cheer went up.

Hal glanced over, leaning to set the mop and bucket aside. "This here meat's done to a turn. I won't have my barbecue blackened 'cause you gals can't hold up your end."

Jess stood. "We're all set, Hal. Didn't want to rush the making of a masterpiece."

His cheeks ruddied. "Well, bring on the fixin's. The masterpiece is done. You kids git washed up at the hose, now."

They scampered away.

"Say, Jess," Sleet said, easing his hat from his head. "When you get a spare minute, I'd like to talk to you. Privately."

Nerves skittered along her back. "What about?"

"It can wait 'til we talk."

Privately, he'd said, his eyes mysterious. Was he going to woo her again? Because if he was, she was just going to have to tell him to wait 'til after the futurity.

"Sure," she said slowly. "Although it's not going to do you any good—"

"Later," he said abruptly.

With a prickly air between them, Sleet and Jess went into the house.

Minutes later, the makeshift table was thronged as hungry workers lined up to fill their plates. They were fatted on roasted meat carved with a flourish by Hal, beans served by Betty, corn bread by Jess, fresh corn tortillas by Josepha and salad by the two Miller boys. Angie Miller served up slices of the five lemon meringue pies she'd baked during the afternoon, and soon those were gone.

When the company had eaten and relaxed into quiet discussions, and a small bonfire crackled in the cooling air, Jess stood up from the group of women who'd clustered around her. Betty was seated in a folding chair to her right. She stopped sipping coffee and angled a questioning glance at Jess.

"I want to say a few words," Jess told her.

Hal was tilted back in his cook's chair, gabbing with Charlie. Betty jabbed Hal in the ribs. "Jess wants to say her piece," she said. "Quieten down this bunch."

Hal badgered everyone to silence. Nodding to Jess, he said, "Go on ahead, gal."

"In my daddy's day," she said, gazing into the eager, friendly faces, "this kind of get-together happened all the time. My brother, Josh, and I were raised with the gruff sounds of men moving cattle and cussing a dink horse."

Chuckles rippled around. She smiled and went on. "In those days, there were barbecues—" she glanced down at the rotund Britton "—'though none as tasty as Hal's—" more chuckles "—and picnics in the summer. There were barn dances in the fall, and Josh and I learned the ways of country folk through all of that. Nothing's changed since then. I just want you to know, it feels so good—" The emotions welled, coiled into her throat. A sparkle of wetness danced on her eyelashes.

Josepha, to her left, made a gesture as if she wanted to embrace her, then simply stepped beside her for support. Betty reached up and wrapped sturdy fingers around Jess's forearm. "Aw, now, honey," she soothed.

Jess grasped Betty's hand, put an arm around Josepha and hung on. She felt so *loved*. If only... She caught Sleet looking at her, his face muscled up with a strange tightness. Was he angry at her? She quickly glanced away. So much of the emotion she felt was wrapped up around him; she couldn't risk feeding it by trying to decipher his gaze.

She drew a steadying breath. "What I'm trying to say is, you're the kind of neighbors who make 'country' what it is. Your kindness. Your generosity. Your loyalty. You're the kind of folks who never let a friend down. And I thank you. From the bottom of my heart, I thank you."

Clapping and whistles echoed off the hills, and Jess relaxed in the warmth of their approval. She smiled, bent to hug Betty.

"Hey, Jess," someone called. "That futurity stud of yours. He going to put Hemet on the map?"

The crowd quieted to hear her response.

"A cutter always wants more time," she said. "But, God willing, we'll do all right in Cowtown. Thanks in no small part to your support, and to Sleet's help, of course." She began to turn away, then swung back. "But Sleet better stay loose in the saddle," she challenged, voice raised, grinning. "If he doesn't, Blue and I are bound to whip the pants off him in Texas. That's a promise."

The crowd hooted.

She caught Sleet's glance, and something in her went cold. His eyes . . . they branded her. Had she angered him?

Betty stood up. "What's eating Sleet?" she asked.

Jess shook her head. "Lost his sense of humor, I guess. Can't stand the thought of a woman beating him at his own game."

"You do it for all of us, then. It's time we dragged our menfolk into the twentieth century."

Jess laughed. "Why, Betty Britton. I thought you were an old-schooler."

"Am. But you're not. The times they are a changin'. Haven't you heard that old song, girl?"

A youngster went up on his toes and danced, throwing mock punches at Sleet. He batted them back, twisting, ducking, moving in for a tap on the shoulder. It eased the men into laughter.

In thoughtful silence, she and Betty joined the women who were gathering empty cups and plates.

About dark, the kitchen cleaned, the women straightened their hair and drifted back outside. Jess went down among the neighbors and said some personal thanks, working her way toward Sleet. Someone turned up the music. The local station was playing a whole weekend of oldies, and this one was Doug Kershaw's famous "Orange Blossom Special." The fiddle whittled at you 'til you were feeling so good you had to move. Engaged in a gab session about the fine art of making corn bread, Jess drummed her fingers against her thigh, thinking about Sleet. Every time she headed in his direction, he seemed to slip off to talk to someone. He avoided looking at her. Couldn't he at least stand still for a thank-you? If he didn't like her anymore, why had he worked so hard to put her ranch in shape?

When she heard Britton call his name, she lifted her head. Hal diddled his toe in the dust and challenged Sleet to a clog.

Sleet was slouched against the fender of his pickup, talking to Charlie. Both of them looked up. The burly cutter spit in the dust and went back to the conversation. When Hal called again, Sleet nodded. Settling his hat down around his ears, he began to clap his hands. When the rhythm caught the crowd, clapping rang against the hills behind the ranch, and Sleet shuffled forward in time to the music. Loose-jointed and graceful, he did a series of triple-shuffle-slaps that fired Jess's blood. The circle closed around him, and Jess was pressed to the inner side of the group, watching, enthralled, mesmerized.

Halfway through the number, Kershaw's fiddle changed down almost to a waltz. Dancing around the circle, Sleet ended up in front of Jess. He stood there for a moment, hat over his heart, legs splayed, one boot a-tapping. His eyes glittered as if he'd been drawn to her against his will and it made him angry. Her heart beat wildly, but she met his gaze with all the bravado she could muster.

In response he shimmied a thigh in provocation, eyes seducing her while he held out his hand to her. The neighbors hooted and cheered. She shook her head, then something in his eyes stole away her resistance and he took her with him into the light.

They began to sway together.

At just that moment, the music changed up to double-time. Sleet put his arm around her back and drew her to him, sweeping her into a fast triple-step polka. The world spun. Never did his eyes leave hers, nor did he falter, but whirled her through the steps she'd learned as a child at just such down-home shindigs.

The music changed again, this dance a lilting piece called "Waltz Across Texas," and Sleet pinioned her with a smoky gaze that sent shivers up her back.

"One more," he whispered, breathing hard, and swept her into a series of grapevine maneuvers as smooth as sun-warmed honey. He avoided looking at her and kept his gaze trained on the black ribbon of foothills. The others began to dance but Jess only knew this by a subliminal sense of movement—a patch of plaid, the brim of a hat slid by. She and Sleet did not speak. The heat poured from him, penetrated her shirt and branded her. His breath rasped, slowed, then became long tunnels of breathing as he drew her slightly closer. His right hand roved her back, directing her movements, yet he did not press her body to him.

Instinctively she knew he was holding back. Part of her was glad, but it angered her that he ran hot and cold, seducing her one moment and throwing silent daggers the next. Yet a longing was drenching her, urging her to connect, to merge, and the struggle to deflect it made her tighten her fingers on his shoulder.

There was a sudden giving-way inside Sleet. It was as if he'd fought down the need for distance and given in to a more primitive force. He was sensitive, a healer; of course he would respond to her subtle battle within, her longing! He curved over her, nestled her face in the protective nest of his shoulder and gathered her to him. Now she felt cherished. Now she fit perfectly in the warm curve of his muscles. Her breasts grew taut, the nipples hard, and a hot honey smoothness swept down inside her body and made i ache sweetly.

She swirled in an amber glow. Her right hand crept from his and joined the other to link behind his neck. His hand slid to just above her buttocks and pressed; she felt hi erection, and the honey turned to liquid fire between he legs.

Sleet moaned softly.

Jess nearly stumbled. *Too soon,* clanged a warning bell i her head. *Not 'til after Texas!* But she closed her eyes an let a secret happiness drench her like warm rain.

Her mind was so consumed with the vision of Sleet in he bed, that she ignored a sixth sense that tried to warn her. / scuffle outside the circle of light irritated her but she ig nored that, too. This was too precious a moment.

A shout broke through her reverie, and Sleet turned t stone in her arms.

She glanced up. His jaw jutted granitelike. His eyes wer trained over the heads of other men.

"Trouble," he muttered. He slid one hand down the fror of his jeans and took a step away. Then he gave her a look one glance, and her legs nearly buckled. In his eyes was hunger so vivid, it was palpable. Submerged in desire her self, she took a half step toward him, her lips parted. Hi gaze flicked to her mouth, held. A muscle ticked in his jaw Then the shutter of consciousness slid over his eyes, and h turned toward the altercation.

Still tied by the cord of desire, she followed as Sleet cut trail through the dancers. *Could* she wait 'til December? I he pressed her, would she give in? Tonight?

But the reverie was broken when she came to the ou skirts of the crowd. She stopped, her mood altering t dread.

Chapter Eleven

A tall, raven-haired man in a Western suit and boots was standing over Antonio, his stance aggressive. Antonio's dark face was stoic, as if he'd endured a tongue-lashing many times before and could endure this one. Jess was afraid Antonio was going to be arrested, and her insides clenched in alarm.

"...make you sorry," said the stranger. "...back where you belong."

"What's the trouble here?" asked Sleet.

The stranger glanced at Sleet, at Jess, and the lethal look in his eyes dissolved so quickly, Jess wondered if she'd imagined she'd seen it.

The man straightened, stepping away from Antonio. He ignored Sleet. "Miss Latham?" he queried, staring at Jess.

He was handsome, his face carved from marble by an artist who appreciated high cheekbones and a strong clefted chin. But the craftsman had skimped on the mouth; it was small and thin, as if all the marble had been used up before reaching the lips. His mouth turned up in a spare smile. "Miss Latham?" he asked again.

"Yes," she said, coming forward. "And you are?"

"Bart Devon. I did business with your father a year or two ago."

Like a torero, Noa had said. Of course. The rapier Devon plunged into the hearts of his victims was none other than political power. Her blood froze in her veins. She didn't attempt to hide it. In chilly tones she asked, "What are you doing on my land?"

"Stopping by to pay my respects, ma'am. The community is sorry for the trouble you've had since your father..." He let that simmer in the air. "Well, things have been difficult for you, with the fire and all, and I—"

"What do you want?"

"I'm here on a courtesy call, Miss Latham. I don't understand your antagonism."

"I don't call what you were doing to Antonio Pascale 'polite,' Devon. I call it a threat. You're not welcome here."

She felt Sleet's body slide next to her right arm and stay. "What's this about, Jess?" he asked softly.

"Antonio implicated this man in arson," she said tersely. "Maybe worse." She glared at Devon. "He's here to shut him up."

Devon abruptly pointed to Antonio, who stood ramrod straight among a group of children, eyes front. Devon said in a pitched voice, "I'm here to tell that boy—" shaking a finger in agitation "—that he's one voice in the wilderness. One voice. *Respected* citizens of this town call him a liar!"

A murmur rose. Noa came to Jess's left and planted his feet apart. He muttered something off-color in Spanish. Others moved in to form a shell of work-toughened bodies and grim faces behind Jess and Sleet.

"Miss Latham said move on," Sleet said, low. "Better git."

Devon glanced around, then back at her. "What kind of people are you, taking the side of a greaser against me?"

"Now hold on," said Hal, stepping out of the group, gesturing with a beer can. "That kinda talk's a red flag. Pascale's people settled this land."

Devon pulled himself up tall. "I gave you jobs, put money in your pocket, food on your table," he said, passionately, as if to a jury. "I won't tolerate a Mexican immigrant laborer sullying my name, dragging all I've worked for through the mud."

"He saw you coming onto my land the night of the fire," Jess accused.

"He's lying. Trying to get back at me for firing his thieving cousin."

Pascale stepped forward, looking at Jess, his face skewed with emotion. "My cousin no steal from this man. He lies. I see him. He drive in here in his big Lincoln. Why he do that?"

"*Sí,*" said Noa. "*¿Por qué?*"

"I don't know," Jess said, and turned her gaze to Devon, hardened it. "But when I know, he'll pay."

"You all heard her," said Devon. "She's threatening me."

Sleet stepped close to the man and looked down into his face. "She's not. I am. Now get off this land."

Devon jerked back. He curled his arms like a fighter squaring off.

"C'mon," Jess heard Sleet say softly, lethally. "I've been spoilin' for some action all day. Way I see it, you'd be doin' me a favor."

Jess wondered what he meant, but she didn't have time to dwell on it. Devon's shoulders suddenly relaxed. He chuckled mirthlessly. "Sure," he said. "You and twenty of your friends. I'm not an idiot."

"Just me, sheep crap," Sleet said in that cold near-whisper.

"Another time, cowboy." He glanced at Jess. "Ma'am, I'd advise you to leave the law in the law's hands. Otherwise things could get worse for you. Much worse."

Jess paled.

Sleet butted the man with his chest. Devon put up his hands and backed away. Then he turned and hurried down along a canyon of pickup trucks and station wagons, and disappeared in the darkness.

The neighbors converged on Jess, hammering her with questions and offering opinions about the way Hemet was going to the dogs, what with new housing developments cropping up all over the valley.

Sleet stepped up to Jess, his eyes still arcing sparks. "Now would be a good time to have that talk," he said.

"Thanks for backing me with Devon," she said, still shaken. "He's a real creep."

"Save your thanks. You may not feel so grateful when I've had my say."

She tried to find his eyes, read them, but he turned and started for the house. Curious, wary, she followed.

Inside, he stalked the living room as if he felt caged. He closed the door after her, muting the sounds of the party, and crossed the braided rug. He flipped on a lamp, then stood with his thumbs hooked into the front pockets of his jeans. The stance accentuated his manly assets, and Jess had to force herself to focus on his face. That wasn't hard duty. She found she loved his face, loved its look of experience and its character. What she did not love was the fierce intimacy of his gaze. That, she feared.

Conscious of her vulnerability to his strength, his physical appeal, Jess stood by the front door and made herself sound matter-of-fact. "Well," she said, "what did you want?"

"I want you to sell out, Jess."

Her hands balled. Her breath shallowed out. "You want *what?*"

"Devon's a powerful man. It came clear to me tonight that he's not going to stop at burning your barn and throwing rocks. You're in danger."

"So... just give in to him? Let him win?" Her voice had risen but she hardly cared. *"Sell out?"*

"That's right. Devon's scum. He won't do you in himself, but there's every chance he'll hire it done. You've got to let him win. You can start again somewhere else, where the land isn't so congested, so valuable."

"What are you going to do, make me an offer?"

"No! That is, yes, yes I am."

"So that's it. You want my land." Her control disintegrated like paper in the blaze of her fury. She advanced toward him, eyes flashing, fists raised. "Of all the conniving, underhanded—you bastard! You're his *thing,* you're Devon's emissary. You lit the barn!"

He grabbed the wrists raised against him and held her in place. "For the last time, dammit, I did not light your barn."

The tremor that shook her at his touch had nothing to do with their anger. She was in danger, all right, but not from Devon. "Let go of me before I scream and bring the whole town in here."

"You keep threatening that, Jess. It won't do any good. I'll tell them I was trying to reason with you, make you understand how dangerous it is for you to keep fighting City Hall. They all know how temperamental you are. They'll take my side."

"You sonofabitch! You arrogant, meddling, oversexed sonofabitch!"

His eyes danced with the beginnings of humor. "You keep referring to my sexual prowess, too, but you won't let me prove it. Now settle down and let me explain my terms before I take back my word and seduce the hell out of you."

"To *hell* with your terms," she grated with measured loathing. "To hell with your macho moves and your word. They aren't worth the dust on my ranch. Now let me go and get the hell off my land!"

"You bring out the worst in me," he said. "You give me no choice." He jerked her forward so swiftly, with such rough grace, her breath caught and she fell against him. "I thought to make you the offer so you could fix up the place, live decently again," he said, talking against the swirl of her hair, and holding her so tightly she couldn't move. "But Devon's little visit told me just how vulnerable you are. Not only you, but Josepha and Noa, too. You've got to sell, Jess. Otherwise..."

"I'll never sell," she said through clenched teeth.

"Otherwise, there's no telling what the developer and his cronies will do to you. I can't be here twenty-four hours a day, Jess. I can only make an offer on Blue and give you some cash flow."

Her heart plummeted to utter stillness. "Blue?" she whispered.

For a split second more, he held her firmly against his chest and thighs, so she felt every hard muscle he possessed. But her mind had funneled down to the pinprick of his real intent: he wanted Blue. That was all she could fathom—that and the fact that he'd betrayed her.

His hands gentled, caressed and eventually set her slightly away from him. She barely felt it. He glanced down into her face. "Look, I'm not trying to steal him from you."

While she tried to digest the irony of his statement, he shifted, poked into a pocket, withdrew something that crackled. He brought it close to her. Reflexively she read the amount written in bold black ink on the check, and thought,

It's a small fortune. With that and the sale of the ranch, I could practically retire.

"What do you say, Jess?" he asked gently. "Sell everything and start again where it's safe."

She was suddenly very tired. Staring into the light from the lamp, she drew breath enough to say in a monotone, "I told you, I'll never sell. Now get out, Sleet. Just—" she lifted a hand, moved it vaguely toward the door "—get out."

After a long moment, Sleet took the check and his masculinity and his lies outside, closing the door quietly behind him.

Do I love him? she asked herself woodenly. Is that why the betrayal hurts so much? Or is it just that I wanted his touch enough to believe that his artistry with horses translated to people, too? Perhaps she was that frightened, desperate woman Sleet had called her weeks ago. At twenty-nine, with no long-term successful love affair to her credit, she could no longer argue with him. She felt emotionally battered. Cold and deeply lonely, she moved into the hall and down it to the bedroom. Once there, she closed the door and lay on the soft old four-poster, grieving for the thing that was lost between her and Sleet without ever being named.

Chapter Twelve

For two hundred miles, the rain had dogged Sleet, Hal and the horses they were hauling into Oregon. Sleet took one hand from the wheel and pressed his fingers to his eyes. They ached with strain.

"Jeez," he murmured, glancing across the cab. The schedule was killing him. He needed rest, like Hal was getting over in the corner of the cab, his head bobbing on his chest.

But rest meant a clear head. It meant images of a black-haired spitfire with roots in the ground—a spitfire with passion in her body and turquoise eyes that accused him of being a traitor.

Hell, he tried to tell himself. It hadn't been planned as betrayal, just a business deal. Then Devon had come slithering onto her ranch, and Sleet had stepped up to the sidewinder as if it were his ranch, his woman being threatened.

Then, like an ass, he'd assumed the protector role. He'd told Jess she had to sell the ranch, and his plans to seed his own operation with her stallion, had gone down the tubes along with any hope of possessing Jess. Somehow the two losses felt equally devastating.

Wallowing in self-disgust, he found some music on the radio and watched chartreuse pastures rise and fall along the

Rogue River, the bottomland a velvet carpet that fed dairy cows and horses. He wondered what it felt like to own such lush pastureland. For years he'd traversed the parched Southwest, at one with the endless stretches of dry gulch and prairie, the lavender dusks and the startling myriad of colors when the deserts bloomed.

Here was an Eden of green—pasture, pear and apple orchards, truck gardens of corn and beans, mountains ridged in pine. You couldn't ignore the life it gave; you couldn't just drive on through without thinking of its potential, and your own. Hell, what potential did he have? He'd never really tested himself, never put his name to a land deed and wrestled it into something he could call his own. He stared hard at the countryside. This land was busy growing things, being productive, as if evolution were its chief mission. It reminded him of the family farm in Missouri—now his brother's farm. And roots deep in the land . . .

"Ho!" Hal barked, coming out of his catnap against the passenger door.

Glad of the diversion, Sleet eyed him. "Bad dream?"

"Hell, no, a good one," said Hal, scrubbing his face. "Trouble is, I don't know if it was me 'n' Betty doin' a slow two-step under the stars, or you and Jess. You two made a pretty picture t'other night."

Sleet felt her name slide down into his gut and sear it. He narrowed his eyes on the gray screen of rain.

Hal looked over. "What's eatin' you?"

"Nothing. Why?"

"All I said was 'you and Jess.' You act like I threw you in a patch of poison oak."

"Just tired, boss. Nothing to it."

Hal grunted and reached for a thermos of coffee he'd refilled at a truck stop ninety miles back. He unscrewed the cap. "Want a pull?"

Sleet shook his head.

Hal drank the steaming tar-pit brew, recapped the container, then set it on the floorboard. "Been meanin' to yak at you about somethin'."

"What's that?"

"The colts. You been neglectin' 'em lately, ain't you?"

Sleet's conscience rared up and shook him. Firming his mouth, he edged about a produce truck. As he came back into the slow lane, he formed his words. "What's on your mind, Hal?"

"Don't get all riled, son. I think highly enough of your talent to assume you know what you're doing, otherwise I wouldn't have asked you to come out to my place. But I'm worried about the Doc Tari colt. He ain't gettin' around in his turns like he should by now. And the bay filly. Seems to me she was showin' plenty of cow and you had her stoppin' pretty good. We figured she and the colt was futurity material. You ain't finished 'em yet, that's all."

"November is still ahead of us, Hal."

"Time's running out, son."

Sleet sighed. "I know. I've been restless lately. When we get back I'll see to them. They're close to being ready."

"All right, son." Hal slid the Oregon road map from its slot in the door, unfolded it and began to run a thick finger up the main highway. "Jenk's place is beyond Grant's Pass," he said. "Take the last exit and follow it north for ten miles."

"Roger."

The wipers thunked back and forth across the windshield, and Garth Brooks crooned softly on the radio.

"Some nice land here in Southwest Oregon," Hal said.

"They get more rain here than you do."

"Yeah, Betty 'n' I like the sun, I guess."

"Reckon I do, too."

"You figure this fella we're going to see is in trouble?"

"Word is his apple trees got the blight. That's his money crop. Cutting horses are a sideline, like they're a retirement hobby for you. If he won't be reasonable on the price of the San Peppy colt, at least we have Checkers and your palomino with us. We'll catch the regional show."

Hal nodded, gazed out the window for a time, while Sleet wrestled with his rebuke about the colts. If he didn't put the colts back on a rigorous program, they were going to look like they'd been trained by an amateur, come December. A prickle of stress assailed him.

The futurity was five weeks away, and the competition was going to be fierce. As world champion, he was going to be in the spotlight; his livelihood depended on showing well.

The image of a muscled-up black swinging nose-to-nose with a sour cow flitted through. Blue. He was going to be ready.

Sleet's fingers tightened on the wheel, and something in his gut ached. Blue was the kind of young horse a cutter dreamed about owning—stupendous lines, incredible speed and stopping ability, lots of cow. But he had more than that. He had that rare sensitivity called "try." He wanted to please. His willingness had only increased since they'd done the massage therapy. In losing his fear of abuse, Blue had gained more try. Sleet had no doubt he'd bust his heart for Jess.

The Doc Tari colt had win in him, too, but he was more inclined to enjoy a challenge than please his rider. Sleet was going to have to ride better than he'd ever ridden before—and finish off that colt to perfection—to beat Jess's stallion.

How many others would have his talent? How many riders would have Jess's determination to win?

Sleet felt a jolt of adrenaline go through him and he flexed his arms. He was the champ. He had that edge, and years of seasoning. What was he worried about? A woman? No way. If she wanted to waste the win potential of a stud like Blue by riding him herself, that was her business.

Jess, my lovely, he mused, the contest isn't over 'til it's over.

"We going to give Jess a lift to Fort Worth?" asked Hal, uncanny in his ability to slither into Sleet's mind.

Sleet glanced over. He wanted to say no. Let her find her own way to Texas. But the crime of the century would be to steal the opportunity to compete from a stud like Blue.

"We got room," Hal added. "I was thinkin' Betty 'n' I would take the Caddy. Drive in comfort. You could haul my trailer and Jess could be company for you."

His gut did a whirligig. Maybe there was a way to patch the break between them, get back on track with his original goal. Did he still want her?

Hell, yes.

"Don't believe we'll need your rig, Hal," he said with a calm that was a lie. "Checkers is particular to her slot, and your two colts and her stud will fill the other three."

"When we get back, give Jess a call. See if it sets well with her."

"Okay." Sleet was aware that Hal would normally make the call himself. He was handing the job to Sleet.

He angled a probing look at his friend. Hal folded the map and met his gaze. "It's just a phone call," he said.

Sleet smiled. "Yeah," he said. "Just a phone call."

It was a three-day drive to Texas—three days of rugged wild territory he knew like the palm of his hand—every road stop a haven where he'd have a chance to seduce her. Manipulative? he reiterated, remembering what she'd called him. Baby, you haven't seen manipulative 'til you've seen me with all the stops pulled out.

Sleet had to quell the urge to pull over to an emergency roadside phone and call her now, before she asked one of the other cutters to give her a lift.

IT WAS 6:50 A.M. on Friday. She parked the pickup on Florida Avenue in front of Warner's Rest in Peace Mortuary, and walked up a wide sidewalk. The brickwork and shrubbery of the entrance alcove provided camouflage, like the calm resolve in her expression hid the rage.

Choosing a spot in the shadows, folding her hands, she watched a chickadee flit among the branches of a shrub that shone with morning mist. "Come on, Warner," she whispered with venom. "I'm ready for you."

The chickadee chirped.

Jess shivered. She'd worn business clothes—a simple navy-blue suit and matching heels—and tied her hair back with a blue ribbon. The navy was unrelieved except by a small V of white blouse at her throat. Conservative was best in dealing with a mortician/city father, she'd decided. The business clothing, once her style, felt constricting. She missed her comfortable jeans, chafed at having to waste time with Warner.

"Damn him," she muttered, adjusting the skirt. She meant Sleet. The anger welling up from the initial crush of betrayal had stayed with her for five days, since Sleet had departed from Latham land. Now it washed her again. She couldn't stop thinking about him; nothing had changed there. But now it was with loathing, not the crippling obsessive-compulsive need to bed him.

She believed he had not set fire to the barn. Evidence pointed to Devon and a workman of small proportions, the quintessential opposite of the man with quarterback shoulders, lean horsemen's hips and masculine, craggy features, whom she'd nearly allowed to share her bed.

It was just that Sleet's uncanny timing—producing a check to buy her stallion on the same night Devon showed up with his threats and his oily smile—had reignited her earlier suspicions.

With the return of reason the morning after the barbecue, she'd realized Sleet had done much worse than burn her barn. First, he'd put his hands on her, his intimate stamp on her heart. The galling thing was that he hadn't done it for romantic purposes or even for conquest, which she could excuse from a rake who thought he was God's gift to women. He'd done it to finagle his way into buying her futurity horse. To compound it, he'd tried to scare her into thinking Devon might try to kill her, or Josepha and Noa; he'd used Devon's threats to try to steal something more precious than momentary pleasure: her dream.

"Blue's mine," she whispered vehemently. "Mine!"

She clung to the satisfaction that she'd foiled Sleet's plans.

The only other good to come of events the night of the barbecue was her anger. It allowed her to confront Warner and get him to stop protecting Devon. She used her rage against Sleet to feed her courage, used it to remain standing in the shadowed doorway, waiting...

AT SEVEN EXACTLY, Warner arrived in a late-model Chrysler sedan. He parked precisely between the lines in the deserted parking lot, near the entrance, and unfolded himself from the car. Turning, he reached in for a brown leather briefcase that matched his suit and the green-and-brown swirls in his tie, and straightened to close the door. He was tall and spare and tan, efficiency even in the simple task of pointing an antitheft device toward the vehicle to secure it.

A beep sounded. Starting for the entrance to the mortuary, he flipped the key chain in midair and caught it with a key at-the-ready. His reflexes and his concise but long-legged stride told her he worked out regularly. She already knew he played golf.

He was abreast of her when she said, "Councilman Warner?"

He stopped, turned to gaze down at her, his gray eyes narrowing. "Yes?"

"I'm Jessica Latham. I'm sorry to surprise you like this but I tried your secretary several times. You were so busy."

"I'm busy now, Miss Latham. I've no time to chitchat about your personal problems, even if I had the inclination, which I do not. Now if you'll excuse me?"

She felt as if she'd been slapped. Anger flared. "I won't, Councilman. You'll hear me now or I'll air my thoughts to the city council. That's up to you."

His face lost a little color. "I—I'd think your personal psychologist would be more appropriate."

Did he think she was deranged? "What is this?" she asked, waving. "I've had trespassers and arsonists on my property of late and you're telling me I've imagined it?"

"Certainly not. The fire at your place is a matter of official record. But—" he chose his words "—emotional entanglements come back to haunt us in the most unusual ways. We sometimes create a situation that gets out of hand, gets . . . ugly."

"You're saying I *deserve* what happened to me?"

"I don't pass judgment that way," he said, stepping away to put the key to the dead bolt. "Bart Devon is a business associate and a friend, but I don't meddle in the personal affairs of my acquaintances. That kind of thing is—" he wrinkled his nose "—distasteful. I'm sorry, Miss Latham, you'll have to work this out on your own."

"So you admit to covering for him?"

The key jingled, scraped on metal. He cleared his throat, evidently to cover his sudden awkwardness, and finally drove it home. A metallic click echoed in the small enclosure. Warner slipped the keys into his right pocket and faced her, his features composed and forbidding. "As I said, Miss Latham, I don't get involved in messy sordid affairs. Devon was with me during the hours Sheriff Sanford asked about and that's the end of it. Whatever you and Devon have to work out about your private lives is of no concern to me. Now I must go. Please leave or I'll call the police."

"Affairs?" she said. "Private lives? Do you think—" But the ridiculousness of the insinuation was too ludicrous for words. She laughed dryly. "You don't think—that Devon and I—for God's sake, that we had an affair?"

Warner straightened visibly. His nostrils flared. "That's your business, and his. Good day, Miss Latham."

He turned to step into a flagstone entry.

She grasped his sleeve. "That's a lie! He's invented something completely untrue!"

The soft wool-blend sleeve slipped from her fingers. The gaping doorway began to swallow him up. Still the enormity of the situation assailed her.

"Please listen to me, Councilman Warner," she said on a shrill note. "I never met Devon face-to-face 'til last Saturday night. We had a barn-raising dance. He came uninvited, to threaten Antonio Pascale. And me!"

"It's of no concern to me," said Warner, beginning to close the door.

She pushed against it, hard. "It is to me! He's using you. You're a city official. He'll drag you down, ruin your career—he's a snake that way, he's lethal. He's a greedy land-grabber."

One disdainful eyebrow arched. "If you claim to have known him less than a week, Miss Latham, how is it you know his character so well?"

A breath of a chance was left to her. "My father," she said, gathering her thoughts. "Devon bought half my father's land and put the Sundance Community all over it. Those places sell for upward of three hundred thousand dollars apiece. They're nearly all sold. Devon must want the other half of my property, but everyone knows I won't sell. The ranch is my life, Mr. Warner. It's my *life.*"

The plea was too emotional. Warner drew away, put pressure on the door that remained wedged open by her body.

"I'm not making this up," she said, the door closing on her inch by inch. "It's a matter of public record. Look it up, please. Ask to see Devon's long-term expansion plans."

The heavy portal shut. The dead bolt clicked. Fury and frustration swept through her and she pounded on the door. "I haven't slept with a man in six years!" she shouted.

Expensive men's dress shoes tapped away down the flagstone. Then, silence. Jess sagged against the hard, polished wood.

Chapter Thirteen

She didn't need a love affair, she fumed days later, sitting on the oval rug in the living room, surrounded by leather tack and oil rags—least of all a love affair with a ruthless, conniving womanizer. It was her favorite subject of late; it gave the struggle toward success, the terrible grind to survive, an edge. It made her feel alive.

To think she'd dreamed of seducing Sleet, the litany continued. She rubbed a silver buckle 'til it shone, and threw it down to pick up another. She wasn't a one-night-stand kind of woman. What was love anyway but the need to quench the thirst of loneliness? She could do that by visiting the neighbors.

Though she was loath to admit it, it shamed her to think she'd come close to making a fool of herself, sleeping with him on the flimsy excuse that she'd have memories to last a lifetime. What bunk. The idea was childish, and unforgivably grasping. She flung down another polished buckle.

She hadn't missed his presence at the show on Sunday. She was relieved he wasn't there, hadn't witnessed the dismal showing she'd made. At least he couldn't gloat over Sienna's diminishing career, damn him.

But the display she made of detesting Sleet was merely a front that hid a more serious problem: she couldn't scrounge wheels to get Blue to Texas. She'd called Charlie, but he wasn't going. He suggested she call Hal. She thanked him politely and called someone else. Sandy Letterman, wife of the retired Riverside stockbroker, said they were hauling some colts to the lucrative auctions affiliated with the futurity, and had no extra room. Jess had dialed five other cutters she knew from San Diego to Seattle, but none of them could accommodate her.

She was righteously into the anger, taking it out on Blue's bridle, rubbing harness oil into it furiously, when the phone rang.

It was a natural extension of the anger to leap to her feet, stride to the telephone at the desk and say tersely into the receiver, "Latham Ranch."

"Jess?"

The anger had such a grip on her that hearing the cowboy's voice fueled it—though something she used to feel for him put a catch in her voice. "What the devil do you want?"

"You okay?"

"What business is it of yours? I'm busy. State your case or I'll hang up." She took the receiver from her ear and held it against her chest, as if that would stop the furious beating within. Dear God, she thought, I don't want to talk to this man.

As she put the receiver back to her ear, she heard him ask, "How're Josepha and Noa? Doing all right?"

She drew rein on her fury to answer, "Tolerable. Devon hasn't made an attempt on their lives, if that's what you're asking."

There was a brittle silence. "I'm glad to hear it," he said tersely.

"I don't know why you're bothering with the amenities, Freeman. We already know what motivates your neighborly concern."

"You took that wrong, Jess. You took everything wrong."

"Sure I did. You got Hal to report on my operations out of pure human concern, right? Nothing to do with protecting your 'investment.' You taught me everything you know about massage, out of the goodness of your heart, right? No thought about the fact that I'd use it to beat you at your own game." She laughed in derision. "No, because you wanted to take me entirely out of the game. You must be running scared, Freeman. Very scared."

She could imagine the fury leaping from his eyes when he said, "I train on the best ranches in the Southwest. I have access to the best tools, medicines, feed and equipment money can buy. You scrounge to buy grain. Do you really think you can beat me, Jess?"

She smiled with venom. "I know I can, Freeman. You're going to eat my Texas dust."

"I hear y'all are having a little trouble getting there. Any truth to that rumor?"

Jess's face blanched, then flushed with anger. She firmed her shoulders. "It's nice of you to ask," she said sarcastically, panning her overheated brain for backup ammunition. He obviously knew she'd canvassed the circuit for a ride. "I considered using Noa's trailer."

"That piece of crap? You won't get two hundred miles on those tires."

"I said I *considered* it." She let out an impatient breath. "You didn't give me the chance to say I rejected the idea. He's too big. He'd have to keep his head bowed all the way to Texas."

"Hal's offering to give you a lift. His feelings are hurt you didn't call to ask."

Now the sarcasm dripped from his words. But the mighty lure of Cowtown took its toll on her pride. "Tell Hal I'm grateful," she snapped. "Tell him I'll let him know."

She heard his harried breathing, then, softly, with evident control, "I surely will. And, Jess?"

The timbre of his voice burrowed into her, tried to loosen her shoulders. She waited, ramrod straight.

"Y'all will have to ride like hell to beat me."

"No problem," she shot back. "I'll be mounted on the son of Satan."

She hung up.

For long minutes she stood near the desk, wishing for triumph to fill her with strength. All she felt, though, was a desolation deeper than tears.

FEELING ALONE in her battles but for the anxious watchfulness of Josepha and Noa, Jess devoted herself to the ranch. When she wasn't training or feeding or washing the horses, she was making runs to the feed store, picking up loads of hay herself to save the cost of delivery. She spent the evening hours oiling tack, patching her old cutting saddle in preparation for the futurity, massaging her frugal finances and refusing to dwell on the challenge Sleet represented to her dreams. His betrayal and Warner's rejection had sealed her heart. There was only work now.

November was nearly spent; Thanksgiving was tomorrow. Josepha had planned a special dinner—had paid for it against Jess's protests—in celebration, she said, of Jess's coming success in Texas. Josepha was trying to show her concern, trying to break the deadlock of Jess's gloom.

On one level, she appreciated the care and concern; on another, she hated to lose the time away from work. She'd become obsessed with the notion Blue wasn't ready for the futurity, after all. She lost sleep over it.

IT RAINED LIGHTLY on Thanksgiving. Protected from the drizzle by an Army Surplus slicker and an old felt hat, Jess worked the tired cattle relentlessly. She urged Blue back and forth, schooling him with a sharp bite of the bit when he overstepped his calf, touching a spur to his flank to get him around with more speed.

She was deep in a cut when the brindle cow turned tail and zipped by Noa, crashing through the sawhorse barrier.

"Noa!" she called sharply, frustrated, billowing the slicker. "I just had him working good!"

When there was no response, she lifted Blue's reins and glanced up. She saw the reason for the lost cow.

Looking like a traditional Mexican doll in his striped poncho and straw hat, Noa sat slumped astride Sienna, talking to Josepha at the fence. Josepha had slipped on oversize rubber boots to come down to the arena; they looked incongruous with her Sunday best: a flowing burgundy dress, and a delicate gold crucifix pinned to a snow-white lace collar. She had dressed for the meal. Now she'd come to collect her family.

Jess trotted Blue over to the couple. Leaning to the side, she tipped the brim of her hat, releasing a trickle of rainwater. "We're almost through, Josepha," she said, breathless.

"Time to clean up," Josepha said firmly, eyeing Noa. "The turkey she is nearly done."

"*Bueno,*" Noa smiled in approval. "*Tengo hambre*—I'm hungry."

"Another couple of cows," Jess pleaded.

Noa lost his smile.

"Jessica," Josepha scolded, the authority of years of mothering in her tone. "You come in now. Get washed up. Is time."

Unused to orders from Josepha, Jess stiffened.

"Your stud is tired, *mi'ja*," Noa said, softening the words of his wife. "The mare, she is exhausted."

Jess glanced at Blue's shoulders; they trembled—*trembled!* His breathing sounded like waves rushing the shore. Sienna was in worse shape. Her muzzle, chest, belly and legs were stained dark not just by rain but by sweat. Her powerful forequarters heaved. Her nostrils flared to drag in air. Guilt washed Jess so suddenly, her face reddened. "Oh," she said on a moan. "What have I done?"

Silence from her companions. She turned to them, shame eating its way through her like acid. "I-I've worked them too hard!"

"*Sí,*" Josepha said gently. "And yourself, too, *mi'ja*. Come inside. It is time to rest, laugh, have fun. It is time to celebrate your trip."

Jess nodded, stepping Blue over and beginning to walk him to cool him down. In a moment Noa joined her, leading Sienna. He said nothing. They moved like phantoms through the drizzle, Jess reaching periodically to take the stud's pulse, and casting worried glances at the mare.

After currying the horses and treating Sienna's legs for swelling caused by excessive stress, Noa and Jess left the barn side by side. The rain had abated; the air was pungent with barnyard smells.

"She just want you to be happy," Noa said, speaking of Josepha. He shook moisture from his hat and set it on his head.

"I know," said Jess. "I should have been inside helping her with the dinner instead of running you and my horses into the ground."

"You work too much lately," he said.

"I guess. It's all there is, anymore."

About to head for the cottage, presumably to change his clothes, Noa stopped. Jess drew up beside him. He took his hat off and held it against his chest, rolling the brim. The moisture in the air gave his hair a silver sheen. The overcast darkened the lines in his baby-soft face.

"Mi'ja," he said, gazing at her with affection. *"Tu padre*—he is dead now. I think you still try to please him, no?"

"No, I—" She clamped her mouth on the lie.

"I think so. He would be very proud of you for what you have done here." He swept an arm toward the ranch. "But he would want you to be happy, like Josepha and me. He would not want to see you all the time sad. It would make him cry."

"He never cried!" she burst out.

"In his *heart*. He always cry inside, *tu padre*. He never show how he feels, like Josepha and me show it. But he feels, just the same. You know?"

She nodded. He'd been tough as old leather. She'd learned to be tough by his example. She knew, now, how safe you felt, locked behind a facade of gruffness. Sleet had temporarily melted away her shield, and then when he'd let her down, she'd constructed it again. If you were vulnerable, life would tear you to shreds. She'd remembered that rule just in time. "It's best to just keep forging ahead," she said firmly, with intentional vagueness.

"But is not healthy, your way," Noa said.

"Maybe not, Noa, but right now, I need to be tough. Everything we hold dear depends on it."

"Not everything, *mi'ja*. Josepha and I can live with relatives in Mexico. We could live like *peones* in a shack if only we know Jessica is happy."

"Oh, Noa." He was telling her that happiness was more important than saving the ranch. She rejected the wisdom but was touched by his generosity. In a rare display of love for the man she'd known all but three years of her life, she went to him and hugged him. In a moment, she held him apart, letting her eyes tell him the words she couldn't say, the gratitude for his loyalty, his caring, his years of toil. His eyes were moist. She hugged him again, briefly, and stepped away, saying, "She's going to kill us if we don't get washed up for dinner."

"*Sí, querida. Voy pronto*—I'm coming very quick."

He swiped at his eyes and Jess turned away, heading for the main house, with each step shoring up the facade she'd rebuilt over the weeks.

When Jess came indoors, she was assailed with scents that harked back to her youth. Josepha was rustling around in the dining room, so Jess toured the kitchen, taking advantage of the lack of supervision to nibble on her favorite delicacies. The house smelled sweet with roast turkey, dressing, *tamales*—pork-stuffed *masa* wrapped in cornhusk leaves and boiled—and *buñuelos,* the crispy, fried flour tortilla sprinkled with cinnamon sugar and cut like a pizza into pointy wedges. Despite her own meager finances, Josepha had not stinted on the shopping, Jess noticed, swiping a *buñuelo* from a plate. She munched the flaky treasure, and slipped back in time ten, fifteen years.

The Thanksgiving and Christmas dinners Josepha had prepared for the Lathams for more than two decades had always yielded food enough for thirty. In the days when the ranch was at its zenith, it was the custom of her father to seat the hands at a formal dinner with the family. The roasting of the turkey had always been a concession on Josepha's part to the American traditions of the Latham family, and the *tamales,* and *buñuelos,* a gift of her culture. At the holidays, she had been treated like royalty by everyone; her dinners were famous in the community. Poor dear, Jess thought; she misses the frivolity and homage of those days.

Evidently Josepha had forgotten there were only three mouths to feed. The only concession she'd made to the current economic crunch was to buy a twelve- instead of a twenty-pound turkey. Jess shook her head. What extravagance! They would eat richly for the first time in months.

She wandered to the dining room. Josepha had dusted the massive table and chairs and laid out an ancient lace tablecloth. The rose-patterned dishes were stacked on one end, and Josepha was taking water- and wineglasses from the cherrywood hutch, clustering them near the plates. Jess offered to set the table, but Josepha shooed her away, told her to "wash and dress for dinner." The trimming of the table was Josepha's domain and pride; Jess would not usurp her pleasure.

In the bathroom, she stripped and filled the tub, adding a few precious drops of scented oil from a bottle she'd bought in L.A. more than a year ago. Then she let the hot water trickle into the fragrant bath while she lay back in it and closed her eyes.

Perhaps she wouldn't need the stiffened hide of self-protection today, she mused, running a washcloth languidly up her arms. Maybe she could be human for the first time in weeks. Josepha and Noa, who'd been her parents when her own could not be, deserved her consideration.

In twenty minutes, she was in her room, already wearing hosiery, skimpy black lingerie and heels. As she was stepping into a turquoise silk, flair-skirted shirtwaist from more luxurious days, a vehicle arrived outside her window. As always, she felt a slight tingle of alarm. Trouble? she wondered. Tucking up a tendril of hair that had come loose from the chignon she'd pinned high to create a romantic look, she went to peer from behind lace curtains drawn open to let in the light.

It was Sleet! Softened by her own will to be human, her heart leapt and clattered with joy. How handsome he looked stepping out of the truck, dressed in a gray Western suit and bolo tie. He ducked back into the truck to retrieve something—his hat, she thought, he always wore a hat and it would be a gray beaver felt. He liked nice clothes; he had a good sense of style and color. Sure enough, it was a gray. A smile curved her lips as she watched him adjust his hat in the rearview mirror, tilting the hat lower. He was vain. Funny how she'd begun to know his personal traits, as if they'd been romantically involved for months instead of the few brief days so long ago.

She started slightly. What was she thinking? She disliked Sleet Freeman, knew him for the opportunistic womanizer he was.

And on the heels of joy, came anger and a sense of betrayal. Josepha had planned this! Jess whirled away from the window, fisting her hands. Sweet, motherly Josepha had come down to the arena demanding she and Noa stop work on the pretense her turkey was done, and all along she'd wanted Jess to primp and pamper herself for the itinerant cowboy. Of all the low-down things to do!

No, wait, she theorized, zipping the dress in a flurry of temper, buckling on a wide turquoise belt. Josepha wouldn't have called Sleet and set this up, Noa would have. All that talk of happiness and how proud her father would have been of her—Noa had wanted to soften her up.

He and his wife were playing matchmaker. It made her furious.

Cutting a glance toward the window, she saw Noa, white shirt buttoned to the throat, hurry from the cottage to join Sleet, who walked toward the porch with his arms full of a brown paper bag and an immense bouquet of fall flowers and oak leaves. Josepha's centerpiece, no doubt, she thought sourly. Josepha always finished off her holiday table with a touch of beauty.

Jess turned away in disgust, went to her bureau. Here she opened the lid of the jewelry box and pulled out sapphire earrings—a gift from Josh and her father when she'd graduated from high school. She should put on jeans and a work shirt to spite them all, she thought. It would serve them right, tricking her this way. But she knew she would not. It felt too good to wear silk after more than a year of denim.

She heard the tramp of men's feet as Sleet and Noa entered the living room. Sleet would take off his hat, walk to the far wall and hang it on the hat rack. He'd smooth back that still-damp chaff-gold hair....

She looked into the mirror, squared her shoulders, and mentally erected her protective wall. Her black-fringed blue-green eyes flashed with ire. She would show them nothing of what she felt, she decided.

After arcing on rose lipstick, she put down the gold case and picked up a cheek brush. With deft strokes, she applied rosy blush. Done with the basics, she arched her eyebrows at herself, turned to glimpse the lustrous upswept chignon and left the room.

She emerged from the hallway at the moment Sleet was passing in Noa's wake, the two men on their way to the kitchen. Sleet paused as she stepped out, their gazes darted together, held, and she was sent speeding backward in time.

She'd worn the same color that night, a teal-blue lamb's wool sweater, and when she'd pushed open the screen door, there had stood a long-legged, broad-shouldered cowboy, the lamplight catching silver threads in his golden hair. She had owed him the life of her stallion and probably her own, but she had battled with him as if he'd stormed the palace gate to steal her treasure. It had been a breathless moment then, and it was again.

He stared at her as if she were a gem he hadn't expected to find in his pocket.

"Well," she said archly. "Come to swallow your weekly mouse? I suppose dinner's almost ready."

"I switched to wildcat." There was a glimmer of humor she didn't like. "Tastier than mouse." He motioned to her. "After you."

She turned and walked down the wide hall, conscious of the tapping of her heels on the oak boards, conscious of his hungry eyes. She'd be damned if she'd weaken to them again.

When they entered the kitchen, everyone carefully ignored the minor detail that Sleet's arrival had been a surprise to Jess. They carried on awkwardly, stiffly, saying their hellos, until Sleet put the grocery sack on the counter and turned to Josepha.

He made a flourishing bow to her, said "*A sus ordines—* at your service—" and presented her with the bouquet.

Josepha blushed prettily, Jess rolled her eyes and Sleet dug into the sack. He brought out two bottles of white wine and handed them to Noa. Noa immediately offered to open a bottle for dinner, and then Sleet reached in again. This time he was holding a black, velvety material. "For you, Jess," he said. "For Texas."

Reflexes carried her through. She took the item, rubbing her fingers over luxurious leather. "It's a little late for peace offerings," she said in an unyielding tone.

"For Texas," he insisted, the familiar commanding look telling her not to refuse. "And for my rude behavior this past month or two."

Irritation tried to surface in her gaze. She firmed her lips and looked down at the treasure she held. It was so supple, it slid open to drape down the front of her. Chaps. A pair of deeply fringed suede chaps for the futurity, black as Blue-bar-Satan. How magnificently they would show with his glossy beauty. If she wore black at the show, nothing would detract from his lines, his pure gift for the cows. Sleet had known black chaps were the perfect foil, and she closed her eyes briefly, aware, despite her resentments, that this gift was a true peace offering. She wanted to hug them to her, bury her face in the soft leather. Instead she walked to the counter. Folding the chaps, she lay them inside the paper bag. "You ought to know I can't be bought," she said, pushing the bag to a corner—hating to do it. "You can take them with you when you leave."

Josepha frowned at her. *"Mi'ja..."*

"I don't approve of the trick you all played on me," she quipped sharply, drawing her hands together in front of her. "It was a low-down thing to do."

Sleet ducked his head to hide a half smile. "I was told you wanted to discuss the details of the trip," he said. "I realized as soon as I saw you, my coming was a surprise."

So he had been unprepared for her chilly reception, she realized, thawing minutely toward him. She supposed courtesy and the Latham legacy of generosity compelled her to make him welcome.

By now he understood she was no longer starry-eyed and infatuated with him. The beautiful chaps were an attempt to take her off guard again. It wouldn't work, but they did need to talk—she had called Hal to accept the ride to Fort Worth.

"I suppose we should make arrangements," she said, her gaze glancing off him and over to the paper bag containing the chaps. "It'll take us three days to make the trip?"

"Right, and I have to get there a day or two early to polish up a couple of colts I trained before coming West."

She bit her lip. Two additional days of expenses. She'd sold the burned trailer to a rebuilding outfit, earning enough to pay the utilities before she left, and food for the trip. Two extra days would stretch her to near nothing. But she was lucky to get Blue to Texas at all; she wouldn't quibble if he and the Brittons wanted to leave early.

"That going to present a problem?" he asked, including Noa and Josepha in the query.

"No," she said quickly. "That'll be okay."

Sensing Jess's capitulation, Josepha gave her the coveted task of arranging the centerpiece for the table. She set Noa to uncorking one of the bottles of wine, and asked their visitor to arrange kindling and logs in the fireplace in anticipation of a visit in the living room after dinner.

In the dining room, as she placed the vase of flowers on the table, Jess heard Josepha and Noa whispering. Then the radio came on. The strains of a mariachi band played gaily. That, too, was custom in the Latham home. Jess lit the candles, admiring the reflected gleam on leaded crystal goblets. For Josepha's sake, she resolved to be pleasant for the duration of the gathering.

TOWARD THE END of the meal, Josh called, and Jess spent several minutes in the living room, exchanging greetings and news with his family.

When she returned to deliver Josh's holiday wishes to Noa and Josepha, she found the couple plying Sleet with questions. With a swish of silk that brought Sleet's gaze to her, Jess sat down. She smiled, waving them to continue the conversation. It had been a lovely dinner. Music, nostalgia and the warmth of her stand-in parents had eased Jess into the pleasantries, and once she'd recounted stories from former Thanksgivings at the ranch, Sleet had needed little encouragement to entertain them with anecdotes about the horses he'd trained. Now Josepha asked about his younger brother and mother, and the farm in Missouri.

Sleet warmed to the discussion, his face relaxing with memories. Once or twice in the past, he'd lent a hand with the taxes, he said, but for the most part, these days, the farm was faring well.

"Why you no work the land yourself?" Noa asked, tucking the last tortilla-wrapped bite of turkey into his mouth and pushing away his plate.

At the query, a strange shadow of thought moved over Sleet's face. "That's better left to my brother," he said in a low voice.

"But you are the elder son, no?" Noa persisted.

Jess folded her napkin, wondering why Sleet seemed ill at ease.

"Too restless, I guess," Sleet said, shrugging a shoulder. "No taste for settling down. Besides, my brother couldn't just work for anybody. He was blinded in one eye when he was fifteen."

"*Pobrecito*—poor thing!" Josepha exclaimed, her face showing sympathy. Jess felt it, too.

"*Lo siento,*" Noa said.

Sleet spread his hands. "He's fine. Puts in a full day like any other man. Does a damned good job around the place. No need to feel sorry for him."

But Sleet did, Jess knew, though she didn't understand *how* she knew it; intuition, perhaps, or that weird emotional link she sometimes experienced with him. How did the accident happen? Was Sleet involved?

Suddenly it didn't matter. He was a guest. You didn't put guests on the hot seat, make them uncomfortable. She raised her glass. "A toast," she said brightly, urging them to join her.

They raised their glasses. Sleet caught her glance and thanked her for the diversion. She ignored the intimacy.

"To family," she said. "Josepha and Noa are a great blessing in my life."

They drank to family, and then to Noa's "*Buena suerte*— good luck—in Texas."

Sleet hailed Josepha's cooking as the best since the good old days in Missouri, and they drank to that. Then Sleet cocked his head. "That almost sounds like a waltz," he mused aloud, and they all listened to the guitars and plaintive singing of the mariachis. "But not quite a waltz tempo."

"*Sí,*" said Josepha, rising beside the table. "Is a waltz. I show you." Lifting a bit of her skirt, she performed a few dainty steps.

Sleet rose, grinning. He went to Josepha and held out his hand. He glanced at Noa. "With your permission?"

"*Seguro*—of course. I am too full to dance." He patted his stomach.

Jess and the others laughed.

Sleet took Josepha in a loose embrace and, looking down at their feet, began to match her steps. Soon he had the rhythm. Slight, feminine Josepha, her face glowing, danced around the table and into the hall with Sleet.

Reminded of that moment at the barn dance when she'd been held in those strong arms, Jess felt something go through her—a stab of jealousy or nostalgia or longing, or perhaps all three. Absurd, she thought, riffling the edge of her napkin—trying not to envy Josepha's breathless, "You dance good, Señor Sleet. *¡Perfectamente!*" Seduction was the need to quell loneliness.

She stood up abruptly. It was utter nonsense, that sickening lurch in her stomach. She reached for her plate, took Sleet's and stacked it. She dared not look at Noa. He would read her as easily as he read temper in a horse.

The dancing couple were returning, waltzing their way back to the table, Josepha laughing gaily. Mouth firmed, hands full of china and silverware, Jess stepped toward the kitchen, desperate to submerge with busywork the rippling tide of emotions she was feeling. Where was control? Where was the grim anger that had driven her the past weeks?

"You try," she heard Josepha say to her. "Is easy."

"No, I'll just clean up. You enjoy—"

A sharp *crack! zing!* sounded from outside. Jess froze and turned to the others. They each wore expressions of confusion, of question.

"Did you hear it, too?" she asked.

"*Sí,*" said Noa.

Sleet said, "Yeah. Did a car backfire down below?"

In answer came another report, followed by a squeal that turned to a high whinny. The equine cry rose to a tortured scream.

Jess felt the color leave her face. "Brisa!"

"*Ay,*" wailed Josepha in alarm.

The four of them were suddenly in motion. Jess shoved the dishes to the table with a clatter. Glass shattered but she didn't stop to see what she'd broken. She wanted to take the time to rush to the bedroom closet and unearth the thirty-ought-six she'd planned to store under the couch but never had; the urgency to get to Brisa was too great. Sleet was opening the front door by the time she emerged into the living room. Noa and Josepha were right behind her, following her and Sleet outside.

Dusk was about to fall on a gray day. The sky was hung with clouds so pregnant with rain that the air felt suffocating. Sleet jumped off the porch, heading for the arena, casting glances toward the hills, the valley, the barn. Jess, mimicking him, saw no movement in any of those directions. Slipping off a shoe, tossing it, hopping 'til she had the other one off, she shoved her feet into the pair of muddy boots near the door and bolted after Sleet.

Blue called from the barn. He wanted his night feeding, and sensed people about. He would have to wait.

Sleet arrived at the far corral first and as he climbed through the rails, Jess, a few yards behind him, heard the oath he uttered.

Shocked by what he witnessed, Sleet stopped and stood with his legs apart. Jess arrived, climbed through and flew past him. Then she, too, stopped and stared at the filly, her heart clutching in fear.

Brisa recognized her and whinnied pitifully. It was an agonized, pleading call. She hobbled forward, swayed and tried again to come to Jess. She was bleeding from the shoulder.

Jess's eyes filled and she ran forward. "Brisa!" She stopped close to the yearling and raised her hands in a helpless gesture. "Oh, Brisa, who—?"

Shot you, she finished silently. She cast a fearful glance toward the foothills. With darkness falling, she could see nothing among the scrub oak and rocks, nor along the spines of the ridges. The filly nudged her. Jess turned back in time to see Brisa swing up her muzzle to nip at her left shoulder. Blood ran in a wide sheath down the sorrel hide. "No," Jess urged, choking back the tears. She put a hand on the soft nose, holding it away from the wound. "Easy, Brisa. We're going to help you."

Sleet was beside her, reaching out to heal, to sympathize, to judge the extent of the wound.

"Is it bad?" Jess asked, holding Brisa's halter.

"Surface, maybe. Can't tell." At his exploratory touch, the animal squealed, crab-stepped away. "Easy, girl. Go her easy."

Jess clung to Brisa's halter.

Nearby, Noa was embracing Josepha, who buried her face in her husband's neck. She was moaning soft Spanish words to God, to Mother Mary.

"Noa," Jess said, sharpening her voice to penetrate Josepha's grief and fear. "Phone Doc Brady. And the sheriff. Josepha, get me towels. At least a dozen. Quick."

The couple hurried away. She turned to Sleet. "Do we need to close the wound? I don't have needles or gut. Do you?"

"No. Some salve, some cauterizing powder, some rope. My bandages won't help. We'll strap towels on her 'til the vet gets here." He moved out of her vision.

Jess felt alone and frightened. There was so much blood! Hurry, please, all of you! Was Brisa shot through? Bones broken? Would she have to be put down? *Brisa! I'm sorry I resented the food you ate, the work you required! Stay. Please stay with us.*

She left the filly's head, ran her fingers into the wound and probed, unmindful of the warm slick liquid that coursed over her hands, her wrists. Brisa shuddered. "I know it hurts," Jess soothed. "Stand easy, girl."

Her fingers tracked a long diagonal rift in the hide, the hard surface of a bone that had a sharp edge to it, probably a fracture, and a little soft tissue. Jess wasn't skilled in physiology and there was too much blood to tell what damage had been done. If only she could stop the bleeding. She lifted her skirt, but the wound was too high to reach. For seconds that felt like minutes, like hours, she cupped her hands to the wound, murmuring to the filly, willing her not to bleed to death before help arrived.

The anguish of waiting ended when Sleet came to her, touching her shoulder lightly. A white, folded towel was pressed to the backs of her hands, and she removed them to help hold it in place. It was sodden immediately. Another towel replaced it, and another, and there was no sound from anyone except Brisa, who trembled and groaned out each breath.

After the seventh towel, a gleam of white bone appeared, and Sleet dumped half the can of powder into the wound and slapped three towels over it. Brisa jerked back, whinnying in pain. "Quick," he said. "The rope."

Jess looped one end of the rope under Brisa's belly. Noa grasped it and brought it up to Sleet, who laid it over the towels and ran it down to Jess again. They wrapped the rope three times around the yearling's belly and she only flinched once, though she'd never felt the cinch of a saddle in her life. It's the massages, Jess thought. The massages had made Brisa trust them enough to tighten a rope around her for the very first time, without a fight. For that small miracle, she owed Sleet. Again.

The filly staggered. She was going into shock. Sleet, Noa and Jess propped her up, Noa tucked under her chest where Jess couldn't see him, Sleet facing Jess as she leaned in on Brisa's right side. Sleet glanced at Josepha, whose face was streaked with tears.

Josepha wrung her hands. *"Por Dios,"* she implored, *"por Dios."*

"We need a blanket," Sleet told her. "Josepha, can you bring a blanket? Two blankets?"

Josepha nodded, wiped her face and went back to the house.

In the ensuing silence, when there were only Brisa's groans to listen to, Sleet and Jess looked at each other. The gaze was long, his filled with compassion, hers with fear. The gut-searing anger she usually felt toward him had drifted away, obliterated by an overwhelming gratitude that he was here.

"As always," she murmured, "you have such impeccable timing."

"Glad to oblige," he said softly, his mouth curving in a ghostly smile.

From some distance above the ranch, stones clattered down the slope.

Sleet swiveled toward the hills.

Heart thudding, Jess followed his gaze. The foothills were dark gray, obscure. "Up there, do you think?"

"I don't know. Sniper would have a good view. The doc may know which direction the shot could have come from."

They listened for a time, but silence prevailed once more.

Josepha came running with the blankets. They covered the filly with one, and Josepha spread the other on the ground nearby, according to Sleet's direction.

"If she falls," Sleet explained, "let's try to get her to fold up on that blanket. It'll keep the dirt away from the wound."

In the distance a siren moaned. Then they heard the crunch of gravel down by the live oak, and a pickup truck ground its gears, coming up the hill. Headlights glanced off their tense faces.

Doc Brady parked the pickup so the headlights illuminated the scene. Carrying a battery lantern and a medical box, he climbed through the rails and strode to them, his gait snappy. He bent to open the box on the edge of the blanket, and set the lantern to shine across his tools to the white terry cloth covering the wound. Doc was a short, grizzle-faced man with keen blue eyes.

"Evenin', folks...Jess," he said gravely, hanging a stethoscope on his neck and approaching the filly. He pulled a short lead from his belt loop, clipped it on to her halter and eased her head down. Gently he pulled up each eyelid and stared in. Grunting, he let her go, fitting the ear tips to his ears and laying the diaphragm casually against her chest, as if he were going to give her a friendly rub. Brisa arched back and tried to peer down at him. "Settle down, now," he told her idly. "How's she holdin' up?"

"Staggering some," Jess said. "Lost a lot of blood. Sleet put some cauterizing powder on the wound."

Doc slid a quick look at Sleet, nodded approval. He put the stethoscope away, said to Jess, "Her ticker's working hard but it's in good shape. Her age?"

Jess told him.

"Name?"

"Brisa."

"Somebody shot her, Noa said on the phone. Who might that be?"

"Sniper," said Sleet, his voice flat, angry. "We've had trouble here lately."

Speaking as if he had a stake in her ranch, Jess noted. She sent him a probing look but he was focused on Brady.

"Heard about the fire," said Doc. "Damned lousy business."

"Damned low-down lousy," said Sleet.

Doc jabbed a thumb toward Brisa, the preliminaries clearly done. "Somebody hold her head. Let's take a look at that wound."

Jess went to Brisa's halter and grasped the chin strap. While she stroked the animal's nose, she craned around to watch Sleet ease the blanket and rope away. Brisa quivered as Doc grabbed the towels, handing them to Josepha, who tossed them down near Doc's case. The inside fabric had been soaked but the bleeding had abated to a steady ooze. The white powder had caked in thick slabs, like a mud puddle dried up in flakes. Jess felt her stomach turn over.

"Uh-huh," Doc mused, probing the bloody wound with his fingers, making Brisa toss her head. "Somebody get me the towels from the front seat of my truck."

Noa went for them.

"Chipped the outside of the shoulder bone," Doc pronounced, turning to Jess. "Shot must have come from high up, behind her, judging from the angle of the tear in her coat. The foothills, maybe. No muscle damage but she's going to be lame for a while."

At Jess's beseeching gaze, he said, "She's young. She'll be scarred but whole. Won't interfere with working cattle or giving you lots of baby Brisas."

Jess pressed her face into Brisa's neck and hugged her. *Like a soft wind,* Jess thought, remembering the day the filly had arrived. Brisa was like her name—gentle, lovable. Who could kill such a darling?

It was then that Jess felt the first stirring of hatred. It fueled a need to take action.

Chapter Fourteen

Wrath seemed too mild a word for what she felt. It had been building for an hour, this tight-gutted rage that made her feel omnipotent. It had simmered each time Brisa quivered from the prick of an injection. It had glowed red-hot as the patched-up youngster staggered across the barnyard and into the barn, collapsing on a fresh bed of straw, panting, grunting, frightened.

A stall was where Brisa should have been for many nights past, Jess thought, easing into light traffic on the field-bordered expressway. But she'd been paranoid that Brisa might be carrying a strain of equine strangles or some other dread disease that would contaminate her contender for the futurity, so she'd kept her quarantined. Then she'd gotten busy and forgotten her—and she'd been nearly killed. Jess struck the wheel. Sleet had been right, and she should have believed him. She should have known the attempts to destroy her operation would go on.

Somewhere behind her, Sleet and Sheriff Sanford and a deputy were climbing the foothills, looking for clues to the enemy's whereabouts. The thought of Sleet up there in the dark, armed with her father's rifle and a flashlight, added to her agitation. She should have insisted on going with them.

But time was of the essence in picking up clues. When the doc finished with Brisa and they'd settled her, he'd given Blue and Sienna their quarterly vet check and care, telling Jess there was no rush in paying the bill. Josepha was soaking the bloody towels, Noa was feeding the cattle; there'd been no one else to assist with the doctoring. So Sleet had headed out with the lawmen, telling her to keep the coffee hot for him.

She would, and glad to do it, but that would have to come later. First, she had business in town.

Taking a corner too fast, she whipped the wheel to straighten out the truck, barreling down Hacienda Lane. The bullet could have been for Blue, her pride, her cherished stallion, she was thinking. It could as easily have been for Sienna, whose loyalty and ebbing stamina had seen her through these past critical months, months when every dollar counted and she'd needed a proven cow horse to get her through her first cutting season. Instead, Brisa, new symbol of productivity at the ranch, had paid the price, and the guilt of it lay on Jess's heart.

Loathing flamed in her afresh. Only a subhuman coward would have shot a helpless creature like Brisa.

That thought was burning a hole in her as she swung the truck into a driveway, shearing off the corner of a waist-high, precisely trimmed box hedge. She shoved the gearshift into neutral. Jerking on the emergency brake, she tore out of the truck, leaving the door ajar and the engine running.

She pounded up the concrete walk and steps, pressed a doorbell and hammered on a lacquered oak panel. "Warner," she shouted. "Warner!"

A light came on in the entryway, and above her head. The door swung open.

Warner wore slacks and a dress shirt, and, ever the neat freak, was cinching up his tie. He stopped, one hand in midair. "What the devil—"

She took in his expression—horror—and the frightened face of a child about ten, behind him. Wearing pajamas, the boy paused to stare, then darted out of sight, calling, "Mom!"

Jess realized why they were horrified. She pushed tangled strands of black hair from her eyes, looked down. Rust-colored blood tinted her hands, her sleeves, and large splotches covered the silk skirt. She was wearing muddy rubber boots. She looked crazed; she looked like a murderess. But it didn't matter.

"I have to talk to you," she said, chest heaving.

"Clinton," said a feminine voice behind him. "Clint, what's wrong?"

A slim woman appeared beside Warner. She was right out of an ad for golf clubs, down to the knee-length skirt and knit shirt. She put a hand to her short blond hair, sucked in her breath. "What on earth?"

"What's happened?" asked Warner, sounding rattled. "Miss Latham, are you . . . ?"

"He's shooting bullets now," she said, knowing the councilman understood she was speaking of Devon. "You're protecting an assassin."

Warner's eyes darted to his wife.

"Clint, what does she want?" she asked, voice rising. "Who's shooting? Should I call the police?"

"They've already been called," Jess said tersely. "Sheriff Sanford's up at my place now, looking for the sniper."

"Sniper!"

"Mommy?" said the child, peeking around her, his eyes huge. "That lady's bleeding."

Warner's shock wore off abruptly. "Caroline," he snapped. "Take Jimmy into the kitchen. I'll handle this."

Things're getting untidy, Jess thought; he needs to take control.

Caroline backed away, hesitated, biting her lip.

"Caroline!"

She collected the boy and withdrew into the house.

Warner glanced over his shoulder, then faced Jess, his gray eyes seeking injuries. "Who was shot?"

"A young filly. Devon shot her. Or had her shot."

The relief showed in his face—*only a horse,* he was thinking. He narrowed his eyes. "How do you know it was him?"

"No one else has been implicated in what's been going on at my place, and you're his only alibi. Why would he come to my place and try to intimidate Pascale? Why would he threaten me? You're shielding a criminal."

"That's a wild accusation. You don't have proof."

"Not with you holding out, I don't. My yearling was shot tonight because Devon's conned you into lying."

"Now, hold on." He stepped outside and closed the door behind him, his voice a stage whisper. "You can't lay that kind of blame on me!"

She eyed him in contempt. "It's getting messy, isn't it, Warner? You like things clean and tidy with all your ducks in a row, don't you?"

"Get to the point."

"Two thirds of the way through med school, you took a left turn, right? Too many emotions involved in doctoring the living? Cadavers are perfect for you. No emotions, no messy relationships, no need to get *involved.* How did you ever get into politics, with that aversion of yours to *people?*"

"Look here, Miss Latham, that's enough." He nudged the knot of his tie, evidently seeking self-control. "I'm sorry about your horse, but I don't have to stand here and listen to crass innuendos from you."

"No? I had to listen to yours."

He pulled to his full height. "I told you before. Your personal business isn't anything to do with me. Now, get off my property."

"And I told you—" she jabbed a rusty red finger at him, till he arched away "—I'm not 'involved' with Devon. Did you bother to check? You get one witness who'll claim I was—besides him and his paid criminals—and I'll pack up and leave Hemet in a heartbeat. In the meantime, you tell that creep something for me." She drew a harsh breath. "You tell him I'm going to Texas to win that futurity. Then I'm coming back here to get the ranch on its feet. He's not going to run me out. I'm going to get foals on my brood stock 'til they're coming out of my ears, 'til the whole valley's filled with the Latham brand—and known for it— and *proud* of it."

She took satisfaction from the distaste she saw on Warner's face. She poked him hard in his bony chest again, smudging his white shirt. "You tell him that, Warner. And you tell him if anything happens to my own while I'm gone, I'll take my daddy's gun and blow his brains to Riverside."

Warner paled.

She smiled. "I guarantee you, you won't like cleaning up the mess I'll leave behind."

She pivoted and marched to the truck, the rubber boots thudding heavily. Turning back to Warner, she called, "Don't expect to get any sleep, Councilman. I'm going to rattle your neat little world 'til you tell the truth!"

SHE PARKED THE TRUCK next to the barn and shut off the ignition. She'd seen a deputy parked under the live oak at the property line, and Sleet's pickup was still gleaming in the porch lights. Both vehicles had lifted her spirits. She had protection, and Sleet was still at the ranch.

Why should you care? asked a niggling voice in her head. *He betrayed you, tried to steal your dream. You hate him.*

But tonight, she did not. Tonight she had needed him and he had been there for her, like a trusted old friend.

Wearing his good hat, and a corduroy jacket over his stained gray suit, Sleet hurried out of the barn. He came to the door of the pickup and held it open for her. "Where'd you go, Jess? Noa said you tore out of here like you were angry. Said you had to go to town."

"I went to see Councilman Warner," she said, noting the exhaustion and worry on his face. "I wanted him to know what kind of low-life he was protecting. I wanted him to see my anger."

At dinner she'd told Sleet about her first confrontation with Warner—leaving out the innuendo that Warner believed she'd slept with Devon—and now she told him what she'd said to him tonight.

Sleet eyed her as they walked toward the barn doors. "Don't be a fool, Jess," he said, the macho barely restrained. "You want to go making night calls on a jerk like that, I'll go with you."

"No you won't. This is my ranch. I protect my own."

He swore. "You're so damned self-reliant, how come your filly was shot?"

She jerked to a stop, and so did he. She glared at him. "I sure as hell wouldn't want to rely on you to protect the 'little woman.' You'd steal her blind and call it duty."

His face went bleak as meadowland under snow. He glanced into the shaft of light coming from the barn. "I guess I deserve that," he said. He took off his hat, spun it once. In a moment, with quiet conviction, he added, "I wasn't trying to take advantage of your situation with Devon that night, Jess."

She tilted her chin and started to argue but he urged, "Wait, hear me out. I think my point about your being in danger has been justified."

"You used that to your advantage, Sleet," she said bitterly.

"I did some things wrong, Jess, but not that. I should have come to you with a straight business deal when I knew I wanted to, weeks before I made the offer. Waiting screwed things up between us pretty badly. I regret that."

Ignoring the reference to their relationship, she said, "Forget it. I'll never sell Blue and that's that."

"All right. I realize that. But I won't apologize for wanting him. And I won't apologize for wanting you."

A tremor shook her. *Wanting* me, she thought. *Present tense?* Was it all going to start again? "You've got to be kidding," she said in amazement at his gall. "Do you think I'd ever trust you again?"

He smiled. "You never trusted me before, Jess. That doesn't deter me. It strengthens my resolve."

"You said that before," she snapped, hiding consternation—and a trickle of foreboding. "You're wasting your breath, Sleet. You should take all that macho sweet-talk and tell it to someone who gives a damn."

She strode toward the lights.

"Too bad about that," he murmured, following her, replacing his hat. But it didn't sound at all like a concession.

Josepha was coming from Brisa's stall, carrying a thermos and cups. Her presence put an end to the conversation, for now.

Voices lowered, they looked in on the filly. Brisa lay stretched out on the straw. At the hushed conversation, she raised her head. It swayed; her eyelids were at half-mast. "Groggy," Sleet mouthed, and Jess nodded.

Noa rose from a pallet of blankets along the wall of the stall, explaining he was going to sleep there to watch over Brisa. He felt responsible for the vet bill and the trouble he'd caused by bringing the filly to the ranch, he said. He offered to pay her expenses. Jess refused, and Sleet told him it was no use arguing with her. An independent woman like Jess couldn't even hear such talk.

She was about to jab him in the ribs when Josepha, with convenient timing, handed her a cup of steaming coffee. She took one for Sleet, too, and threatened him with it before handing it to him.

"Behave yourself," she said under her breath. "Healing this filly is serious business."

He raised his eyebrows at her and grinned. So much for his exhaustion and worry. It had vanished.

In a few minutes, Sleet said he'd better get down the road. Jess walked him to the truck.

"Did you and the guys find any clues up there?" She indicated the black hills.

"Sheriff Sanford picked up a spent shell casing behind a boulder," Sleet said, removing his hat, tossing it into the cab. He raked his fingers through his hair. "It's been taken in for analysis. The sheriff's going to post a deputy at the live oak for a couple of days."

She caught a sparkle of lightning blue in Sleet's eyes as he spoke and marveled at their color. She shifted, uncomfortable with the sudden intimacy of the darkness.

He touched her cheek. "Jess?"

She lifted her face away from the caress. "I should get inside and clean the kitchen for Josepha. She'll want to be with Noa. Thanks, cowboy. For helping with Brisa."

He gazed at her for a moment, a question in his eyes. Then he leaned down and grazed her lips with his. It was a light kiss, a caring kiss. It made her long to cross the bridge, get to more intimate ground.

Instead she stepped back, her expression unmoved.

Sleet grinned, saluted, climbed into the cab. Twisting on the ignition, he backed the truck 'til he could head down the driveway.

When he disappeared off her property, she walked to the house. She must remember who he was, she reiterated. She must hold fast to the knowledge that defenses were best fortified by reality.

ON DECEMBER SECOND, dawn was just breaking over the foothills east of the Latham ranch when Sleet drove his rig toward the sign swinging on rusty hinges. It was the next-to-the-last time he'd see the place. The last time would be when he brought Jess home from the futurity.

In between lay a river of experiences—two long drives, some grueling workouts, the competition and the exquisite pleasure of Jess's seduction. He thought maybe he'd save that for last, give himself time to rekindle that light he'd seen in her eyes the night they'd danced before the bonfire.

He'd failed to grub-stake his ranch, but he'd be damned if she'd beat him at the other game he'd mastered as well as he'd mastered cutting.

The rig bucked over the pothole just inside the Latham Ranch gate, and that negative voice that had been pestering him lately said, *She'll be nice to you because you helped her out some and she needs this ride to Texas. Anything else you*

think you'll read in her eyes is pure ego on your part. Take
her to Texas, bring her home, then get the hell out of Dodge.

He ignored the warning. His mind was set. He was going
to be the picture of gentlemanly charm—until the night
when he took her to bed. Then all bets were off. When it was
over, it was going to be worth all the grief he'd suffer at the
lash of her viperous temper.

Eager to begin the adventure, he eased the truck and
trailer past the corrals, and when he did, he did a double-
take on the corrals. Gray and black goats munched feed
where the cattle used to be.

Cutters held opposing views on the use of goats to train
cutting horses. They were quick and they didn't eat much,
which was probably why Jess had gotten them, but a dyed-
in-the-wool cutter hated to work anything but cattle. Cows
were the natural adversary of the modern horse; man had
made it that way with sprawling ranches and the hunger for
beef.

A sudden tingle crawled up his back, and Sleet knew why
Jess had done it. She'd needed the extra money the cattle
would bring. She'd traded down to goats, giving Blue
something new to work against, so he wouldn't be lazy on
the fresh cattle she knew he would face in Texas, and had
pocketed the difference for the trip.

Sleet shook his head. Her determination was as pathetic
as it was admirable. He'd polished his colts to perfection. He
might face some competition from the real legends of the
industry, but Jess? No greenhorn, especially a woman, was
going to unseat him from his title.

Sleet glanced at the house, smiling. There was a small
mountain of gear on the front porch. Jess pushed through
the screen door and tossed her red sports bag onto the pile.
She glanced down into the cab, frowned and went back inside. Fresh as a lily in deep shade, he thought. She was

wearing faded blue jeans, running shoes, a white cotton blouse and a white ribbon catching her midnight hair in a high ponytail. She looked young and eager.

This is her first futurity, he reminded himself. *Don't ruin it for her with your real opinion of her chances.* He parked, collected his hat and climbed out of the truck.

Bending to look into the rearview, he settled his hat on his head, straightened up and walked into the yard. He drew in the woodsy scent that drifted down from the low brush that carpeted patches of the rocky hills. It was nippy. He liked the air here. It was clean, and the robin's-egg blue of the morning sky made him feel strong.

At a sound from the barn, he turned. Noa ambled out of the barn leading the filly and the mare. *¡Hola!''* the stockman called, smiling.

"Hey, Noa," Sleet said, watching Brisa limp slowly toward him. Seeing her, seeing the bandage on her shoulder, he felt his gut tighten. He wanted to shoot the sonofabitch who'd done this to her. If he'd had a gun two days ago, when he'd paid a visit to that Warner jerk, he might have used it. He might have waved it in Warner's prissy face to underscore his point.

"If anything happens to Jess Latham or anybody or anything connected with her," he'd promised Warner, backing him against the wall of bricks outside his funeral parlor, "I'll personally come back and break bones. If you know what's good for you, you'll get your butt down to the sheriff's office and tell him what you know about Devon."

Warner hadn't even known who Sleet was. He hadn't needed to know. He'd gone white as a frozen pond and ducked inside his sanctuary, scurrying like the rat he was.

Sleet only hoped it had done some good.

Noa was abreast of him. He stopped, and Sienna nuzzled his shoulder. Reaching to her nose, rubbing absently,

Noa looked soberly at Sleet. "You take good care of Jessica, Señor Sleet. Okay?"

"You bet, Noa. We'll be fine."

"No let nothing happen to her."

Sleet thought he and his wife were in more danger than Jess; she'd be off the property, out of harm's way. "You keep your eye peeled for felons—guns and such," he said.

Noa grinned. "Jess going to give me Señor Latham's rifle. She say I should keep watch over the horses while they graze in the paddock. Keep watch every morning, every night, 'til dark. This old mare, she retire now." He raised Sienna's lead rope, used it to scratch her on the side of the face. The filly pushed her muzzle in under his hand, her large eyes surveying Sleet.

Sleet reached over, cupped his hand beneath Brisa's chin and stroked. She was a lovable little gal.

Jess came outside, slamming the screen door, making the horses lift their heads. She was carrying the rifle. "Hi, Sleet," she said, looking preoccupied. "Noa, I'll put the rifle here for you." She leaned it against the porch newel. The barrel gleamed dully.

"You retired Sienna?" Sleet asked, filling his eyes with her lithe form, like a man dying for sunlight.

She smiled. "Ulterior motives. I'm going to fatten her up for the spring breeding season."

He and Noa chuckled. Jess's enthusiasm was contagious. He indicated the pile of gear. "All this stuff going with us?"

"That and a picnic Josepha's packing." She bent to heft a sack of grain. Then she let it sag to the porch, gazing toward the truck. "Where're Hal and Betty?"

"Driving the Caddy. They're not leaving for a couple of days."

"Not . . . coming with us?"

He thought he read panic on her face. He went up the steps and took the sack of grain from her, resting his eyes in the blue-green depths of hers for a moment. "I'll take that," he said. "It's heavy."

Saying he'd be back to help as soon as he'd put the horses in the paddock, Noa moved off.

Jess ignored him, her gaze staying on Sleet. "Nobody told me."

"They wanted to drive in comfort. We knew you'd want to travel with Blue."

"Oh. Right. I do."

Aware of the rapid rise and fall of her breasts and the high-strung quality of her body, Sleet moaned in silent anguish. To keep his distance from such a woman 'til after the futurity—how could he manage it? But he'd known it would be hell. It heightened the pleasure of the conquest.

So she wouldn't guess the gist of his thoughts, he turned and stepped down off the porch.

He stored the grain and her tack in the forward compartment of the trailer, and instructed her to put her suitcase behind the front seat. He was making a third trip to the porch when he saw her coming back to the truck with a large roll of canvas in her arms.

"What's that?" he asked, stopping in front of her.

"My sleeping bag."

"You won't need that, Jess."

"Yes I will. I've got to sleep somewhere."

"You'll sleep in a motel or at the ranches of friends, like me."

"I'm going to sleep in the truck," she said, obdurate. Then, sarcastically, "If that's all right with you, sire."

"It sure as hell isn't." The very notion of it roused his ire. He'd allowed more anger to creep into his voice than he intended, and he saw an answering flash in her eyes. "Look,

Jess," he temporized, spreading his hands, "I'll pay for the motel rooms, okay?"

"No!"

Patches of pink showed on her cheeks. Her fingers dug into the canvas. Her pride was up like a flag.

It riled him. He leaned down and said tersely, "I won't have you camping in my truck while I'm sleeping in a comfortable bed. Is that clear?"

"No, it's not clear and don't you raise your voice to me!" She backed away.

He followed. "Listen to reason! Do you think I'd get a wink of sleep with you out in the truck in a parking lot? I've got to acclimate my colts. I've got clients meeting me in Fort Worth who'll need coaching on how to compete. The press'll be on me like ticks on a hound. There are fancy breakfasts and cocktail parties and black-tie auctions 'til the cows come home. I've got to be sharp for all that. I've had little rest 'til now and I can't afford to worry about you!"

"And *I* can't afford more than a few nights in a hotel!" Evidently hating to bend her pride to the admission, she took a step back and glared at him.

He thought she'd handled the finances with the cattle change, the cheaper cost of the goats. Maybe he'd misjudged just how broke she was. Think, he ruminated, studying her defiant face. Think of something.

And then he had it; he'd use her pride to convince her. "Jess," he said, "let me stake you to the expenses. You can pay me back with your winnings."

She looked up, her mouth open in surprise. A light flickered in her eyes. "Yes!" she said suddenly, vehemently. "That's it, Sleet. That's what I'll do. But I'll pay you back, every penny. I swear it."

Pivoting abruptly, she took the sleeping bag into the house.

Sleet stood there for a moment, congratulating himself. He'd never seen a woman change her mind so fast in all his life. And he knew how to make it pay off.

SEVERAL HOURS LATER, Sleet's shoulders ached from driving, but he hardly minded. A new feeling had settled in him and he was worrying the edges of it, trying to figure out what it was. It had something to do with the pleasure of having a companion on this southeasterly trek he'd made so many times alone. Well, not just a companion, he corrected. Hal was a decent buddy it you didn't mind lots of cryptic sentences and miles of silence. That was fine, but Jess was another matter.

She was drinking in the sights, asking questions, making him feel brilliant in the areas of Indian history, land use and flora and fauna. As a rule, Sleet didn't drive through an area nonstop. It was his custom to stop at landmarks, at scenic lookouts, at local museums and cafés where the indigenous citizens offered trivia about bugs, fishing boats, how to fix a fifteen-year-old refrigerator and where he was likely to glimpse a rare Gila monster with its beadlike skin of black-and-yellow patterns. Although time didn't permit such luxury on this trip, his listener tapped his vast body of knowledge about the Southwest, and he reveled in the telling.

They had already crossed the arid Mojave Desert with its ocotillos rising in lone, spiky silhouettes, and he'd told her where the scorpions and sidewinders dug in to avoid the blaze of the summer sun; how the hawks circled patches of creosote, angling for a dive on kangaroo rats, squirrel or mice. They'd stopped to picnic above the sheer sandy gorge of the Colorado River, that wide flow of gold bisecting California and Arizona, and he'd told her about the decades of bloody disputes and political plea-bargaining over its use.

Now, back on the road, Jess seemed sated with descriptions and information. She had fallen silent, watching the saguaro and saltbush give way to the stunted juniper and piñon of the Upper Sonoran zone. They were rising from the desert to the low foothills, making their way along Interstate 40—old Route 66—climbing toward that lovely town at the foot of the Rockies, Flagstaff, in the center of Arizona.

"I thought we'd stop for the night at a spot I know east of Flagstaff," he said, consciously avoiding thoughts of sharing a room. The plan was to get her to relax her guard. Besides, he thought, angling to get a hook into this new contentment he was feeling, it was pretty decent to just have her around. "The motel's right next door to an outfit that'll let us corral the horses for next to nothing. It's pretty. Ponderosa pines all around, a view of the San Francisco peaks."

"Sounds great," she said, turning to gaze at him. She smiled, and didn't say another word. Strands of black wavy hair had loosened from her ponytail, and the cool breeze from the partly open window feathered them against her temples and neck. She looked mellow and young in the lowering afternoon light. Her eyes had softened to a warm blue, the color of the desert at dusk. He'd never seen her so lovely.

"It'll be too dark to ride, but I figure we could exercise the horses, get their blood stirred," he added. "It's going to be better than a twelve-hour haul to Amarillo tomorrow."

"Fine. My muscles are so used to exercise they feel jumpy. Are yours?"

"Yeah. I don't usually make this trip so pressed for time. Normally I'd saddle up, scout around some of the old pueblos or something. Walnut Canyon, just east of town, has some interesting cliff dwellings of the Sinagua people from A.D. 1120 to 1250."

"Sinagua, as in Spanish for 'without water'?''

"Right."

"I'd love to see them. Maybe on the trip back?''

Something sharp pricked his gut. Coming back meant the end of him and Jess, whatever they represented. By then he'd have run his mouth over every inch of her body. "It's a thought," he said, pushing away the erotic image. "If y'all win, y'all pay expenses, how's that?''

She grinned. "You've got a deal."

And she leaned back, unconsciously pulling the white blouse taut against her breasts. His eyes lingered. She was watching the scenery again, her face relaxed, her profile pearly in the low light. The contentment he felt was whirling around with another thing—an unnamed feeling that spun through the contentment and put a crispy edge to it. It was pleasantly achy, but what was it?

JESS WOKE in the hard queen-size bed with a mild headache, no doubt brought on by the seven-thousand-foot elevation, and tried to ease it a bit with a familiar drug—thinking of Sleet.

"One room or two?'' the desk clerk had asked last night, looking from Jess to Sleet. Into the pregnant pause Sleet had said crisply, "Two." She would have insisted on separate rooms, of course, but he'd still surprised her. Knowing how libido-driven he was, she'd expected him to at least raise his eyebrows at her.

All in all, he was being a total gentleman. For the first time since she'd known him, they weren't fighting. With the passion of a confirmed traveler, he'd regaled her with minutiae about everything from Gila monsters to pueblos. He'd given her the room with the best view—according to the night clerk—and they'd exercised and fed the horses. When it came time to eat dinner, he'd offered her Mexican,

Southwest, Oriental or down-home, going right along with her appetite for a rare steak. Back at the motel, he'd walked her to her room and waited 'til she'd gone inside and locked the door.

If he wasn't pursuing her, neither was he shutting her out, and the friendship that was developing between them was balm to her work-ravaged soul.

She rose and looked outside the window. It had snowed in the night. The Ponderosas were dusted with white powder, and a gray half-light was riffling up the bark of the coffee-brown trunks. Miles away, the San Francisco peaks glistened in a pink dawn light. To the left of the motel, fifty yards away and framed by pines, the horses tossed their heads as Sleet scooped grain from a burlap sack and poured it into their feeders.

As always, her insides leapt at her first glimpse of him. His lean, long-legged appeal, his seasoned face—each trait stirred her and made her remember the plans she'd once made to seduce him. She half wished, watching him caress a glossy equine neck as Blue dipped into the grain, that she'd not forsaken that plan. But she had, and it was hard. His eyes still found vulnerable spots in her armor; accidental touches as he brushed by shook her intent to remain reserved. In certain moments, lulled by his beautiful drawl and the splendor of the Great Southwest that he'd brought to life for her, her will could melt away as swiftly as the hot sun melts the snow.

He did not pursue it and she was grateful. The respect she'd once felt for him and lost was beginning to rebuild.

She was coming fully awake now, and seeing him dole out grain to the horses reminded her of Noa. Wondering if he and Josepha and the horses were all right, she reached for the telephone.

In Hemet, it rang four times, making her headache throb anew. Then Noa answered, *"¿Bueno?"*

"Noa? Is everything all right?"

"Ay, Jessica! *Sí.* Brisa, she like the pasture very much. The mare is taking care of her, like a daughter. She stay very close to the little one. I am in the barn, getting them a salt block. How are you, *mi'ja?"*

"Fine," she said, relieved. "It's beautiful here. We made it to Flagstaff, Arizona."

"When you get to Texas?" He pronounced it *Tey-haas.*

"Today, hours from now. You're sure everything's okay there?"

He assured her it was. Eagerly he added, "I have some good news for you."

"I can always use good news, Noa."

"This I know, *mi'ja.* Señor Hal called. He say to tell you Mr. Warner, he quit heez city job. The paper say he is in scandal."

Her heart fluttered. She gripped the receiver tighter. "Quit the city council? Warner?"

"Sí. I get the newspaper, try to read it. It say something about an investigation and a confession. It no say what for. Señor Hal going to bring the paper to you in Texas. Maybe when you visit this Warner *cabrón,* you scare him, eh?"

She let out a pent-up breath. "Oh, Noa, I hope so. This is wonderful news. But Noa?"

"¿Sí?"

"Don't take any chances. Devon might still be lurking."

"No worry, *querida.* I have your daddy's gun. I can shoot real good, too. I learn when I am a *muchacho."*

She smiled. "Give Josepha my love. *Y que las vayas bien*—keep well."

"Igualmente—the same—and say hello to Señor Sleet for me and my wife, eh?"

They hung up.

Jess dashed around the room, bundling up a red sweater, shirt, socks, jeans and running shoes, and heading for the bathroom. Warner, confessing! It was too good to be true. She couldn't wait to run out into that pristine morning and tell Sleet. He would be bowled over with surprise.

THEY DISCUSSED IT over breakfast, and again as Sleet carefully eased the rig down out of the mountains. They dropped to 4800 feet in Winslow, and a wintry sun replaced the heater. Sleet had a habit of leaving the windows open and the heater on, and it pleased her. She stayed warm yet could still smell the spice of chaparral or the sweet hay scent of native grasses.

As the day ripened, they peeled off their warmer clothing, Jess slipping out of her sweater and wool peacoat, and helping Sleet out of his Pendleton. Reaching around his shoulders to grab a dangling sleeve, she tugged, laughing, 'til the sleeve came free of his arm. When he poked her in the ribs and cast a quick glance at her, she laughed. Impulsively, she lay her head on his shoulder. "This is a great trip, Sleet," she said. "I'm so relaxed I could do the first go-round in Cowtown blindfolded."

He reached up to filter his fingers through her hair. She'd left it loose. It crackled with static electricity.

"Ow!" he said, jerking his hand away. "Is that your hair or a mine field?"

She chuckled. "Just a reminder to keep your mind on the road."

"You started it," he complained.

"I know," she said. She folded the Pendleton and laid it over her coat and the luggage in the backseat. Swiveling, she slid down into her seat and faced front. "I'm just so excited about the Warner deal."

He eyed her, his gaze teasing. "I'm sure y'all were far more convincing than I. That bit about blasting Devon to Riverside was good, Jess. I just threatened to break bones."

"We're just hell on wheels with the bad guys, aren't we, pardner?"

She'd said it in a drawling wry tone, making a joke, but he swung his head to her, his eyes narrowing.

She grinned. "Well, forget the partner bit. We'll never be that. We're just hell on wheels with the bad guys."

Without speaking, he turned his gaze back to the road, and she settled down to look at the scenery, wondering why he'd gone silent all of a sudden.

In Gallup, New Mexico, they climbed again to 6500 feet, then dropped 1500 feet down to a wide commanding valley between the Scandia Mountains and the west-sweeping plateau country that paralleled the Rio Grande. The place was called Albuquerque, where one-third of the state's population dealt in a blend of science and aesthetics. The townspeople, Sleet commented, were a vigorous lot who chased the American dream in some of the most sophisticated R & D labs in the country. Yet they cherished the environment nearly as much as the Hopi, Zuni, Taos and Cochiti of the nearby pueblos.

She had not felt such wanderlust since she'd explored Victorian London, she told Sleet. She wanted to visit museums and squander time in Old Town, picnic on the banks of the famous Rio Grande and visit the pueblos north and south of the town.

Sleet bent his head and looked into her eyes, as if to reassure himself that she was real. "Maybe we'll do it, Jess," he said. "Just remember. If y'all win, y'all pay."

They laughed and pressed on with the journey, and she wondered how it was possible to like someone as much as she liked Sleet Freeman, yet know they did not have a future.

TWELVE AND A HALF hours later, Sleet donated another piece of local gossip. "If it was light out, about a hundred yards off the road you'd see a bunch of Caddies stuck head-first in the prairie."

"What for?"

"That's been the source of arguments and gossip between the farmers, ranchers and oilmen hereabouts since the sixties, when old millionaire Stanley Marsh III buried 'em there."

"Seems a grandiose statement, whatever it means."

"That's Texas," he said, rubbing his neck. "Bigger is better. It's a way of life."

Jess wanted to reach over and ease the tension from his shoulders. He must be about to scream in agony, he'd been driving so long. "I wish you'd let me help with the driving," she chastised softly. "You have more pressure on you than I do, with all you have on your plate in Fort Worth."

"I don't fancy sittin' there with nothing to do with my hands," he said. He said it plainly, but he gave her a wolfish leer, adding his ounce of humor. It made her laugh.

"On second thought, you'd better keep driving," she said, smiling, her own exhaustion easing.

Gusts buffeted the truck, howled around the rearview mirrors. She felt cozy. They'd finally closed the windows because the blasts of icy wind, hurling across hundreds of miles of open prairie, were chilling their noses, turning them red. The heater pumped warm air on her legs. A bizarre and catchy tune by the name of "Achy Breaky Heart" galloped along to the thrum of the tires. The dash lights flickered over the stubbled chin of her companion, hollowing his eyes and grooving his cheeks, and she liked the intimacy of the cab.

The vast dark nothingness outside pressed them together in a funnel of comfort, their headlights cleaving the darkness ahead. Sleet's travelogue had long since died out, and they were united, mentally willing themselves to stay awake 'til the horses were fed.

Lights glimmered as Amarillo rose up out of the flat grasslands of the Panhandle Plains. Heralding the Christmas season, billboards advertised Amarillo's Festival of Trees, which seemed silly since she hadn't seen a tree for ages—oil pumps, yes, but not trees. Several signs, pure Texas in flavor, called to the hungry, "The Big Texan, Home Of The 72 oz. Steak—Free If Eaten In An Hour!"

"I don't think I could handle another steak," she said. "Do you want one?"

"I want a bed worse than food," he said. "But we should eat before we go on out to the ranch."

Back at the New Mexico/Texas border, Sleet had phoned a friend who would put them up tonight. He was a member of the Will Rogers Range Riders, a social and philanthropic group devoted to horses; a man, Sleet had said, with a heart as big as his 25,000-acre ranch. She couldn't fathom owning so much land. He'd told her the operation was small by Texas standards. She glanced at her driver; his eyelids were drooping, and she questioned whether they'd make it to the ranch in one piece.

"Fast food?" she suggested, trying to keep his groggy mind focused.

His head snapped up. "Fast food? Ugh, but I guess so. I'm too bushed to sit down to a meal."

After eating, they gassed up and headed for the I-287 South. It would take them to the ranch in the Palo Duro Canyon.

Amarillo had struck Jess as a gritty place. The women wore home-spun hairstyles and every man wore a duckbill cap—the Dallas Cowboys and John Deere Tractors were favorite insignias. Economic depression wore a grizzled face in this town, Pop. 157,600, Alt. 3,672'—according to a road sign—but it hadn't whupped it. "Y'all" and "Shoo-oot" and "Hey, girl" were catchall phrases that softened the grim reality of the oil slump and made you feel welcome.

The town wasn't cosmopolitan, like Albuquerque, with its skin of civilization stretched over a heart that beat to many drums. It wasn't built from the tourist overflow of a great natural wonder like the Grand Canyon, or spiced with the fervor of the downhill skier, like Flagstaff. And it wasn't remotely like Hemet, set in a sleepy-eyed sunbelt greened with citrus and walnut and apricot trees, where snowbirds and city-dwellers came to nest in discordant flocks among ranchers and indigenous Indians.

Amarillo rose up from the plains with its unpainted face, like a monolith from the void in space, and it said to the bleary-eyed traveler, "Here I am. I ain't got much, as any fool can see, but you're welcome to what you need."

Big heart. Big Texas. Jess was moved by the bravado, and she felt a kinship with this place she had come to conquer.

Too numb to absorb any more sensory input, she only knew a vague sense of relief to be leaving the immense tableland and dropping down into limestone canyons marked by promontories of white-striated mudstone and the beautiful silhouettes of brush and trees.

There was no energy left to be hopeful Warner had taken back Devon's alibi and stopped him from terrorizing her ranch. There wasn't a shred of inner tension about the coming competition, or a drop of passion left in her body. *Tey-haas,* with its bigness, had drained everything but the instinct to rest.

Chapter Fifteen

The blue norther dogged them all the way through the famed Red River Valley and down into the rich blacklands that undulated around Dallas and Fort Worth. But it was the best blue norther he'd experienced, Sleet decided, driving along a straight, narrow road that would take them to the work ring and stables he'd hired for preshow workouts. Jess had made it an adventure, a fun, sexy, mind-stirring adventure.

Right now, just before dusk, she was on a weather kick. The slanting rain had finally stopped and the grass lay flat on the hills, buffeted by strong winds.

"Look at that bluish cloud bank," she commented, turning three hundred degrees to check out the view. "What makes it blue?"

"Pure orneriness," he answered, cutting a glance at her curves as she angled around, stretching the sweater's red stripes where they banded her breasts. Lord above, but she was a sweater girl! What was the topic? Oh, right, blue northers. "These are the coldest danged storms I've ever been in," he said.

"It's kind of pretty, in a wild way," she said. "Don't you think so?"

"Mmm," he mused. "I think something else is a sight prettier."

"What?"

"You, darlin', with your jeans and your ponytail and your turquoise-blue eyes. Y'all look scrumptious as apple pie on the Fourth of Ju-*ly.*"

She flashed him a feisty look. "The closer we get to cow town, the thicker your drawl gets. And that's not all, cowboy. The bull's getting near to waist-high."

"I mean it!"

"Sure you do. Where's all that fine egalitarian behavior I came to enjoy these past three days?"

"Well, that's me, too, hon'." He winked. "I'm a man of many facets."

"You're reverting to type, pard-ner." Pursing her lips—they looked so tempting he wanted to pull to the side and kiss her just to taste them—she said, "I suppose it was inevitable."

"Are you really disappointed? Or egging me on?"

"Don't flatter yourself. We both know it's not going to amount to anything."

She flopped back on the seat and folded her arms—a rather astute protective gesture, he thought.

Oh, baby, he wanted to tell her. *You have no idea what it's going to amount to. But I do.*

A gust punched the rig, jerking him out of the discussion for a moment. He glanced into the rearview. The trailer settled and tracked again.

He put a dart of challenge into his teasing. "Eve tried the apple and found she liked it, Jess. At least she had the guts to go for what she wanted."

Jess snapped around. She was going to flay him with her temper—but she changed her mind. "We're too different," she said, and sat back to stare out the window, closing up on him.

Not that different, he thought, noting the heightened color in her cheeks.

He drove silently for a time, enjoying his fantasies. Rough barns and neat houses and flat fields of wet fodder passed by. Rain began to pelt the windshield. Sleet turned on the wipers, listening to the blades beat in time to a Randy Travis song. This time he'd kept his cool. They hadn't fought like a pair of starved dogs. During the whole trip, he hadn't put the facts of life in her face about her chances of winning the futurity, and he hadn't done more than titillate her about sleeping together. Both were inevitable, but he hadn't rubbed her nose in it. Maybe he was maturing. He liked the dignity, the sense of control he felt.

"I imagine you'll change when you've made peace with the past," she said, her voice coming disembodied from the far side of the cab.

Inwardly, he blanched. "What's that supposed to mean?"

"Just that you're touchy about your brother, his accident and all. I imagine your footloose life-style stems from that."

A quake shook his body. A swirl of emotion flooded his mind, drenching his limbs, his face with hot color. His brother! What the devil did she know about that part of his life?

"Everything's fine with me and my brother," he said gruffly, shifting his shoulders to dislodge a vague pressure there. "We're tight. He's the best. He and I have nothing to do with you and me."

Facing him, she taunted, "Are you sure?"

His gut twisted like rusty wire. "Leave it, before I tell you the facts of life."

She started to speak, and instead laughed dryly. "Oh, for Pete's sake," she said. "Here we are in Fort Worth, about to try to turn the world on its ear with our colts, and we're finding excuses to tear each other apart. Let's hold on to the good times, Sleet, and leave the rest to destiny. Tell me something about Fort Worth."

He wanted to tell her he was going to make her look like a pretender to the throne in the coming trials. He wanted to tell her that no matter what she accomplished in the futurity, he was going to find a way to make that sweet body of hers cry out in ecstasy, and she was going to do the same for him.

He hesitated. Was he about to blow all his plans on an ego trip?

Hadn't he worked the magic he'd intended, on this drive? Softened her up for surrender? All it was going to take was a picnic at a remote abandoned pueblo, maybe some heartfelt sympathy at her losses and she'd be clinging to him, begging him to take her over the threshold into paradise.

The more he conjured the fantasy, the dimmer grew the ugly memories of home, of Missouri and the lost legacy of the farm.

"What are those stockyards in the downtown area?" she prompted. "What are they all about?"

Suddenly he was relieved at the diversion she presented. Between now and the win, he needed a clear head. She was offering a truce. He grabbed it and began to talk about the great cattle drives that had built Fort Worth to prominence after the Civil War.

On and on he rattled, about the university and the Water Gardens and the Trinity River snaking through it all, but beneath the travelogue, his attempt to forget the unwelcome subject she'd broached was fruitless. He was un nerved by their relationship, her comments about his life-style and his brother's memory.

Finally he spotted the green-and-white Butler's sign he was looking for, and in silent relief, turned off the road onto an easement lined in cattle pens. Along the track, cow pies and horse manure were melting in the muck. Herds of red cattle huddled against the wind-driven rain inside their enclosures, bedraggled and miserable. The white-railed arena was deserted, telling him the great rush of cutters hadn't yet descended on Butler's to prepare for the futurity.

Eager to be free of the cab, where his emotions had spun like tumbleweed through the long hours of confinement, he grabbed his slicker from the backseat.

"Stay here and I'll roust someone who can show us our stalls," he said, settling his hat and opening the door to the storm. "No need for you to get wet."

"Sleet, I don't mind—"

"Stay here," he ordered, the sound harsh with the growing frustration he felt. He slammed the door and ducked, running back toward the office.

Your brother...make peace with what happened.... There was nothing to make peace with. What kind of mind game was she playing? Would she try to sabotage his concentration with a low trick like that?

He was going to have to forget her seduction for a time, keep on his guard. If she would stoop to emotional blackmail to keep him from the win, he'd better treat her with the polite courtesy of any other competitor, and keep his distance.

Striding up two chipped wooden steps, shouldering into his slicker, he knocked on a weathered white panel and turned the doorknob. Hesitating, the rain sheeting against the right side of his body, he racked his brain. What was the nameless thing brewing in him, tightening his gut?

"Close the danged door!" hollered Butler from inside, a gruff man who'd spent sixty years around livestock.

Grimacing, Sleet went in to register and hear the latest gossip about who had the hottest colts in town for the futurity. Whatever was bugging him was going to have to take a backseat. Cutting was his business, and he'd come to defend a title that said he was the best in the world.

TWO DAYS HAD PASSED since they'd arrived. The storm had blown on through, but there was another one brewing between Jess and Sleet. She put his short temper and businesslike attitude down to preshow nerves, decided to avoid him when he was grouchy and worked Blue on the feistiest cattle she'd ever seen. Personally, she was glad to be left to enjoy the unadulterated thrill of being in Cowtown.

They'd checked into the Glen Oaks Motel, where she'd met five-time futurity champion Buster Welch, her father's contemporary, and the younger Welch, Greg, also a futurity champ, as well as half a dozen other heroes of the cutting world. At the motel and at Butler's, every cutter she met was gossiping about bloodlines and "try" and stopping ability. Jess soaked it up. It was heady stuff.

Hal and Betty arrived on the third morning. Sleet had gone down to Butler's early, leaving her to greet the Brittons. She needed to let Blue rest, anyway. Tomorrow was their first trial.

Once settled in their suite, the Brittons ordered breakfast from room service. Afterward, Hal sluiced his travel-parched throat with an icy beer, while Jess and Betty sipped coffee.

"How is that jughead of yours?" asked Hal. "The long haul take any of the edge off his personality?"

"Matter of fact, yes, for about a day. But the elevation's only 610 feet in Fort Worth, and the feed and the air are both good. Blue's in fine fettle again—better shape than ever."

"That right?" he responded on a higher note.

Jess thought to egg him on a bit. "Your trainer taught me some massage techniques awhile back. They helped me finish my colt to perfection. Couldn't be more pleased with his progress."

"I'll have to get after him." Hal scowled. "Givin' away his secrets to the competition."

The three of them laughed, enjoying the good-natured rivalry.

Jess pictured her colt at the finals. There wasn't much to be done about the fire-damaged saddle, but she'd clipped the worked-silver decorative medallions back on his bridle after oiling it to a dark mahogany. He was going to be a flashy contestant. "I rubbed Blue's coat 'til it shone like polished hematite," she said. "I even painted his feet black."

"What'd you do a silly thing like that for?" Hal asked.

Betty came between them. "What do you think, you old range rider? She wants him lookin' sassy for the judges. Don't they count eye appeal in the points?"

"They're looking for animation in his personality," Hal argued with mild chagrin, impatient with women's concerns. "He's got plenty of that. We got more important business to discuss."

Jess's nerves came alive. Leaning to set the coffee cup on the carpet, she sat at the edge of the chair. "About Warner?" she asked.

"Among others." Hal slugged back into the couch and tilted up his beer for a long pull, letting the tension rise. He was paying her back for teasing him.

She wouldn't let him buffalo her. She waited in silence.

Finally he said, "You already know Warner stepped down from his post on the city council."

She nodded, her hands bound together, her body tense with anticipation. "Noa told me."

Hal grunted. "He admitted to Sheriff Sanford that Devon hadn't been with him after their golf game, the night of the fire. He'd lied at first, he claimed, because Devon had complained of woman trouble with 'a rancher in the valley.' Guys protectin' each others' backs. Some nonsense like that."

Jess waited, praying her name hadn't been mentioned.

Evidently it hadn't. Hal would have quizzed her about it. Instead, with relish, he continued, "Once Warner had lied, told the sheriff that Devon had been with him, he felt uncomfortable about it, the way I hear it. But the slimeball kept to his story because Devon pressed him to it. Anything I hate worse, it's a crooked politician."

"Get to the good part," Betty urged, coming to sit on the arm of Jess's chair.

"Don't rush me, woman." Hal took a slug of beer. "I couldn't call it a conscience, but something got the better of Warner."

Me, Jess thought in elation—and maybe a bit of Sleet's intimidation.

"He wiped the slate clean at the Sheriff's Department, and stepped down from public office," Hal added. "The papers put it that he was going to spend more time with his family, and that creepy beauty shop for dead people. I figure he was running scared."

Hal stretched, rubbed his paunch affectionately—drawing out the suspense.

"Did Sanford find out anything about the sniper?" Jess asked, to keep him talking.

"All that blubbery lawman would say is that a skinny lit-tle fella had been taken into custody because his finger-prints was all over that shell casing they found at your place." Hal furrowed his eyebrows and squinted out from under them. "Sanford mentioned the guy was bargaining his way out of a prison sentence. Said he was singing at the top o' his lungs..."

Jess's heart picked up its pace. "About?"

Hal grinned. "About a certain local developer who put him up to his dastardly acts. Fella name of Devon."

"Yes!" Jess jumped up from the couch so suddenly, Hal uttered a panicked oath. She went to him and threw her arms around him, heedless of his flustered protests. Laugh-ing, thanking him profusely, she held on and gave him the hug of his life.

"Well, shoo-oot," said Hal, sounding like a native of Amarillo. "Betty, git this crazed woman off me, 'fore I can't be held accountable for my actions."

"Serves you right for teasing her," said Betty, and they laughed together in relief and enjoyment.

AN HOUR LATER, when Betty dropped her off at Butler's, Sleet was working the Doc Tari colt with some other cut-ters, so Jess went on to the barn. She wanted to take Blue out on the road, let him stretch his legs. When she got to his box stall, he was munching alfalfa.

"We've beaten Devon," she told him. "Hurry up and eat. I want to tell Sleet."

Blue snorted chaff particles from his nostrils and went on munching. Many horses ignored their trainers when they spoke conversationally. Not Blue. He was always talking to her. She could walk by his stall or the wash rack or even the trailer, and if he saw her, he'd nicker. He was a people-pleaser. She was lucky.

Would he please the crowds at the show? A bead of anticipation laced with fear tried to race along her back. She dodged it and kept her mind liquid, free of the jitters. When Blue was finished with his hay, she saddled him and went wandering to find Sleet.

From early morning to sunset, Sleet was always seen mounted, exercising the four colts that were his responsibility, training the two men who'd hired him as their private futurity trainer, or riding turn-back for one of the handful of cutters who were polishing their futurity prospects at Butler's. His face, she saw as she entered the arena on Blue, was deeply scored. He was showing the strain of his packed schedule.

At a break in the action, she rode up to him.

"Hey, girl," he said evenly, adopting the Texas greeting for a woman.

She glanced at Tari's Baby, a stocky animal that reminded her of a locomotive. His flanks were heaving with exertion. "How's it going?" Jess asked casually, hiding the deep curiosity she felt.

"Good. It's going good." Sleet slipped off his hat and scrubbed his sweat-plastered hair. Her heart went out to him; he was tired, driving himself too hard. If he didn't get some rest, he'd be too wired to ride decently tomorrow. If he hadn't been her rival, she'd have offered to exercise one of his colts for him.

He replaced the hat, and didn't elaborate on the details of his workout, as a cutter would to a friend. She kept the disappointment out of her eyes.

"Hal brought me news," she said.

He tipped back his hat and waited.

She told him about Warner and the arrest of the sniper and that he was "singing" about a certain developer.

"Well, I'll be," Sleet said in apparent surprise, watching cows mill around. "I'm happy for you, Jess. Now you won't have that worry hanging over your head these next few days."

"I wanted to let you know so you could stop worrying, too."

He cut her a quick look. "I wasn't worried. Like you always told me, it's your ranch."

Her chin lifted at the outright lie.

One of the cutters called to him, forestalling the crack she was going to make about that three-sided personality of his—the courtly tour guide, the manipulative womanizer and the seasoned cutter. She never knew which she'd be facing.

Sleet glanced up, waved and looked back at Jess. "That all you wanted?" he asked.

She felt the urge to slap him but she quelled it. She wasn't going to foul up her concentration by waging war with him. She nodded coolly. "Betty and Hal invited us to dinner at some place in the Stockyards, after that auction at the Hilton." She picked up her reins. "Go her easy, Sleet."

He didn't answer as she left the arena.

Taking Blue out to the road, she began a series of warmups—walk, trot, lope—working him lightly along the fences and fields of the neighborhood to give him a break from the gridiron of training.

Oh, hell, she thought in chagrin; leave it alone. It was playing with dynamite to get riled at Sleet when so much was at stake. Maybe he was scared, his confidence shaken. That was to her benefit, wasn't it? It gave her an edge over him. She was feeling confident—why spoil it with regret for the loss of something she couldn't even rightly call friendship?

INSIDE THE BIG DOME of the Will Rogers Coliseum, her practice cutting went badly. Her first cow was sluggish, making Blue look lazy, and the second was lost and returned to the herd. Face flaming, Jess eased Blue into the herd for a third cow, cut her out and set Blue down on her a fraction too late. The calf ran to the fence, collided with the turn-back man's horse and fell down, bawling. Additional seconds were lost when the calf scrambled up on the fence side of the turn-back horse and darted for freedom.

Shaken by the experience, Jess left the arena and rode for half an hour in the warm-up area, head down, mind churning around the awful possibility of going home without a win.

In four hours, she would face that possibility.

She finished the cool-down and led Blue back to his new stall, where they'd moved him last night. Unsaddling him, she let him loose in the sawdust to roll, then brushed him clean and fed him lightly.

That done, she headed for the concession stands to eat a hamburger she didn't want. Her stomach was in knots. A faint headache pulsed behind skin that felt too tight across her forehead. She propped an elbow on the shelf along a concrete wall and took a bite. It was tasteless. She forced herself to eat.

Sleet appeared out of a crowd of men, walking over to her with a Coke in his hand. "How'd it go?" he asked.

She put down the half-eaten burger. "My worst nightmare."

"Lose a cow?"

She nodded, feeling ashamed.

"That's lucky," he said, scanning the hall.

She tried to meet his gaze but he kept threading it through the crowd. A past champion's opinion carried a lot of weight when her confidence was dashed to pieces—even if the champion was arrogant. His arrogance put more spice in her tone. "Glad to know all's not lost," she said wryly.

"Losing a cow in practice shakes out the jitters. You deal with the worst up front."

His tone was abrupt. The lines were still grooved deep into his cheeks. He hadn't rested well, she thought. The workouts, the auctions, the late but obligatory dinners with the owners of his colts—it was telling on him. Sleet was burning the candle at both ends, and that definitely gave her an edge.

"I drew numbers one and fifteen in the first set," he said, straightening to move away. "Got to get my colts ready."

"I suppose we ought to wish each other luck," she said archly. "After all, for three days out of three months, we were practically friends."

At this, he met her gaze. His was stormy. "Did I get to you on the trip, Jess? Make you hot to sample the goods? Make you think twice about the sacrifice you're making to your almighty pride, turning me down?"

The half-truth of his words sent her advancing toward him, face bright, tight with anger. "You'd like to think so, wouldn't you? Your towering ego *needs* to think so."

"I don't think—I know. You're so hot to have it, your jeans are probably wet." He started away. Then he came back and pointed a shaking finger in her face. "Make no mistake, Latham. When it comes to my work, nothing stands in my way. Not your underhanded ploy to sidetrack me by mentioning my brother, and not your tight little body with its teeming sex appeal. When it comes to the competition, I'm going to steamroll over your pathetic attempts to beat me, and I'll carry the pieces of your wounded pride back to Hemet and dump them on your front porch!"

She swung hard, aiming for his craggy, arrogant, furious face.

He caught her hand and held it three inches from his cheek. "Damn you," he muttered. He twisted her arm behind her back, snugged her against him and held her while she struggled. He leaned in and kissed her, a hard, quick kiss that told of the frustration and rivalry between them.

Abruptly he let her go. "For luck, Jess," he said, and walked off toward the barn.

She glanced around, embarrassed to see a couple of cutters smirking, looking like they were proud of the manly thing Sleet had done, putting her in her place.

"You're all macho creeps," she retorted and strode away wiping his kiss from her lips.

A RECORD THREE HUNDRED and ninety horses were entered to compete against the animals Sleet and Jess had brought to the futurity. The purse for the Open Division had jumped to over a million dollars, with the lion's share going to the winner.

Every walk of life was represented in the crowded warm-up area where Sleet worked the Doc Tari colt, loosening his bulky power muscles.

In addition to a staggering number of world champions, there were baby doctors and beer distributors and backyard bricklayers, a bartender/trainer from Oregon, some stockbrokers, bookkeepers, book editors, barbers and at least fifteen barristers, who seemed drawn to the grandstanding that went on in the business.

That wasn't even counting the actors, TV announcers and political types, some of them decent riders, Sleet ruminated. The Celebrity Cutting stood out as one of the most popular events of the futurity.

And there were horses with confirmation so perfect it choked Sleet up to watch them move.

Anxious to shore up the confidence he'd nicked in his run-in with Jess, Sleet nudged his colt up alongside a chestnut mare.

Her rider was the slim, slow-talking Oklahoma boy, Joe Heim, who'd snuck up on all of them a few years back, stealing the futurity on a late-great comer by the name of Docs Okie Quixote. He was slouched in the saddle he'd won that year.

"Hey, Joe," Sleet said, nodding to him.

"Sleet," he said, offering that shy half smile of his.

"How's it feel to be back?"

"Oh..." A sun could set in the distance between his phrases. "Like I never left, I guess. You did all right last year. Congratulations."

"Thanks, but today feels like the first time, just the same."

The horses plodded for a minute. "It always does," Joe said. "I figure I'll just go on in there and do my workout. Let her find the calf. She's better at it than I am."

His humility was characteristic. So was the easy camaraderie of opponents who would be vying for a small fortune in winnings. For some reason, he and Jess didn't share the same ease. Sleet tried to tell himself this inner whirlwind that was chasing his courage was felt by all; Joe had admitted as much. But the whirlwind spun on, blowing Sleet's confidence to somewhere beyond Amarillo.

Inside the arena, the announcer was listing the sponsors of the futurity—airline and feed and hat companies, Purina Mills, Chevy trucks; the list went on. A tingle along his backbone told Sleet it was time to put some hot licks on his colt, let Joe gather his concentration. "Say hey to Joice for me," he said.

"I will."

Sleet moved away and took his stout colt into the center of the ring, where he backed him up and stepped him over, then backed him 'til his hocks were buried in the dirt and he was fully alert.

At last it was time to ride to the gate. Sleet's heart pounded and he thought of Jess. She'd deserved that kiss, gunning for his pride like she did. He let the memory of it stir his blood.

"Ladies and gentleman, get ready for the action," the announcer crooned. "The first set opens with a special treat. First up is Sleet Freeman, last year's winner and ranked tenth in the nation in NCHA winnings this year." There was mild applause, whistles. "He's riding Tari's Baby, owned by Hal and Betty Britton of Hemet, California."

Sleet snugged his hat down. *For you, Jess,* he thought. *If you're watching, this ride's for you.* With the memory of her kiss to hold him, he went in through the slatted gate, hips loose, shoulders relaxed, and put his mind on selecting a cow.

JESS SAT HIGH up in the bleachers in a seat nobody wanted because it was so far from the action. Heart in her throat, she watched Sleet cut a burly red cow that reminded her of Refrigerator Perry. The cow, a testy hulk, put a few trial moves on Tari's Baby. The colt was quick, dodging left and right, stirring the crowd's enthusiasm. Sleet had no cause to worry about his mount's interest in the cow. It was a battle of wills from the beginning.

Moments later, Refrigerator lost his temper and tried to dive for the opening between the horse's legs. Baby would have none of it. He crouched, blocking the cow, sending the crowd to its feet applauding.

Sleet sat loosely, face carved in stone, hands still as a dead man's, and rode the roller coaster for a full forty-five seconds.

When the cow gave up the contest, he lifted Baby off and turned him toward the herd. The crowd cheered.

Knowing his colt needed a dicey challenge to show well, Sleet selected another fighting cow. This one was a rangy gray Brahma with its horns stubbed. Sleet chose well. The animal was quick and twisty, contorting itself to outmaneuver the bay colt. Baby wheeled and pitched as if he had Brahma in his own blood, and he shut down every move brilliantly.

The run was so hot, Sleet had no need nor time to cut a third cow.

When he left the arena, raising his hat to the whistling, cheering spectators and flashing them a grin, his score was 219.

You bet he deserved to smile, Jess thought. He'd done the impossible; he'd drawn that unlucky first slot, and rather than be eliminated in his initial go-round, had logged a score the field would have to struggle all day to match, her included.

Instead of the jealousy she expected, Jess felt pride. It welled up and spilled over into her eyes. Frustrated by it, she lifted her head and said, "Please, God. Let me stay in the competition. Give me courage like his."

Chapter Sixteen

Jess needed him, he could feel it in his bones.

He stepped out of the shower and wrapped a towel around his hips, reaching for his shaving cream. He lathered his face and picked up the razor, whisking away blond stubble with deft strokes.

He wondered if she was crying, alone in her room.

When she'd come through the gate after Blue's go in the semifinals, her face tight with held-back tears, he'd ridden over to her. He could afford a little kindness, he remembered thinking. Leading on points going into the finals, he'd never felt more confident. He'd said something soft to her. "Go her easy, girl, you slid in by a hair." Something like that.

"It's just not working!" she'd snapped, her eyes ablaze. "Blue's acting like I abused him his whole life. He's jerky in his moves. The crowd scares him."

The rear end of a big bluish stud slid against Blue's hindquarters. As if to prove her right about his mood, he squealed and kicked out. Jess snapped up the reins. "Hey!" she shouted. "Stop that."

Blue danced and pulled at the bit.

The owner of the grulla said, "Keep that stud under control, girl. I don't want my investment stove in."

Jess glared at him.

Sleet reached over to lay a soothing hand on her arm. She jerked away. "I've got to go cool him down," she said.

"You made it to the finals, Jess," he said. "A newcomer hardly ever does."

"I'm not exactly a newcomer, though you'd never know it by the showings we've made. I was born to cut cattle. So was Blue."

She had kicked her horse and sent him into the circling stream of warm-up riders, her chin lifted and her eyes boring a hole in the air between Blue's ears.

Shaving, Sleet slid the blade carefully along the downward groove in his right cheek, still concerned about her. She'd stood beside him at auctions, danced with him at the champions' party—albeit unwillingly since he'd been prickly as a boar's head—and stayed out of his way when he was dragged out with work. In short, she'd been a trooper, a true pro, in every encounter they'd had. The only time she'd crossed him was when he'd egged her to it. Once he'd scored high, his head was clear enough to see he'd provoked her. He'd said some pretty rough things in that confrontation. Practically told her she was going to lose. She was, he had no doubt about that. But she was good enough to qualify for the finals against men who already had the seasoning of a world championship under their belts. How much of her misery was his fault? Didn't he owe her more respect than that?

Sleet set his razor on the counter and sloshed warm water on his face, drying it with a hand towel. She'd worked so damned hard to get here.

The thought crawled into his head and stuck there. Why hadn't he settled down before now, taken over a spread like she had? He wanted it, didn't he?

Hell, yes.

In the shower, he'd experienced recurring flashes about his younger brother, Hank. The day of the accident, Hank had been hassling him, grumbling about having to distribute the hay as Sleet pitched it into a stall in their barn. "Ever since Dad's plane crashed, you been lordin' it over me, man," Hank accused bitterly. "I'm bigger 'n you. I get an equal say in who does what chores."

Burdened with responsibilities, Sleet had lost his temper. "You'll do as I say, dammit! Now get that hay spread out so we can bring in the colt."

He'd swung the pitchfork full of hay at full force.

Behind him, his brother had clutched his face and screamed. . . .

Sleet shuddered. He could thank Jess for the recurring flashes of memory. She'd seeded his mind to the idea that he was restless because of his brother's accident. She was right. He just didn't know how it had made him a wanderer.

Or how that related to her and him.

TV shows always discussed relationships as if all you had to do to get along was talk to each other. He and Jess had done that. On the trip, they'd talked for damned near twenty-six hours, and found out they were compatible as kittens with a yarn ball. And still they couldn't get past whatever was keeping them apart. Linked in spirit, polar-opposed in life, he thought.

Why was that, anyway?

He slapped cologne on his face and dried his hands, ran his fingers through his hair and went into the bedroom. He stretched out on the queen-size bed and closed his eyes, relishing this rare break from his grueling schedule.

He saw Jess as she'd been two nights ago, hair up in that feminine style he liked and dressed in a black silk number that sculpted her fine figure and fell in soft folds to her knees. She had great legs, especially in heels. When he'd walked her to her room after the champions' party, he'd told her she did. How he'd wanted to make love to her then.

But she'd rolled her eyes at him and said, "Good night, Sleet. Good night before we find something to fight about. I need my wits about me tomorrow."

She'd slid right into her room and closed the door, not giving him a chance to kiss her good night.

She's busted up about the way her go-rounds are turning out, said a voice in his mind. *She should be overjoyed to still be in the running, but she's devastated to be trailing the pack.*

Should he go to her? No, he decided. She'd resent the intrusion. Her privacy and independence were precious to her.

With plenty of time before he had to get dressed, he ruminated on his accomplishments. Hal's filly had lost a cow in her first go, disqualifying her from further competition, but Tari's Baby had won the top score in every single go-round. Two other colts he'd trained had made it to the finals in the Non-Pro and $50,000 Limited Classes, and he was basically the talk of the town. He'd been interviewed by *Texas Monthly, Cutting Horse* and the local papers. It felt good. Damned good.

In contrast, Jess was scraping by. Blue had qualified for the finals by only half a point, which was why Jess had been so torn up afterward. Sleet put just about every trainer of standing in the country ahead of her on points. The work of more than a year, the sacrifice, the long days, the scrounging for a dime—it was all coming down around her ears. Her dream was slipping away... like she was likely to slip away from him.

He sat up abruptly. His mouth went cottony. Something clutched him in the loins and squeezed.

Hadn't he planned it that way? *Take her to Texas, best her at cutting, seduce her, bring her home and get the hell out of Dodge?*

Hell, no, said his heart. Hell, yes, said his head.

He swung his legs over the side of the bed and stood up, scrubbing his fingers through his hair.

He pictured life without Jess, and that vice in his loins squeezed tighter.

Her dreams are breaking up in her hands. She needs you.

Whatever was speaking to him, this time he obeyed.

Slipping on jeans and a rodeo shirt of caramel-and-black stripes, he pulled on his boots, pocketed his keys and left the room.

They were supposed to meet Hal and Betty for dinner in the dining room downstairs, but something told him Jess wasn't going to make it. He was a fool to worry about her, he told himself, striding the short distance down the hall to her room. She was tough as nails and she was going to laugh in his face when he showed up looking worried. But the voice in him said she was falling apart, and he hurried to knock on her door.

JESS KNEW SHE'D COME farther than she deserved, being new at the game. The very worst she could do if she lost in the Finals was take home enough money to pay her taxes and living expenses for a few months; it was seed money. She'd have to get a part-time job, but at least she could eke by for another year.

Somehow the pep talk depressed her more. She gazed around the room, trying to remember what she had to do to finish getting ready.

She'd bathed and dried her hair, leaving it full around her shoulders, and slipped on her black lace underwear. Lacy things draped from the chair, the dresser. Ah, she thought, spying the sheer black panty hose. She smoothed them on, then bent to pick up a black spiky heel. Without touching it, she stared at it and lost interest. What was the use of keeping up the facade? She was holding on by her fingernails and they all knew it. Let them eat dinner without me, she thought, morosely peeling off the panty hose. Sleet deserved the accolades people were showering on him; he'd done superbly in the competitions.

She would have room service, go to bed early.

A tear ran down her cheek and she brushed it away. Folding the panty hose, she laid them in the top drawer of the dresser. Why cry? she chided, sitting on the edge of the bed, balling her hands in her lap. A scraping sob escaped her. She clamped her mouth on it.

Winners don't cry, said her father's voice in her head.

And Lathams don't lose, she answered back. They win.

Except she wasn't winning. Blue was jerky on the cattle. The crowd frightened him. He was barely managing to stay with his cows.

To top it off, Sleet was probably going to win and be on the road all next year, chasing the cowgirls in those honkytonks and breaking hearts all over his beloved Southwest. Another tear fell. Mechanically, she wiped it away.

She'd planned his seduction so carefully, dreamed of it so often, then changed her mind and built up walls. He'd torn them down with his travelogues and his humor and his charming ways, and she'd wanted him so bad she could barely stand next to him.

There would surely be dancing after supper tonight. She just couldn't do it and keep from blubbering all over the Brittons, Sleet and herself. The Latham pride wedged itself up her backbone, and she reached for the phone, intending to call Betty.

Someone knocked on the door. She drew back her hand and stared. She swiped under her eyes and said a tremulous, "Yes?"

She rose and went to the door on bare feet, then dashed to the chair and swept on the emerald-green robe.

"Who is it?" she called.

"It's Sleet, Jess. Can I come in?"

She panicked, pressed her fingertips beneath her eyes, smoothed her hair. He was early. He wasn't due to get her for another hour. Hell's bells, was she supposed to let him in?

Of course, she thought in quick decision. She would tell him she was canceling dinner, and save herself the explanations and inevitable urgings from Betty.

Swallowing, she cracked open the door, then swung it wide. He walked in, looking around. She closed the door, slanting a look at him. A shaft of light from the bathroom lifted the gold in his damp hair. The face that haunted her dreams turned to her, and her heart stalled and hung suspended in the intimate, searching look he gave her.

"You okay, Jess?" he asked softly.

His kindness loosed the pain in her. The Latham pride deserted her. She choked back a cry and nodded, unable to speak.

"Aw, Jess," he said.

She bowed her head, fighting back the tears.

Suddenly he was close in front of her, reaching for her, folding her into his arms. A sob rose within her and she buried her face in the curve of his chest, biting her lip 'til it hurt, and shaking with unreleased grief.

"Let it out, honey," he crooned.

"I-I can't," she said.

"It's not over 'til it's over tomorrow," he said, holding her tightly.

"Oh, Sleet!"

She clung to him while the sobs racked painfully up through her body and burst from her, like the cracking of a whip against an aluminum wall that winnowed with reverberations. She wept for the dedication and drive that were slipping away and might never come again, and for Blue and Brisa and Sienna, who had each paid a price for her ambition. She wept for the torment she'd given Josepha and Noa, and for the pathetic patch of land that held her in its iron grip and now might not be saved.

And she wept for herself and Sleet. That, too, was lost because of who she was, and who he was.

As her tears subsided, a thought crept in. She tilted her head to look up at him, asking the question mutely, letting it speak itself, through the mist that glistened on her lashes.

For a protracted moment, Sleet held his breath. A strong current bonded them and his mind probed hers while his gaze roved her face, lingering, darkening as he watched her parted lips. When he searched her eyes again, she trembled.

With a soft, indrawn keening sound, he lifted her bodily to him and brought his mouth down on hers. It was a hot, wet, seeking kiss. It was a moving, molten kiss, and their tongues collided in a frenzy to know at once the depth and meaning of this moment.

His hands began to explore her, bunching her buttocks, while her hands cleaved to and followed the twin arches of muscle ridging his back. He lifted her again, groaning into her open mouth, and she felt her body tilt and swing horizontal, cradled by him as he moved to the bed. He shoved something off the spread, leveraged her down, freed one hand to whip the coverlet away, and swayed with her onto the pliant mattress, still kissing her.

Sleet eased away from her lips to watch her eyes darken when he loosened the belt of her gown, pushing fabric 'til he could see her torso, lacy bra and black panties. He dipped to her breast and covered it with his mouth, making a throaty sound that peaked the tip of it, beneath the lace. He looked into her lidded eyes, then did it again. Pleasure arrowed down between her spread thighs; she writhed, eyes closed, and was wet, aching with desire and urgency.

After flicking the clasp of her bra and pulling her damp panties off, he glanced down, muttering, "You're so beautiful," as he caressed her shimmering flesh.

It was the touch of his hands there, just there, that she'd imagined so many times. "Ah!" she cried, moving to each caress, hips bucking against his lean length. He plied her with his lips, a forearm, his chin, his hair, reveling in the shape and texture and taste of her, and when his work-roughened hands grazed the tips of her breasts, she arched and cried out.

He reached back, behind him, and a boot thudded to the floor. Turning, lips roving hers, he got free of the other.

A wild, feverish thought crept in. Grabbing his hands before he could shrug out of his jeans, she stayed him.

There was a fantasy she wanted to fulfill, had imagined, in the countless times she'd glanced below his waist as he walked across a patch of earth. She had wondered if he had other talents besides horses. She was a hot-blooded woman when she let her hair down, and she measured men in a number of ways, not the least of which was their prowess at satisfying a woman's biological urge.

Twisting her body, Jess pressed him to lie down. There wasn't a thing the two of them couldn't do while kissing, she thought in wonder—even contortions like this. They twined and undulated like the blackland prairie, tumbled like tumbleweed caught in a vortex of wind. When he lay on his back, she slithered against him, the source of her nearing orgasm pressed against the ridge of his erection and the rough texture of the half-open zipper. Again his hands roved over her flesh. He knew. He understood what she wanted, and she rode him 'til the vortex spun her out beyond the prairie to the void.

But it wasn't enough. Their bodies, kept tortured but apart by reasons neither of them fully understood, begged to join... to meet flesh with flesh... to revel in the freedom they had given themselves this night.

She reached for his buckle, and after that there were the sounds of snaps, zippers and falling coins. She helped him out of his jeans, his jocks, and ripped open the snaps of his shirt to bare his chest, nuzzling the golden down.

He wanted her mouth on him. He asked with his breath and his hands, and she gave, loving him willingly. She had never been a servant to any man. Now, she was joyfully, powerfully, his.

He cradled her head as she worked over him. Gentle hands. Encouraging hands. And she was inspired by his hands to put her own on him, below her moving lips, so that she felt the flick of her tongue, and she enveloped him and swallowed part of him and felt spiritually his.

He was a benevolent, emoting, expressive protector, cherished friend, considerate lover. He arranged her just so in order to pleasure her; he wooed her in a thousand supple maneuverings. She and Sleet were like the entwined branches of a tree moving in the wind, touching and bowing and glancing. 'Til she whimpered and quivered in anticipation of his entry.

He took her by the shoulders and pushed into her like a train moving into a station, until he was fully inside her. They both cried out with the sweetness of it. Again he plunged, again—only three, four thrusts, as she crossed her ankles behind his back, and he was ready to pour himself into her.

Something stopped him. He was utterly still for a heart-beat or two. He opened his eyes and looked down at her. Her eyes were just fluttering open, and in them he could see molten desire. It faded in an instant, replaced by a question so eloquent he read it easily in the aquamarine depths. *What's wrong?* she wanted to know.

She took her hand from his arm, made a tiny movement—another mute question.

"Time," he said, his voice husky. "Don't move, don't breathe."

A tremulous smile tilted up one corner of her mouth.

He withdrew and slid in, once, twice, easing into a rhythm that was controlled and would not send him into mindless-ness. If only she would not move.

Her face tensed. A small cry escaped her. "Sleet," she begged. "It's hell to lie still. Please!"

"Easy," he soothed. "Go her easy."

Laughter bubbled up from her, and she said, "Like riding..."

"Like nothing ever before," he said, and gathered her close, rocked her, letting the passion dwindle simply to have the pleasure of cherishing her. There would be time to build the mighty forces again.

THEY LAY IN passive completion, Sleet cradling her, telling her about Hank. "I was in a rage. I didn't know he was so close behind me, or that the pitchfork..."

He swallowed. The guilt was thick in his throat.

She turned, traced his cheek.

"I didn't know 'til this moment what a blow it was to give the care of the land to him," he said. "How it crippled my ambition."

"Are you sorry?"

He shook his head. "I did it willingly. He's good to Ma and good to the land. We're close."

"You can love someone and still not give up your dreams."

Was she telling him something about herself? He nuzzled her silky shoulder. "So wise. So beautiful. I love you, Jess."

Her eyes darted to his face.

He met that wary, probing look steadily. "I love you," he said, muting it to a tender pledge. He'd known it the moment she'd allowed him to comfort her.

She wriggled out of his arms, scooting to the edge of the bed. "We'd better get moving if we're going to make the Owners' Finals Draw Breakfast."

"Did you hear me, Jess?"

"I heard you. I just don't trust what I hear."

She rose and walked toward the bathroom, her firm rear delighting him like strawberries for breakfast on a Sunday morning.

He lay back and folded his hands beneath his head, smiling.

He'd known all along that a woman who rode like she did and danced like she did would be hell on wheels in bed. He recalled thinking he'd gentle her, back when the barn had burned. He never would. But he knew he was going to stick around and try.

For starters, think of the comforting she was going to need when he aced her out of the win today....

JESS SLID OUT of the saddle and checked the cinch, thinking it was too loose. It was perfect. She climbed back aboard and pressed Blue to a trot, throwing her weight to left and right, settling the rig.

Beyond the gate, the crowd roared. Tommy Lyons was doing his best to steal Sleet's lead, from the sound of things. Sleet had been second in the draw, and had put the crowd on their feet with what must have been the cut of a lifetime. She wished she could have seen it. But her job was to prepare Blue for the two and a half minutes when his future and hers would be written in the history books.

She found a spot against a wall and finished off his warm-up, putting his hocks in the dirt and polishing his spins.

About thirty minutes ago, riding up to her after his cut, Sleet had slapped Blue on the rump and told her, "Break a leg."

"This isn't the entertainment business," she'd quipped, nervy and snappish, still simmering over the endearments he'd offered her this morning.

"Sure it's entertainment," he'd said, grinning. "Go on out there and show 'em a good time. Enjoy yourself. Give 'em their money's worth." He dropped down into twang and said, "They ain't never again going to see a show like you'll give 'em, mark my words. And y'all ain't never going to be cherry again, neither." He did Groucho with his eyebrows.

His humor didn't dent the little grudge she held against him. "You can be nice and crack jokes all you want," she returned, "but I'm still going to put my heart into beating you."

A spark of fight lit his eyes for a moment, but evidently he chose not to voice it. He tipped his hat. "Give 'em hell, Jess."

He'd ridden out of the building, leaving her to question his motives and the meaning of his postcoital confession.

He hadn't had to tell her he loved her this morning, she thought sourly, smoothing a sweaty palm on the velvet black chaps she wore over her jeans. She was a big girl. She didn't need polite niceties to soothe her feminine ego. Nor did she want thanks of that kind just for being tender to him when he revealed his feelings about his brother. Let the culmination of all they'd been to each other stand on its own merits, and the night they'd shared be a keepsake to treasure for a lifetime.

Her number was called. She settled her hat down tight. Thoughts of Sleet fled in the momentary terror of approaching the gate. It swung open, and the great sandy arena floor spread out like the Mojave, blanched by the lights. Two levels of white fencing corraled the tiers of spectators, mere dots of color in the huge domed building.

Blue danced, throwing his head.

"Easy," she said, patting his neck. He quieted and walked through the opening. In seconds they were among the cattle, cutting deep into the herd, Blue flicking his ears and Jess searching desperately for one that hadn't been worked too much in the early runs.

Trust Blue's instincts, she told herself. *Relax. Break a leg.*

The herd peeled around her, filing back to the greater number bunched behind her. The herd-holders kept well back, and the turn-back men, too, giving her plenty of room to prove Blue's abilities. In front of her, facing the herd, was a collection of stands, and the judges....

Seconds ticked off the clock. There were only five cattle left to file by. She'd be marked down if she chose the last one. *Think! Choose!*

Blue quivered. He was watching a surly-looking chocolate with one white target eye. That was his cow. It had his name on it.

She pressed him forward.

Her father's voice echoed out of the past. *The horse that wins is the one that does something spectacular, and dares to be great.*

Suddenly she remembered what she'd known for months, but had forgotten in the awful tension of the go-rounds. Blue had greatness. He was the most talented animal on the face of the earth. All she had to do was sit back and stay out of his way.

She set him on the cow and did just that, sat back, rubber-limbed and easy, the reins loose.

The critter blinked his target eye and tried to duck around Blue. Her horse tripped over, quick as you please, and turned him. The cow tried to run the other way. Blue stopped him. They played that game a few more times, racking up points because the runs were short and centered near the herd, but far enough out to avoid disturbing them. Blue kept his ears and eyes on point-lookout and went gunning for his target. The cow was quick and mean-hearted. He faked a left and dived right. Blue was headed the other way.

Jess's heart went to her throat. Blue was in trouble! He scrambled his legs beneath him, turned on the power and lunged, turning the calf. Jess rolled in the saddle, clinging to the horn and wondering what the distant roaring implied. *Breathe,* she commanded herself. *Breathe! Stay with him. Blue's in charge.*

Target tried the trick again, but with a twist. He did a double-take, then dived for Blue's belly. Blue was ready for him. He backed on his hocks, pattered the sand with his front hooves, tucked his head, flattened his ears and stopped the calf cold. That wasn't enough. Target wanted to play Ping-Pong. They went back and forth in a four-foot span of churning sand, the calf looking for a hole, the horse filling it, seven, ten, twelve licks. After that, Jess lost count, and her horse was turning so fast, he was drilling holes in the sand.

He was doing something spectacular, he was daring to be great. That roaring in her ears was the world cheering him on.

The contest ended abruptly when Target, a beaten cow, flipped around ninety degrees and hauled for the judges' stand. Blue stayed where he was, feet planted, sides heaving, watching his adversary's retreat.

Jess's heart sang. With more pride than she'd felt in her life, she lifted the reins and went in for another one.

If Blue could do it again, the Doc Tari colt was going to eat his dust.

After the second cow and thirty seconds of pure rodeo, Jess thought her heart would burst. But there were still forty-odd seconds left. Cutting the herd shallowly, she selected a compact brindle that had showed no fear and looked like it had some speed. *Go for broke,* she urged, setting Blue down on her. *Give 'em a show.*

He did.

The wily cow twisted and darted and bucked, then did a one-two-three hot-lick smack-dab in the center of the arena. Blue's mane was flying and his ears were flat as he tap-danced with his front hooves and side-passed with the rear. She'd have given half her winnings just to see the fire in his eyes.

At the corner of her vision, she saw the fringe of her chaps feather the air as Blue lurched left, and she knew a keen pleasure in the picture they painted, she and Blue, writing cutting horse history together.

The buzzer sounded, hoarse as a Canadian gander. While the roaring thundered down from the stands, Jess let Blue patter back and forth in a dandy finish. Finally the cow bawled and backed away. She picked up the reins and left the arena, body erect for the first time in two and a half heart-stopping minutes, her face flushed crimson with pride.

Her score was announced. She didn't hear it, didn't care. Blue had taken this futurity with greatness.

One of the contenders murmured "Congratulations." She bobbed her head in automatic acknowledgment and kept on to the center of the warm-up field. The next competitor's number was called, and it floated through without registering.

Reining in, Jess collapsed against her mount. She flung her arms around his neck, panting, "Blue...Blue."

She lay there for several minutes, listening to the thud of her heart, feeling the wild pounding of his. He snorted heartily and she giggled. There were tears in her eyes. "You're the greatest, Blue. You're the greatest."

"As long as y'all are talkin' to a horse," someone drawled. It was Sleet. He'd come back to get his colt, tied at the far end of the field, and ridden over, reining in close to her. His leg brushed her chaps. She pushed up from Blue's neck and looked long into Sleet's eyes. He wasn't smiling.

"That was just about the finest cuttin' it's been my life-long pleasure to watch," he said, pushing back his hat. Respect was there; grudging respect.

"I beat you," she murmured.

"That you did."

Still there was no smile. Her heart clutched. "Will you hate me for it?"

He nudged his chin with a knuckle and looked far down the arena, his mouth pulling pensively. The grudge she'd been holding muscled up and tried to shoulder aside her victory. She could understand his disappointment. After all, he'd lost the thing she'd risked her life, the lives of her loved ones, to take from him. But did he have to make a federal case out of it? His indecision hurt.

"I've got to cool him out," she said, picking up the reins.

Blue surged forward under leg pressure and began to walk the great circle of the field. Sleet rode up next to her and put his hand on the reins, stopping them. "Not this time, Jess," he said, his voice flat.

She tried to ease the reins away, but he held them fast, his fingers pinioning hers—like last night, at a certain point, but then she hadn't minded. Now, she didn't mind too terribly much, either, except that there would come a time when the memory of his touch would be torture.

"Jess, listen," he said urgently. "I want to try."

"Try what?"

"You and me. Us."

"You want to try it?" Her throat was dry. "Try it how?"

"In Hemet."

"Us?" Her fickle heart began to rattle the bars of its cage. She felt the clatter throughout her body. "Us?" she asked again, disbelieving.

"I'm not asking for commitment."

"Of course not," she said archly. "You wouldn't."

"Maybe not now, but someday. We could do the circuit together next year. Raise colts. Collaborate on training. If y'all will have me."

He stepped his colt up next to her and let go of her reins. Leaning over, he put an arm around her, and Blue miraculously stood still, eyeing the stud beside him in uncertain wariness. Sleet squeezed her arm, sending thrills up her back. "What do you say, Jess? Will you have an old has-been world champ in your stable?"

"Stable?" she retorted. "Sleet Freeman, if I have you anywhere, it'll be in my bed!"

He laughed and hugged her.

Behind them, the announcer named Blue-bar-Satan, owned and ridden by Jess Latham of Hemet, California, the new world champion of the NCHA cutting-horse futurity.

"Soon as you take your bows," Sleet said, eyeing Blue covetously, "let's ride down along the banks of the Trinity and work out the details of our new association. Checkers would make a mighty fine brood mare, don't you think? Let's see...." He tilted his head. "Checker-Blue, Satan's Check—has possibilities—Blue-bar-Check. No, those aren't quite right. Their young 'uns got to have classy names. Ah!" His eyes shone with teasing lights. "Got it, Jess."

"What'd you come up with?"

"Sat-on-Checkers."

She laughed, and he rode with her toward the slatted gate, his arm circling her waist.

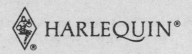 **HARLEQUIN®**

THE TAGGARTS OF TEXAS!

Harlequin's Ruth Jean Dale brings you
THE TAGGARTS OF TEXAS!

Those Taggart men—strong, sexy and hard to resist...

You've met Jesse James Taggart in FIREWORKS!
Harlequin Romance #3205 (July 1992)

And Trey Smith—he's THE RED-BLOODED YANKEE!
Harlequin Temptation #413 (October 1992)

And the unforgettable Daniel Boone Taggart in SHOWDOWN!
Harlequin Romance #3242 (January 1993)

Now meet Boone Smith and the Taggarts who started it all—
in LEGEND!
Harlequin Historical #168 (April 1993)

Read all the Taggart romances!
Meet all the Taggart men!

Available wherever Harlequin Books are sold.

Where do you find hot Texas nights, smooth Texas charm and dangerously sexy cowboys?

COWBOYS AND CABERNET

Raise a glass—Texas style!

Tyler McKinney is out to prove a Texas ranch is the perfect place for a vineyard. Vintner Ruth Holden thinks Tyler is too stubborn, too impatient, too...Texas. And far too difficult to resist!

CRYSTAL CREEK reverberates with the exciting rhythm of Texas. Each story features the rugged individuals who live and love in the Lone Star State. And each one ends with the same invitation...

Y'ALL COME BACK...REAL SOON!

Don't miss *COWBOYS AND CABERNET* by Margot Dalton. Available in April wherever Harlequin books are sold.
